EIGHT CRAZY *One Night* Stands

A STEAMY HANUKKAH ROMANCE

BETH GELMAN

For information, address Beth Gelman directly at BethGelman.com or at BethGelmanWrites@gmail.com.

ISBN: 979-8-9905873-8-0 (Paperback)
ISBN: 979-8-9905873-7-3 (Digital)

Summary:

The endless barrage of taunts from my mother regarding my single-ness has reached new heights. Being Becca Strauss, patent attorney, is no match for my mother, the Socialite. When she challenges me to find a respectable date—no, boyfriend—before her Annual Charity Hanukkah party, I cringe. My only goal in life is to make partner at my law firm, and I'd do anything to keep that dream alive—including placating my mother.

Our deal is struck, and before I know it, I'm dating eight strangers in one week without a wingman. Actually, that's not true. My lifelong friend Spencer has my back, though sometimes I think he'd like to be in the lineup, too.

I'm doing my best not to hurt anyone's feelings. I just want to have fun, complete my mother's challenge, and put this all behind me. So why does it feel like I'm the one who will be the biggest loser in this charade?

Time is running short. I have eight dates, with eight crazy hot guys, and eight chances of finding a happily ever after. Can I become a partner at my firm and find a life partner all in one week? The struggle is real, but I'm up for the challenge.

EIGHT CRAZY ONE NIGHT STANDS

Wild antics ensue each night, with each date weirder than the last. Stress, confusion, deadlines, and hilarious situations make this the perfect laugh-out-loud read this holiday season.

[1. Romance 2. Contemporary romance 3. Romantic comedy 4. Satire 5. Holiday Romance 6. Womens Empowerment]

Copy Editor: Dione Benson

Formatting Editor: Cindy Ziegelman Enterprises LLC

Cover Design: Miblart.com

First Edition

Contents

Dedication

To Ma Mère:

My rock, my champion, my friend

All my love, Prinny

Author's Note
Non-violent dubious consent

To offer transparency to my readers, I am disclosing a possible trigger warning occurring in Chapter 6 and the first few pages of Chapter 7. (A text conversation discussing the previous night.)

Non-violent dubious consent centered around drinking transpires between adults who have had feelings for each other for over a decade. Even though consent was asked and given four times, the circumstances occurred while drinking was involved.

This chapter can be omitted without affecting the outcome of the story.

Chapter 1

There was a need for all Jewish mothers to control their children from the moment of their first breath to their final one. The joy they must feel when they insert themselves into our very first relationships had to give them a surreal power that enabled them to massage, mold, or, in my case, manipulate my life to bend to her will.

My first relationship with a boy, Steven, was in kindergarten. He saw me in my Sunday school classroom and insisted on holding my hand when we walked to tefillah. He held my hand as we sang songs and learned about Noah's Ark as if we had walked two-by-two with all the other animals. I saw my mother clapping her hands and whispering to another woman, presumably Steven's mother, making googly eyes at the both of us. Need I say more?

My mother's meddling in my personal life hit an all-time high in my high school junior year. It seemed that the "right" date for the Junior Prom "would change the trajectory of my life." *Sure.* For the record, most Jewish mothers doted and *kvelled* over their children. They would encourage their children to be themselves and seek their own fortunes. Just not Marilyn.

Another Steven, *yes, there were many,* was on my mother's radar, and she "happened" to see Steven's mother at the nail salon. The two of them plotted to arrange a trial date several months before prom so that we could meet, fall in love, and give them beautiful babies by the time we graduated from college. While that date was bearable, Steven contracted mononucleosis the week before the big event and couldn't attend. Gleefully, I rubbed the situation in my mother's face and wore my ridiculously expensive dress while sitting all weekend on my bedroom bay window seat reading Jane Austen's *Pride and Prejudice.*

From that moment on, my mother had been *hocking* me to find a suitable man for *me* to make *her* a grandmother. Was it enough that I was a grown woman of thirty-two years with two degrees—one in mechanical engineering and one in law? No. Was it enough that I am now an esteemed patent lawyer in a big city law firm making hundreds of thousands of dollars a year? No. Of course not. All that was *bupkis.* It was a ring or nothing, and, frankly, I'd been happy with nothing for a decade.

With their inflated bank accounts and inflated egos, the guys I'd dated took too much time and energy for me to feed their big heads. All the other men I'd sampled should have kept their mouths closed and their pants on the floor, ready to please me. I had my needs, and, when my mechanical man didn't do the trick, I'd find a reasonable alternative—so long as he bought me dinner and didn't promise to call later.

It was Thanksgiving in the burbs of Detroit, and another painful, predictable dinner was beginning. I dreaded hearing the same accusations and "helpful hints" from my entire family on how to get a man. Their disdain for my lack of interest was palpable. Why did they care that I wasn't in a relationship? *Argh!*

I would try a new tactic this year. "Do any of you recall that we are in a new millennium? Many women put off getting married and having children until *after* establishing themselves in business. For the last time, would you please stop *hocking* me about my life choices?"

It appeared I was chastising six of my aunts and uncles, though mostly my mother needed to hear my pleas. She was relentless in her quest to see me settled. I was a lawyer—one who litigated. You would think my arguing abilities would be superior to hers after spending four years becoming a mechanical engineer, three more to become a lawyer, and another seven years practicing patent law. Unfortunately, Jewish guilt was a more formidable power in the universe.

"I'm not asking you to stop being a lawyer or do whatever you want, but can't you have a partner to help you along the way? Someone to lean on and share your triumphs? Someone other than your parents?" My mother, Marilyn, had a retort to every point I'd ever made. She was soul-crushing.

"Mom. Everyone. I appreciate you wanting to help me find a life partner—to settle down and be a traditional Jewish woman. It's not that I don't want a family. It's that I don't *need* one. I'll do it when the right person comes along or when I want to pursue that chapter of my life. What will it take to get all of you off my back?"

My appeals should have been sufficient. Instead, my mother took them as a challenge.

Saturday morning, my mom called to invite me to brunch on Sunday. I only agreed to go because I was a dutiful daughter and loved Mario's brunch, and she would pay for it. I had three court cases to prepare for today, so I was stuck in my office until they were finished.

My office was my sanctuary, and I surrounded myself in comfortable elegance. A contemporary dark maple desk with classic lines, a wool-blended artisan rug resembling waves of blues, yellows, and taupe by the floor-to-ceiling window, and a memory foam taupe leather couch with a recliner facing a serene forest of green. I could live in my office if I had a small kitchen and a full bathroom. There were many days when having a sink would have made things simpler for me. Instead, I used body wipes to clean up after a long day before going to dinner with clients. Those were the same clients who loved to take meetings here because they could kick off their shoes, walk around, and let their minds open to the creativity it took to make a patent that would stand the test of time and scrutiny.

I had built a solid career in a man's world that pushed gear-headed women like me around. Even the company I worked for had taken a few bites out of my self-esteem until I learned to push back and claim what was mine. My name would be going up on that wall someday, and I wasn't stopping to find a life partner until it was.

"Ms. Strauss," Emily, my assistant, buzzed my desk phone. "Spencer needs to speak with you."

"Send the call through." My voice went higher than usual when Spencer called. He was my ride-or-die guy the moment I graduated from college. Our friendship didn't start that way. On the contrary, when he moved in next door before sixth grade, he did everything he could to annoy me. It didn't matter if he was two years older or flung mud at me at a Fourth of July party at my parent's home, embarrassing me in front of my cousins. My observation of his shaggy brown hair curling at his neck was the first clue I liked boys. From the moment we met, he knew how to push my buttons and how to staunch my tears. Between the taunting and name-calling, he would look at me with hazel eyes, begging me to forgive him. Later in middle school, when no one was around, he would ask me if I needed help with my homework or if he should create a distraction to get my mother off my back. As far as I was concerned, I didn't need a life partner. Spence would always have my back, and that was enough.

"What's up, Red? Did you forget we had tickets to see Clem Striker at Comedy Control downtown?" I could hear his mocking tone, picking on me as usual.

Oh my God! "Spence! I totally forgot. It's my mother's fault. Can I meet you in forty-five minutes at the diner next to the theater?" I rushed to clean up my desk and turn off my desk light.

"Don't bother. I'm outside waiting. Get your ass down here in five minutes, or I'm leaving without you."

His snarky tone was severe yet playful. It took many years to figure out all of Spencer's tells. I figured this out in high school when he drove Nathan and me to school, and I took too long to get ready. He left me once, and I punched in the arm so hard it left a dark bruise. He didn't do that again.

"Speaking of asses, settle *yours*. I'll be there in four minutes." I slammed the phone down, making my desk lamp rattle. I punched the intercom button on my desk phone as I ripped off my jeans and Princeton sweatshirt.

"Emily!" Why did I bother with an intercom when she could hear me yelling through the door? "I'm leaving now. Lock up when you're finished." I looked in my office closet, which was stocked with changes of clothes for just such an emergency and selected a teal sweater dress and black boots. It finally occurred to me that it was Saturday, and why the hell was Emily even here today?

I hit the intercom again. "Don't you have a life? Why are you here?"

Emily barged in without knocking, and I swung around just as I slammed my closet door shut. She glared at me as I clipped a black corded necklace with a geode purple pendant around my neck, then flung a cashmere wrap around my shoulders.

"Knock much?" I snarled at her.

Emily had been with me for five years and knew everything about me, including my many moods. She had developed an arsenal of prepackaged replies that triggered me to chill out or engage in fighting mode. She was my unpaid therapist, personal assistant, sounding board, executive admin, and sister from another mother. I rewarded her handsomely every month with food, theater tickets, or her favorite coffee gift cards, and she bought herself expensive gifts on my credit card when I was incredibly obnoxious. *Touché!*

Unfazed, Emily dropped into a tweed cloth swivel chair and crossed her legs casually.

"I'm here because you requested that I come in for a few hours to read Mr. Townsend's latest patent proposal. I stayed longer because you dropped two more on my desk, frantically begging me to do the same for two other cases on your schedule for next week. And, because I'm the incredible assistant I am, I stayed without complaint. That, and my carpets are being cleaned at home, and I can't walk on them until later." She batted her eyelashes at me precociously. Emily always had an agenda. Good thing for me, they weren't secret, just self-serving.

I winked back at her, "I knew you had something up your sleeve. But next time, would you please remind me of my social calendar events? I totally forgot about this show with Spencer tonight." I pouted for effect.

She countered, one eyebrow arched. "Was it on the calendar?" *Hmm? Was it?* I took two seconds to look, and—what do you know—it wasn't. *Foiled again.*

I frowned, hanging my head in shame, my long, curly red locks falling over my face. "I suck. I'm sorry. I'll do better."

She laughed and stood up, heading for the door, "Sure you will. Go. I'll lock up. Have a good evening." She glided out of my office like the queen she was.

I am many things, but I would be nothing without her.

*tefillah—(pronounced TE-fee-lah) Hebrew word for prayer and reflection

*hocking—(pronounced HOCK-ing) urged, exhorted, pitched, asked excessively

*bupkis— (pronounced BUP-kis) absolutely nothing

Chapter 2

A night out with Spencer was similar to a bubble bath—sweet, light, and sexy. I have stuffed down my feelings for him for the past fifteen years to save my sanity. I might have had feelings for him in the past, but that ship has sailed. Hanging out, watching movies, attending comedy shows, and having a sounding board were more important to me than being someone else's version of who they wanted me to be. *Hello, Mother.*

When I opened the door to Spencer's car, I was gifted with the sweet, sexy smell of his cologne. The fragrance was enhanced by the woodsy smell of his new leather seats, and it drove me wild. Spencer was a car guy. It was always something new and exciting for him, while I enjoyed the broken-in leather seats of my five-year-old Audi A5. Sleek, fun, and always ready for a good time. Just like me.

"Hey, Spence. Sorry, I'm running late. So many deadlines. So little time. And, then there's. . ."

He frowned and cut me off. "Whatever, Becs. Works over. Let's have fun."

He waggled his eyebrows like he wanted more than a corned beef sandwich and a few laughs. I increasingly didn't know what that look meant, but for the sake of my heart, I again pushed down any idea of Spencer and me doing anything more than cruising in his new wheels. Since my mother accused his mom of cheating at Mahjong ten years ago, any chance of there being an "us" was down the tubes. Even a decade later, it couldn't be fixed if we thought there was a chance. Sadly, Yetta passed away two years ago, and hopes of a family reconciliation died, too.

I rolled my eyes, shaking off my work persona, and tried to do as he asked. Staying loose wasn't my forte. Being in the hear-and-now meant that I had to eradicate things like my meddling mother, or my annoying bosses, or the fact I haven't grocery shopped in two weeks. I'm even afraid of opening my refrigerator for fear of a mossy, green-eyed sludge lurking under the sour cream lid or in my applesauce.

"Fine. Tell me about your High Holidays. Did you repent? Ask those in your life for forgiveness? You didn't ask for mine." I huffed out, crossing my arms under my ample bosom.

He chuckled. "Why do I need to ask your forgiveness? I haven't wronged you in any way. If anything, it's you who needs to ask me for forgiveness. Last year, you promised me you'd have me over for dinner, and it's a good thing I wasn't holding my breath since it never happened." His pouty lower lip curled down, and I wanted to suck on it. *No, Becca! You don't. Or shouldn't.* "Yeah, about that. Uh, sorry. Give me a minute. Let me come up with a realistic excuse," I said smarmily.

He snorted. "Don't bother. I know why you didn't invite me over." The way his eyes roamed over my body told me exactly why he didn't push me on this. "You don't have to say it."

My brain seized, and my body shuddered, thinking about what could have happened had I invited him over. For some reason, visiting his apartment didn't conjure up the same feelings. It could have been I had the option to leave his home instead of forcing him out of mine. Or perhaps I had suppressed my desire for him so well that I didn't see his obvious overtures. Was it possible I truly turned off my desire for him? Even to me, that sounded ridiculous. If circumstances were different, we may have had a future together. Our decision—my decision—to keep things platonic was for the best, and I'd live with the consequences.

The rest of our evening lightened up, and we were back to our normal, buddy-buddy relationship. Dinner consisted of him sharing some new urban projects he was working on. The comedy show was off-the-charts hilarious and just what I needed to purge the stress of work and the impending doom of brunch with my mother tomorrow. She wasn't letting go this time. She wanted a ring on my finger in two weeks before her Annual Charity Hanukkah party. I would disappoint her—again. Before the end of this year, I was drawing a line in the sand about my personal life and my mother's involvement in it. It wasn't for lack of trying. I was one degree from being a bonafide bitch to her. I've fought the good fight for twenty years—since reaching adolescence— and now it was time to hold the line.

Spencer was watching me. I could feel his eyes checking me out through his periphery.

"What?" I said as if accusing him of something.

"Your mouth looks like a raisin, all scrunched up. Oh no! Have you been talking to your mom again? What does she want now?" He pulled up to my building and killed the engine.

I unbuckled my seatbelt and shifted to face him. We knew each other too well, and I sighed, knowing I had to come clean. "I may have agreed to something I don't want to do."

His exasperation was evident. "You may have? What did Marilyn make you agree to?"

I pulled my lips back, gritting my teeth. "That's the problem. I'm not entirely sure. My whole family at Thanksgiving chastised me about my dating life one minute, and the next, Marilyn announced, 'You have a deal.'"

Spencer's glare bore down on me. "Why don't you tell her to fuck off already? She's been running your life, your whole life. You're a grown woman, Becca. Enough is enough."

I sighed deeply. He was right and I was wrong. I think about this all the time, but something keeps me from cutting the cord. "Spence, I am. January first. It's an only-daughter thing. She has this idea of what a perfect daughter should be and who I should be spending my life with. It's not mine, I know. But I'm working on it."

My pathetic plea sounded like a child. I'm so strong and focused on everything in my life, but this. Next year, I would break free from Marilyn's hold on me. Something had to change.

I reached across the center console and lay my hand open to his hoping he would take it. He threaded his fingers through mine like we'd done forever. This time, though, he turned mine over and kissed the back of it. His soft, plump lips lingered over my hand, and when he placed another sweet kiss on the inside of my wrist, I felt my belly tighten. *This was new. What was happening?*

"I have a plan. Please give me a few weeks to see it through, and by New Year's, this nonsense will be over. I promise."

He didn't let go of my hand. The gleam in his eyes told me all I needed to know. Hope. Hope for us. I couldn't let myself think about a future with him, only that I would have the freedom to choose us if I wanted. I just needed to play this right.

I reluctantly pulled my hand free. "Thank you for being my friend, Spencer. Having you in my corner means so much to me. I hope I won't let you down again. Thank you for a fun night." I opened the car door and stepped onto the sidewalk. I turned and waved, only to see a combination of dread and disgust. I hated hurting his feelings. I had plenty of my own.

I went to bed that night feeling ridiculous for not being able to put my mother in her place and disgusted with myself that I let it go on for as long as I had. By two in the morning, I still couldn't sleep. I managed to put those negative feelings aside, only to keep thinking about how Spencer kissed my hand. The wonderment of what those lips could do to me kept me up another two hours. Dear God! I have to sleep. War was upon me, and I needed my rest. *Legal contracts. Grocery shopping. Ah, that did the trick. Sleep at last.*

Dressed like a debutant going to her coming out party, I arrived at Mario's, playing the role of a perfect daughter. That may be a stretch for my mother to believe, but for everyone else watching, I was impeccable. Dark oak-paneled walls, dim lighting, and brocade-armed chairs wreaked of old money and questionable business transactions. Goodness knows what deals were being cut in this place over the years, including the one being made today with my mother.

Beyond the incredibly light, flakey croissants, expensive champagne with a single strawberry sinking soundlessly to the bottom of the flute, and eggs benedict so savory and rich my mouth watered, I was bored. I knew what was coming and got up early to prepare my negotiating tactics for the stupid challenge I unconsciously instigated.

"Darling, let's get to the point of this challenge." *Wow!* Way to gracefully slide into the topic, Marilyn.

I dabbed the corners of my mouth with the ecru, linen napkin and placed it gently into my lap.

"All right. I know you want me in a relationship, and, while I don't promise to be in one at your annual charity Hanukkah party, I'll play your game and give it the old college try. Would that make you happy?"

The Cheshire Cat grin that crept up my mom's cheeks was sinister. My mother sensed me breaking down my walls and pounced on the opportunity to capture my capitulation.

"That's most sensible, Becca. We all need help sometimes. Several of my good friends have wonderfully available sons, nephews, or grandchildren I'd love for you to meet. You have no idea how hard it is to socialize with these women when my only daughter isn't married."

Oh, the horror of it all! "Sure. Whatever's needed *not* to make you a laughingstock with your friends," I blurted out shamelessly. I guzzled the rest of my champagne and raised the glass, signaling the waiter to bring me another.

I continued unaffected. "Who am I to meet with? Besides, I can't meet anyone until after December tenth. I have three court cases, and I can't be distracted. I can set aside a week for this charade. How about eight dates in eight days? Like speed dating, but not all at once."

Her eyes closed, and her lips pursed, considering my proposal. "Don't you think that's a bit fast? How can you get to know these men well enough to want to date them?"

She wasn't wrong, but I wouldn't drag this out. I'd made it a point to read my clients quickly and accurately, and if I can't do that in four hours on a forced date, then I have no business being in a courtroom.

I picked at the rest of the food on my plate, settling on a blueberry that I stabbed with my fork and slid into my mouth. The fruit's sweetness complemented my next offering. The trick with Marilyn was to make her think you're doing her bidding while skirting around her directive.

"Mother, I'm paid to vet people all day long. Four hours is plenty of time to know whether I'll spend another minute with them. What if I kiss them to be sure I'm not missing any of their charms? Would that satisfy you?" I folded my napkin on my plate and sat back.

My mother had been a student of negotiations since she met my dad. She set her sights on him and said nothing would deter her. It didn't hurt that he was an amiable guy, but he always reigned over her when she got out of control, and she let him. It was a delicate dance that I not only studied but admired.

She could play cards, lunch, shop, make household decisions, and volunteer anywhere she'd liked so long as she was home by six to have dinner as a family and spend evenings together playing games or holding hands on the sofa while we all watched a movie. Family came first—always.

Her stern look forced my attitude to shape up. She put up with my moods like a champ, ignoring my sass and occasional whining. But I knew it was time to relent when that look crossed her face.

"Don't get sassy with me, Becca. I'll not have my daughter being a *zoyne*," she mouthed quietly, looking around the restaurant. "If it takes a kiss to find your prince, then, by all means, pucker up, but don't degrade yourself on my account."

I snorted. "You sound so old-fashioned. A kiss today is like holding hands back in your day. So blasphemous. Don't worry, Mom. I won't hire myself out to any of these guys, but I won't say no to a little fun." She grimaced. "Eight dates. Eight Nights?" I waggled my eyebrows and leaned over the table.

Marilyn leaned in, too. "Deal. I'll pick five dates for you, and you can find three. Fair?"

My jaw dropped. "Fair? How in the world is that fair?" I waved my index finger back and forth.

"Of course, it's fair. I have five friends with five unwed young men in their lives. I can't choose four and leave one out. I'll never hear the end of it." She harrumphed and shook her head as if she had already had to choose.

Oy! "You're such a Jewish mother. Fine. Do your worst. Now I have to dig up three dudes worthy of wasting my time." I rolled my eyes back at her. I think I'll check out the mailroom guy. He had a nice tush.

Marilyn stood up, brushed a few crumbs from her ample bosom, and declared, "Great! I'm glad that's settled. I'll have five names for you by the end of the day."

She didn't wait for me to stand, walked away, and, dare I say, sashayed across the dining room, leaving me with the check.

zoyne –prostitute, whore, or harlot

Mahjong —Mahjong has been a cultural touchstone for Jewish American women since the 1920s, when it was a nationwide fad. During World War II, Jewish women found the game to be an inexpensive form of entertainment while their husbands were away at war. Mah-Jongg, a betting game that requires matching domino-like tiles into rummy-like patterns, has had many sets of rules that have been changed over the years and have become a point of contention from group to group.

Chapter 3

The real problem I'm having is not whether I can find a date for my mom's stupid party, but whether I should put myself out of my misery by hiring a date for the night. Or two or three. Or play her game and find my own three eligible bachelors with whom I could tolerate one evening.

I considered myself a reasonably pretty woman. My red hair had a habit of capturing the attention of every person I'd ever met, mainly because my curls were out of control. I wore it in a bun for business meetings and a ponytail for the rest, saving myself undue stares. When I knew no one was around, I freed my locks and let them swirl around my head, hiding myself beneath the curtain of red spirals. To make my attempts look promising, I'd have to literally let down my hair and apply copious amounts of hair Industries to coif my mane just so. I went to work tearing apart my modest closet, pushing aside expensive suits and blouses to the meager cocktail section tucked behind the dresses I grew out of ten years ago but couldn't part with. I know I'm not alone in this regard, but I had a mission, and a frumpy old sweater dress wasn't going to get the job done. I needed just the right outfits to make these guys fall at my feet.

My phone buzzed as I exited with two promising choices: red and green.

The phone flashed Spencer's name, and I flopped down on my duvet to answer it.

"Did you miss me?" I teased.

"Not hardly, Red. You left your scarf in my car. Are you home so I can drop it by?"

He's coming here? Spencer had only been at my apartment twice. Once when I made him help me move in seven years ago and another when I strained my back and couldn't get off the floor.

"Uh . . . yeah. Sure. I'm here." I wondered what my problem was.

"Cool. See you in ten minutes."

The phone clicked off, and my heart fluttered. Well, more like a swarm of bees buzzed in my belly. Either way, I was off my bed in search of thrown bras and errant undies lying about. Friends or not, a woman's lingerie was private business, even if he wasn't coming into my bedroom.

Three off-limits items were stashed in my laundry basket, and the rest of my clothes were shoved back into my closet just as I heard the intercom ring. I ran to buzz him in and looked in the hall mirror to make sure I wouldn't scare him, though, given our lifetime of friendship, he had seen me at my worst.

I opened the door and was shocked by what I saw.

"Hey, Becs. Sorry to barge in, but it's getting cold outside, and I thought you might need this." He handed over my turquoise cashmere wrap and stood in a sweaty T-shirt and fitted sweatpants, making it obvious he was cold. Nips aside, Spencer was an all-American guy. Mild-mannered with a raunchy sense of humor, usually wrapped in a casual but fitted suit coat and relaxed slacks. His hard-earned position as Southfield's Urban Development Director gave him the freedom to dress up or down as his business required, but I rarely got to see him like this. I may have gasped a little. *Yeah. I definitely did.* Spencer looked edible.

His jaw ticked as he looked at me, too. I wasn't sure why his eyebrows bunched together, but when I turned to let him in, I saw in the mirror my misstep—I was still in my pajama set, and apparently, it didn't cover much. *Doh!*

"Uh-uh, give me a minute," and I scampered down the hall in search of my robe. What the hell, Becca? You only looked at your hair, ding dong. *Geez.*

I yelled out of my bedroom, "Help yourself to coffee!" Forgetting the robe, I pulled on a dirty sweatsuit from my hamper and smoothly walked down the hall to the kitchen.

Trying not to belabor my faux pas, I asked. "Since when do you workout in my neck of the woods?"

He opened the fridge, removed the skim milk, poured two dollops into his steaming mug, and placed it back on the shelf.

He lifted a single eyebrow, "Do you think I'm so base, I wouldn't have friends in your uppity neighborhood?"

His challenge was adorable and teasing, and I was up to some verbal sparring. It was the next best thing I loved to do with Spencer. The other was whipping his ass playing board games. The smack-talk and glorious victories have warmed my heart for over a decade.

I hoisted myself onto the marble counter, which gave me a more direct line to his six-foot height.

"Now that you mention it, you tend to gravitate toward slumming it in your line of business." He almost spit out his coffee.

"That's low, even for you, Red. Don't forget about when you went out with Ralph Unger in high school, and he made you watch a movie on his flea-ridden couch, and you had to take a literal flea bath to get those bugs out of your hair. I thought you'd have a nervous breakdown when your mom suggested she shave your head." His burst of laughter lit a fire in me, and I punched him in the arm.

"You're so mean! He was nice, even though he looked like a *Snoopy* version of Pig-Pen. You'll also remember I grabbed my mom's scissors and buried them in the backyard when she went to the store for that special shampoo. No one was touching my hair!" My face was inches from his as I spat out my words.

He reached out and slid his fingers into my curls, giving them a slight tug, and those fluttery feelings zipped around my belly again. His voice dropped lower, and that sexy richness I loved bled through. "Yeah, I remember. You let me brush through your hair every day for a week, complaining your mom was too rough." He scrutinized each strand intertwined between his fingers and, when he looked up, our eyes locked, and the air in my lungs froze.

He cleared his throat and dropped my hair back where he found it. "What a pain in the ass that was. I don't know how I got roped into doing it but, lucky for you, I found the last gnats and saved your hair from extinction." He chuckled and stepped to the other side of the counter. *Thank God!*

I slid off the counter, poured myself a cup of coffee, and walked into the living room. My two-bedroom apartment was only a mile from work, and I walked most days when the weather allowed. I wasn't an accomplished decorator, so I hired a friend from college to help me find some feng shui in my hectic life. There weren't any pops of color, but a variety of tone-on-tone beige and white colors with a dark brown sculpted carpet under it all. It was a completely different mellow vibe than my office, and I liked the juxtaposition.

Spencer followed and stood by the window, looking somewhere off in the distance, cradling his cup in both hands. Something was happening in our relationship, and I couldn't quite put my finger on it. He was my best friend, and if I let my guard down it might destroy our friendship.

He opened his mouth to speak, and I cut him off.

"My mother is insisting I date. I agreed to her maniacal plan and will spend eight evenings searching for the perfect man for her annual charity Hanukkah party. I tried to get out of it, but I'll have to cancel our movie marathon next weekend. As a matter of fact, between work and my "manhunt," I won't be able to hang out for a few weeks. It was good that you came over today so I could spend a few minutes with you."

I sounded like a bad news masthead, "Girl Pushes Off Guy on Pathetic Pretenses." I've thought about Spencer in every conceivable way: friends with benefits, friends who see each other twice a year, and Spencer fucking the life out of me. But that's the one that scared me the most. We had a great relationship. We talked about almost everything, and he accepted my grossness and all.

When my dad took our picture at my high school graduation ceremony, Spencer was hugging me hard against his chest. He did it again at my party later that week, though he didn't let go that time and kissed me gently on the mouth. I swooned knowing I'd been pining for him for years and might never be able to kiss him again.

Then, at my college graduation, I got pushed from behind into his firm body, and he caught me by the hips, and I froze, feeling the contours of his big biceps under my small hands. Our eyes locked for the second time, and was mute, waiting for what he'd do next. The possibilities were endless, all ending with me and Spencer spending our lives together in marital bliss. If it weren't for my brother Nathan clapping him on the back telling him to get his hands off his sister, that reality could have been mine Except Spencer never did touch me like that again. Now, I only got short hugs, side hugs, and a tousling of hair. I was safely stashed into the "Friend Zone," and I fought to keep my mind from drifting anywhere else.

Spencer was snapping his fingers around my face, trying to get my attention when I regained focus. "What?" I answered, confused.

"I said, I'm sorry you have to cancel our game night, and that you have to play your mother's games again."

I looked sheepish when I came clean. "It was my game, not hers. I mean, I challenged her, and she accepted, then I countered, and she laid down the final rules."

I threw my head into my hands and leaned over my lap, feeling distraught.

"Rules? This is what your relationship with your mother has come down to?" He set his cup on the coffee table and sat in the chair beside the couch.

"Listen, Spence. I've been laying down rules with her since I went to college. Boundaries. Lots and lots of boundaries. It's how I've managed to have a relationship with her at all. She meddles in every aspect of my life, and it's claustrophobic."

He rubbed his forehead. "I had no idea she was ruining your life."

"Not ruining, just creating obstacles I don't want to contend with—like dating. All I want to do is make partner and get my name on the firm's wall. I'll have time for everything else she wants in a few years."

"I see. So, if I'm hearing you correctly, you date a bunch of guys, find one acceptable enough for the party, and then dump him later?"

Why did that sound so shallow coming out of his mouth? I wouldn't play mind games with these guys and make promises for a lifetime. I would have some fun and maybe a thrill and move on. Guys have been doing that to women for an eternity.

"Don't make me the villain," I spat. "It's a means to an end, and I'm not promising anything to anyone—except my mother.

Tell me you've never had a pity date?" I pulled up my knees and wrapped my arms around my legs, making myself as small as I felt.

He stood up and walked to the front door. "Becs, do what you gotta do. Just remember you're dealing with people's feelings."

I followed behind him and opened the door. I reached for a hug, and he gave me a side version of one. *So unsatisfying.*

"I will," I pouted. "Miss me?"

"Every fucking minute," he mumbled.

What did he say?

Chapter 4

I t took a little finagling, but I found a couple of guys' numbers I had collected over the years hiding in on my phones contact list. Given my line of business, my list looked more like sales mining software—tons of seemingly useless data saved for just the right moment. Using a pivot table, I logged my data points, and voila! Three options of single men to fulfill my promise.

Alan, Larry, and Joshua. I wish I could visualize any one of these guys. The information I logged didn't include anything about their personalities, so I looked to social media to bring me up to speed.

Ah, yes, Alan. One of my patent clients had a buddy who joined us for a drink after we finalized his paperwork for a high-frequency thermal conductor that could detect dinosaur bones. I might have my degree in mechanical engineering, but I didn't understand the intricacies of this invention, only that it would be documented correctly.

My client, Stephan Warrington of Warrington Industries, was the president of a company specializing in radio frequency tools. Alan was the science nerd who learned how to apply it to archeological digs. He wasn't like most nerdy people I had worked with, both men and women alike. Alan's dirty blond hair was cropped short around his head with a crop of curls that fell rakishly over his forehead. The way he quirked his mouth when he smiled was sexy, and his round, tortoise-patterned glasses were surprisingly stylish. You could say he was an enigma wrapped in an enigma.

"Becca, meet my friend and co-conspirator in my latest patent, Alan Morris. What he lacks in social awareness, he more than makes up for in intellect." Stephan went on to praise Alan while he sat there awkwardly, opening and closing his mouth like a fish out of water.

I extended my hand professionally, "Hi, Alan. It's a pleasure to meet you. I'm curious, how did you pair radio frequency with archeology?" It has always fascinated me to learn how people found their inspiration in the world to create something special and unique. Alan was an enigma. He pulled his hand from his pocket to shake mine, staring at me like another of his lost dinosaur friends. His stilted, painful response stuttered out of his mouth. Every hesitation was anguished as if he were just learning how to speak English. His only redeeming feature was his rugged, strong hands.

"Uh, I, uh, could show you more at the, um, Natural History Museum sometime." *Wait a second.* Once he found his words, they were rich and resonated in my chest. There were so many layers to Alan that perhaps spending more time with him would be interesting. In my soon-to-be spreadsheet, I would enter sexy voice, rugged hands, and painfully shy next to Alan's name.

It wasn't a question or an invitation but a pathetic statement, presumably hoping I would jump at the chance to learn more about his work.

"That's kind of you to offer. Let me see what my schedule looks like and get back to you. Okay?" I pasted on a sincere expression and feigned exhaustion. Stephan slid a napkin across the table and pulled a pen from inside his jacket pocket, implying that Alan should write down his phone number. I'd file that away in case I needed to cross-reference his designs to any others that came my way, but there was no way I would sit through a painful date just to be nice. That was until now.

After brunch with Marilyn, I blocked out eight days during Hanukkah to complete this mission. If I could immediately get my three picks on my calendar, I could book the other five around them—no time like the present. I picked up my cell phone and held my breath.

Two rings later, Alan answered in a flustered speech pattern, so I focused more on his low, resonant voice. My breath caught in my chest, not expecting the richness in his tone.

"Hello, Alan," I stuttered out, realizing it was him and not a voicemail message. *I sucked at this small talk crap.* "I, uh, just came across your number and remembered you offering to take me on a tour of the Natural History Museum. Is the offer still good?"

You could grow a beard waiting for his reply. What did I expect after springing this call on him out of nowhere? He probably didn't even remember who I was.

"Becca? Wow, sorry. I wasn't expecting a call from you—ever. How long has it been?"

Shit! How long had it been? Time to stall.

"Yeah, right? Life has been zipping by at lightning speed. I'm sorry about not following up all those months ago, but if you're up to it, we could catch up next week?"

More painful moments ensued. "Actually, I think it's been more like two years than a few months ago."

Why was he fixating on how long it's been? Couldn't he just answer the damn question?

"Really? Geez! I suppose it has been that long. How have you been? Can I buy you a coffee and catch up?" Begging wasn't my style, but this guy wasn't picking up what I was putting down.

"I guess that would be okay. I don't have much time now. I have a paper due at the end of the year, and I need to stay focused." The more I listened only to the sound of his voice instead of the words, the more attractive he became. As low as Barry White's but subtle and smooth like Teddy Swims singing "Losing Control," I noticed the slightest tinge of a Southern accent I didn't recall from before. It was a weird juxtaposition that kept me focused on my mission.

"Terrific. How about we meet at the coffee shop across from the museum next Wednesday at about eleven thirty?" Day dates were always safe, and I didn't promise my mother I'd have dinner with these guys.

"Sorry, Becca. I don't drink coffee and can't leave work during the day." Why the hell didn't he say that earlier? He countered, "Would you be open to an early dinner instead? Say six o'clock at Lester's on Seventh Avenue? I love their burgers." *Finally! A question. Good man, Alan. I knew you could do it.*

"Perfect. I love a good burger, too. You have my number if you need to move our date, but I look forward to learning more about you." I used my sweetest voice and let him hang up first. I chastised myself because he wasn't a smooth operator. Maybe he likes to be led? I'm a good leader.

There wasn't time to ponder the enigma that was Alan, given my short time to turn this carousel of guys around. Onward and upward. Two more dates to secure.

It didn't take long to remember Larry. My friend Annie insisted she bring a "seriously wild guy," her words, not mine, to a cocktail party I threw last spring.

"You won't believe the things this guy likes to do." Annie was a super-fun friend, full of exciting stories about all the guys she dated. She divulged all the gory details delivered extremely fast with animated hands and facial movements. It took practice listening to her, but I was never disappointed. Some of the places she went and the things she did with these guys were pretty cool, too. Last month, her latest, Anak, took her to Niagara Falls for the weekend. I sighed while she told me about the *Maid of the Mist*, wine tasting, and everything they did right up to and through their sexual encounters. *T.M.I., Annie!!*

To be so carefree and animated was something I wasn't. My *modus operandi* was intense conversation, dry humor, quick wit, and getting to the point. I didn't have time for handholding and cajoling. That's probably why my mechanical buddy needed weekly battery changes.

It was time to call Annie and remind me about Larry's "special" talents.

"Hey, girlfriend! Long time no hear. Just kidding. What's up?" Annie was adorable and seriously easy to like. "I know you need something because we just had drinks a few weeks ago, and you're always telling me you're too busy just to hang out." *Guilty.*

There's no sense beating around the bush. "I hate that you know me so well, but I need your help. Remember that guy you brought to my party this past spring? You know, Larry Swisher?"

I tapped my red polished fingernail on my desk blotter and waited for her to peel back the layers of her time when she was with him.

"Weird kink, Larry? Capes, Larry? What do you want with him? I thought he creeped you out?"

So many questions, so little time.

"Yes, that Larry. I need to get my mom off my back again and thought he might fit the bill. There isn't a perfect man in my life, so why not?" *Actually, there was, but he was off-limits.*

Squeals of Annie's laughter grated on me as I kept my composure. Why did everyone think this mission was so funny?

It's a colossal waste of time and energy. "Ha. Ha. Marilyn is at it again, so help a friend out and sell me on Larry's better qualities."

"Hmm. Well, after you screw him while he wears a salon cape while sitting in his personal salon chair, you could admire his superb tight ass or sexy smile but steer clear of his fingernails. I'm not sure what's going on there." Her voice went serious at that last bit, and I considered finding an anonymous guy off the street instead.

"I'm not even going to ask what you mean about his nails. So long as he's not going to kill me, shackle me to a bed, or film me sucking his dick, I think we're good. Thanks, Annie."

She choked, hearing my bottom line. "Girl! You haven't lived until you've done all those things!"

"Stop! Do not tell me anything more. I only need to have one date with the guy, and I don't want images of you doing anything swimming through my mind."

We laughed and promised to stay in touch. I hung up, worried that this challenge would be more difficult than I wanted to admit. Salon chairs and capes were weird but, given some of the stuff Annie had confided in me, this was pastoral.

It was time to call Larry and, *damn it*, Annie's images began swirling around my head.

There wasn't an answer, and leaving a message sounded wrong, but I needed to give him a heads-up about why I was calling, so I left one anyway.

"Hi, Larry. You may not remember me, though you were at a party I threw last spring. It's Becca Strauss. Annie's friend? I was looking through some pictures and saw your face and thought I'd give you a call. What do you think about getting a drink next week and catching up? Here's my number, and I hope to hear from you soon."

I cheerfully left the message, trying not to sound desperate. I left my number and immediately hung up the phone. Maybe I should write out a list of questions for each date so we wouldn't have uncomfortable silences. Most guys I go out with are in my field, so we chat about professional stuff. Personal conversations were way more complicated.

Are you really into cape-kink?

Do you have a big dick?

Do you know how to use it?

Are you just a pretty face, or is there anything worthwhile in that head of yours?

Do you mind pretending to be into me for a party my mom's throwing?

I know. I'm shallow. I have at least twenty points of rationale for being this way, but none of them are the true me. The thing I hated most about myself was that I didn't make time to explore who I wanted to be. A thorough analysis of what made me tick. My turns on, desires, and fantasies. I could state clearly, though, who I didn't want to be, or with, or where. Turning off my analytical brain to be settled in a moment was hard. Previous visits to a therapist made it very clear that I should establish activities that are counterintuitive to my work to create balance. Yoga, for example. *Yeah, no. Not going to happen.*

The best option for relaxation was to jump in my car and drive. When was the last time I did that? I should pick a weekend, turn off my phone, crank up the tunes, and set off for an indeterminate locale. I thumbed through my calendar, annoyed that I didn't have a clear weekend until New Year's Eve. This year, it was on a Wednesday, and four days of zero contact with the world sounded heavenly.

As I blocked off those days in my business calendar, I was reminded of next week's Date-A-Palousa and picked up the phone to make one last call, Joshua. Finally, I met a guy on my very own at the organic grocer a block from my apartment. He was squeezing melons, and my nipples got hard. He had strong, bronzed hands with long, strong fingers. His powerful-looking forearms, dusted with light brown hair, were such a turn-on. Broad shoulders and a slim waist indicated he took good care of his body, and I found myself salivating only steps away from him.

"I can never tell when a melon is ripe," he muttered.

And for the first time in my life, I blurted out, "You could have fooled me." I smacked my hand over my mouth and turned to walk away.

"Well, not these melons, anyway." His laugh was resonant, and I froze. "Hey, seriously, could you help me out?"

This had to be the biggest pick-up line in a grocery store of all time. I could never understand why a rich, low voice from a man was so sensual. My abdomen clenched, and the air in my lungs got stuck, but I knew there was chemistry every time it happened.

Unfortunately, for me, this happened more often at work than anywhere else, prohibiting me from acting on it.

I stepped next to him, perusing the produce, and selected a tan-colored melon.

"My nanny showed me when I was a teenager that if you press the bottom of the melon, the opposite of the stem side, that if it was soft, it was ripe enough to eat. If not, and it's somewhat green, pass on it."

His stare made me blush and I felt like a complete nerd. I suppose I *was* in some ways, though I tried to hide it under stylish, expensive clothes.

He took the fruit I was holding, grazing my fingers as he clutched it, and followed my instructions and chuckled. "That's incredible. Why didn't anyone tell me this before? You're a clever woman." His eyes dropped to my plain, yet expensive long-sleeved cotton shirt, which provided a clear outline of my slightly overflowing bosom.

"I'm Joshua. I work down the street. Would you have time for a lemongrass shake?"

Lemongrass shake? Do people drink that stuff on purpose? "Sure," I choked out, clearing my voice to hide my disgust.

We settled on a date, but work kept getting in the way and my reluctance to drink grass didn't help the situation. In the end, we both let it go.

This time, I dialed his number and looked at my chipping nail polish. I needed to remember to make an appointment for a manicure when I finished this call. Three rings went by, and I was aiming for the red phone icon on my screen when he picked up.

"Hey. Thanks for calling. Who is this?" His long, drawn-out vowels reminded me of a California surfing dude. *And why didn't he have my number stored in his phone?*

I cleared my throat. "Joshua. It's Becca. Remember me from the grocery store?" I gave him a minute to jog his memory.

"Oh, yeah. Hey, Becca. What's up?" Joshua was my complete opposite: chill, casual, and with no cares in the world.

I pursed my lips, wondering how to lock this date down. "Well, last we talked, you had invited me out for a drink, and I've been thirsty lately. . ."

He interrupted, "Me too." *Was thirsty code for—sex?*

"What I meant to say is, how about having dinner next week? You promised me a lemongrass shake." *Ack. Why was I encouraging that?*

He chuckled. "Last time I offered that shake you gagged a littlee. Maybe something else instead?"

I guess I was too transparent. I hummed in response. "Yeah, but I'm not opposed to vegan. Pick a spot, and I'll meet you there. Say, Tuesday at seven?"

Joshua agreed, and I put a checkmark on my agenda for today. My dates were booked, and I emailed my mother in victory. I felt I could get through these dates knowing enough about them not to get emotionally involved but physically attracted enough to give them a proper kiss.

Chapter 5

After successfully securing Mr. Townsend's patent on his new dog collar invention on Monday, I quickly dashed from the courtroom to have lunch with our firm's managing partner, Gary Rutherford. Winning this last case brings my wins to fifty over the past three years, and that was the magic number to be considered for partner status.

Shivers ran up my spine as I hailed a cab across town. I inspected my manicure, hoping it was still fresh enough for this meeting. Mr. Rutherford was a stickler for perfection in all aspects of our professional lives. I had kissed so much ass over the past seven years, and finally, I could step into a senior partner role and make a few people kiss mine. That sounds hypocritical, but law firms are notorious for imposing hierarchy onto their employees whenever possible, and my not doing the same wouldn't change that. At the beginning of my career, I decided to treat everyone fairly and not overly dictate to my underlings. I wasn't a monster, and this new position wouldn't make me one, either.

Five minutes before our designated time, I arrived, and the *maître de* escorted me to our table, where Mr. Rutherford was on his phone. Disturbing a managing partner's call was cause for firing, so I quietly sat, leaning my briefcase and purse alongside my chair to avoid any servers.

I looked through the menu, knowing that, before I got there, I would be too hyped to eat anything. Several more minutes passed before Mr. Rutherford smiled, setting his phone at the corner of the table.

"Sorry, Becca. The missus had an urgent matter to share with me, and I needed to let her vent it out. You understand, right?"

What? Because I'm a woman, I would understand? Or that when people are ranting, it's best to let them get it out of their system before aiming for a solution? I took the high road and went with the latter.

"Sure I do. Sometimes, you just have to let people express what is on their minds before trying to help them." I nodded as I spoke, hoping he would appreciate my level-headedness.

"Right." His eyebrows went sky-high as he held his menu—pompous asshole.

The server came by and took our orders. I pressed my hand on my quaking knee, bouncing under the table, willing myself to keep my emotions in balance. *I could use a drink.* Unfortunately, this wouldn't be a drinking lunch with the boss. This lunch would change my career trajectory.

"Becca, I want to congratulate you on winning another case and securing your seventeenth client since you have been with the firm. Several partners have commented on your dedication and willingness to spearhead difficult situations with terrific outcomes." Mr. Rutherford's countenance was genuine, but I could hear a "but" in his monologue.

"Thank you, sir. I truly believe in our firm's mission and look forward to taking on a leadership role soon." *Okay. That was gratuitous but well deserved.*

"Precisely." He swallowed hard. "Unfortunately, that won't be happening anytime soon. The partners have agreed that ten is the maximum number of partners we should have. You'd be number eleven. So, you see, until a partner steps down, leaves, or dies, you won't have the opportunity to move up to senior partner.

I must have blacked out. Did he say I would *never* make partner? That couldn't be. Two other men in my division had also been talking about moving up. I had more credentials, wins, and clients, and seniority than they had. This was horrible . . .

"Becca? Ms. Strauss? Are you all right?" Through a wave of nausea, I saw him hail a server. "Please, help her to the ladies' room. She's not feeling well."

An older woman walked me across the restaurant as I clutched my stomach. This couldn't be happening. I've sacrificed so much for this company. Rutherford needed to know exactly how much. If he knew, he might petition for a change in the bylaws.

The bylaws. I needed a copy of the bylaws immediately. I grabbed the friendly server by the arm, "Please, would you get my briefcase and purse from my table?" She nodded quickly and exited the bathroom. I dropped onto a suede, taupe settee and leaned against the crepe, floral wallpaper to wait for my things.

When she returned, I pressed a ten-dollar bill into her hand. "Thank you so much."

She bobbed her head and left immediately. I stuffed my hand into the abyss of my purse and found my phone. I shot off a text to Rutherford, telling him I was too sick to return to the table and would catch up with him in his office later. I needed Emily more than ever and steadied my voice as I punched the numbers to her desk phone.

"Emily," I heaved out. *So much for being steady.* "I need your immediate help—discreetly. Please locate the firm's bylaws and print me a copy. I have some light reading to do tonight."

"Light reading, you say? Should I order a couple of bottles of wine sent to your office? Better yet, your apartment?" She giggled, thinking this was funny.

I kept my shit together and played along. "You get me. Apartment, please. Also, order ho fun and eggrolls for two from Wing's. Seven o'clock. You're the best."

"You got it, boss. Will you be coming back soon?"

I hated stupid questions. Of course, I was coming back! How the hell else would I get my hard copy? I put my sarcasm aside and politely responded with, "Four o'clock. I have a few errands to make. I also need my other two case files ready for review when I return. I'm in court again on Thursday."

She signed off, promising to do my bidding. I sat in the restaurant bathroom way longer than was necessary, debating whether to call anyone for comfort. I never had before, except for Spencer. He grounded me, and I knew he'd have the perfect words for my predicament. As for my mother, she'd go on a tirade of "I told you so's" and "This is why you need more than your career." Sadly, her point was becoming clearer by the day. *I hated that!*

My friends knew little of what was going on in my professional or personal life—nothing about the three—no eight—guys I was to date. The only person who would understand my sob story was my brother, Nathan. Two women walked into the bathroom, giving me a pathetic look. I took the hint and pulled myself together.

I took the opportunity to give these chicks some side-eye myself and stuck out my tits, "Life is tough," I declared unapologetically.

The buxom blonde replied, "You ain't kidding, sweetheart." We smiled at each other, and I left with my head held high.

My call to Nathan went to voicemail. I didn't want to alarm him. I crafted a melancholy message telling him to call after work.

I know you're busy, but I have some important news to share. Call me tonight if you can. It's been a while since we spoke. Let's catch up.

I hailed another cab to the law library at Weyland College to research precedence. I was unsure, but I thought Rutherford, Timmins, and Grovner once had fifteen partners. Not all were listed on the wall, as there was only room for the top six founders, but, nonetheless, partners. This girl was no wallflower. After I went on and on about not having a personal life before I became a partner, this was best described as a *shanda*.

I wasn't taking this lying down. After pulling at straws in the library, I did what any good Jew would do—eat! I was starving. Forbidden carbs were consumed a la bagel and schmeer in the park across from my office. Tossing crumbs to chipmunks rolling over each other, grasping at what they wanted to claim, was more my speed of processing the fall of my future trajectory. These squirrels were an exact replica of my professional life, and the irony left me feeling pathetic.

I was back in my building, hoping none of the partners saw me making my Walk-of Shame. I rode the elevator to the twentieth floor as my bagel turned in the pit of my stomach, causing me to want to heave. My boss and I needed to finish our conversation, even if I didn't have all my ducks in a row. I would play the role of obedient employee for now, but, for the love of God, not a minute longer than required.

Lisa, Mr. Rutherford's executive assistant, greeted me and buzzed me back to the executive suites. Gary stood behind his desk, feigning concern, and strode to console me.

"Becca, are you feeling better? I was so concerned when you texted me." *Sure, you were.*

"Thank you for your concern. I can't imagine what got into me. Not to worry, though, I'm much better. I'm ready to finish our conversation." I pressed my hands down my skirt and sat at the end of the chair directly across from his desk, pasting the same calm countenance I used when a client was being outrageous.

"Well, since we couldn't make you partner at this time, I suggested to the group that we give you a sizeable raise and an increased percentage of your revenue for your exemplary service and dedication." His smile assured me that he was buying this shit hook, line, and sinker. If he thought placating me would make this all go away, he was mistaken. Being a lawyer has its advantages when creating strategies that would prevail. I just needed some time to gather the facts and build a solid case first, so I conceded.

"I have to say, Gary," I patronized, "This announcement is quite a blow to me. There wasn't any written or verbal announcement about where the firm stood on this matter, and some of my colleagues will be taken aback when they hear about this news." *Because every fucking junior partner would know before the end of the day.*

His face went white. *Not the pushover you thought I was now, Gary?* Were the partner's hoping I wouldn't notice when they stuck another asshole guy in the position *I* worked so hard for?

"Ms. Strauss, please understand. It's nothing personal. Surely the significant pay increase will offset your hurt feelings?" *Aahhh!!*

I wish I had a pillow to scream in. A payoff? What the fuck! Every time this jerk opened his mouth, he stuck his foot in further. This would be the most straightforward discrimination suit in the world. My fists bunched in my lap, and my jaw hurt from locking my mouth shut.

I was out of here. I stood abruptly and marched over to the door, turning once my hand grasped the nob." Mr. Rutherford, I know you and the partners think you're making the right decision about me, but I couldn't disagree more. You'll excuse me. I have work to do."

It was four o'clock, and my documents were ready to be picked up. The elevator pinged as it hit the sixth floor. I stalked my way into my office, motioning for Emily to join me. She scurried around her desk, trying to keep up.

"Shut the door, please." Emily didn't need to be barked at, so I reeled myself in. "Please, take a seat and relax."

"What the hell is going on with you? First, you win a case, then have lunch with the Big Man, and then call me with a covert mission. Explain yourself, woman."

Her exasperation was well-earned, and I fully intended to disclose everything that happened today—just not everything. As dedicated as Emily had been for the past several years, I didn't want her to have to lie on my behalf should she be questioned about my future plans. *Whatever they were.*

"I did win the Townsend case—with your help, of course." She preened, tipping her head my way. "Lunch, however, was abysmal. Rutherford wants me to review the bylaws to be sure everything in there is relevant to how we do business today. It's been ten years since the board reviewed them, and he stuck with me on his pet project. Did you have any trouble getting the documentation?"

"Easy-peasy, boss woman."

"Did you check the date so you had the most current copy?"

"Sure did. Though it was dated three months ago, not ten years ago." Her face blanched, putting everything together. *Bingo!*

"No, no, no, Becca. What did they do?" Emily jumped up and paced. God love her. She was as much upset as I was.

"Screwed me out of my partnership, it appears."

"This is horrible!" Her eyes teared up, and I let her throw herself onto me in a body hug.

"I need you to find a copy of the previous version as soon as possible so I can compare the changes. Can you do that for me in the next thirty minutes?"

"Consider it done."

Emily bolted from my office and I heard the elevator ding. She was a force in her own right, and I needed to let her do her job before I could do mine. I closed my door and fell onto my comfy couch to review my messages.

From Nathan: *Hey, Sis. Got your message. I'll call you about eight. You better pick up. Love ya!*

From Marilyn: *Darling, you haven't responded to my email. Those gentlemen we discussed will call you tonight to schedule your dates. Please be affable and take their calls. Everything you need to know about them is in my email. Love to you, dear.*

From Spencer: *I know you don't have time for me, but my spidey senses tell me you're having a bad day. That, and Emily just texted me. Call me later.*

Oy! Not only do I have a meddling mother, but my assistant is getting in on the game, too.

shanda —scandal, embarrassment, or something extremely shameful

Chapter 6
Trigger Warning

Man plans—God laughs. My life was living proof of this adage. My dreams of making partner by thirty-five are over. The idea of seeing my name on the wall when I entered the building and exited my floor—or at least on the letterhead—kept me going from day to day. Without that motivation, what the hell am I doing here? The firm certainly didn't give a shit. It was time to shift gears.

I entered my apartment, threw my stuffed briefcase on the floor, and kicked off my shoes into the pile I kept there. My coat fell off my shoulders in the vestibule. Not having the energy to pick it up, I left it there. *Housekeeping standards be damned.* This would be the last time in my life I could be a slob without anyone judging me—unless I marry a worse slob. Moments later, the buzzer from my front door buzzed, firing off my desire to eat and drink myself into a coma.

Fortified with Chinese food, wine, and Milano cookies, my exceptional assistant was thoughtful enough to order for me; I directed my attention to my relationship status. Eight guys in eight crazy nights was a bit of a stretch. I needed a mechanism to quantify them. This was as much of a science project as a social circus, and I was finally in the right mindset to get the job done. I was done fighting my mother. I would embrace this game we designed, and—who knows—maybe I will find my Mr. Right. My first order of business was to create a detailed spreadsheet of these eight guys. Every facet of their looks, mannerisms, financial position, ambitions, and sexual prowess would be cataloged. Every minute piece of data would decide who I would invest my time and effort into by the time I was finished. Cultures all over the world did similar exercises to make matches without either person knowing who they would marry, and their unions produced children and friendships for a lifetime. Love was overrated.

I entered everything I knew about Alan, Larry, and Joshua, then opened my mother's email containing the other five men I was to meet. An hour later, my database grew to include Evan, the financial analyst; Ravi, the telemarketer; David, the licensed practical nurse; Max, the travel influencer; and Joseph, the OB-GYN *(this looked fun)*. Vocation alone, none of these guys, shy of Joseph, were the kind of guys I would voluntarily search out, but I would keep my mind open.

I wasn't a snob like my mother, though more a hoarder of my time. Social engagements had to have some value for me to attend and, therefore, were limited. The last time I dolled myself up was for a charity event at the Ritz-Carlton downtown. I was a sucker for a puppy or kitten, and our firm was a major sponsor of this year's Bark Ball. The name was cute, and so were the furbabies that were set up in play areas. Compassionate, affluent future owners could adopt a sweet animal on the spot, and the adoption agency would arrange for delivery at a mutually agreed upon day and time. Like window shopping, I had adopted twenty of those cuties but left with none. It wasn't fair to have an animal when you were only home to shower, sleep, and do your laundry.

By nine o'clock, I had drunk half a bottle of wine, called five men out of the blue—I didn't have time to wait for them to contact me—and peeled off my skirt and pantyhose. My silk blouse hung just below my torso, and my fiery red curls were set free. I had just unsnapped my bra when my door buzzer sounded.

Great! Right after I got comfortable. I padded over to the peephole, hoping it was my brother, Nathan, so that we could catch up. *Wait, wasn't Nathan going to call me at eight?* Instead, my heart sped up when I saw Spencer pacing outside my door. I slid the chain back silently and cracked open the door.

I cleared my fuzzy head, hoping I didn't sound weird. "Hey, Spence. Twice in a week; I hope everything is okay?" *May I remind you that Spencer doesn't just stop by?*

He stopped pacing and shoved his hands in his pockets, staring at me. "You, uh, didn't return my call. You said you were doing all this dating, and I wanted to be sure no one had tied you up and put you in a closet."

SPENCER

Tied up in a closet? Smooth, Spencer. However, having Becca tied up in my bed would have been preferable.

She stood behind her door protectively, her hair cascading down her arm. Even from this distance, I could see her freckles clearly, and they set evenly over the creamy white skin of her nose. She was my Rapunzel with red, curly hair. *Focus man!*

"You're hysterical, Spence. No bondage or gags tonight, though I couldn't promise that on any other night." *Was she drunk?*

I stepped closer, my head inches from hers on the other side of the door. "Is that a challenge, Becs?"

She hummed, her head tilting to the side, "Maybe."

Fuck, yeah! Finally.

"Can I come in?" my throat croaked out. I felt like a teenager trying to sneak into a girl's bedroom.

Come to think of it, I've already climbed through Becca's window once. She was sleeping, of course, and twelve. I wanted to get to Nathan's room to sleep over without waking her parents up, and hers was the only other bedroom on the main floor. I walked across the room, stopping abruptly when I saw a picture of the two of us swimming earlier that summer. I had both of my arms locked around her belly, and I had picked her up when she tried to run away. Her head fell back onto my shoulder and that's when her dad snapped the photo. What it didn't capture was me whispering in her ear that one day I would kiss her. I don't know if she understood what that meant, but I followed through on that promise.

She hummed again, smiling. "Sure."

She stepped back and let me walk through as she stood behind the door, hiding herself until it closed.

Holy shit! The woman was practically naked.

I scrubbed my chin quickly, thinking through my options and the repercussions of picking the wrong one. Settling on something neutral, I kept walking to the kitchen and stood on the opposite side of the counter. That was a safe place.

"You do know you're missing your pants, right?" She looked down at herself and her hair fell over her ample tits. Her tongue darted out, and she licked her lips slowly and laughed.

"Oops! You caught me. I was moments from going to bed after I finished my wine." Her other hand lifted an almost full glass of the burgundy liquid.

Steering clear of my dirty thoughts, I redirected the conversation to why I was there.

"Tough day? By the looks of how much you've had to drink, my intuition was correct." I reached behind me to pull down another goblet off the rack, and poured the rest of the bottle into it, waiting for her explanation.

She walked across the room and sat down on the couch, not so ladylike, allowing me a clear view of her pink lace panties and big tits pressing through the silky fabric, revealing her red puckered buds. I needed to move—and fast. I power-walked over to the buttery, soft, contemporary lounge chair, angling myself so I saw her profile and not her finest assets.

"Spill it, Red." I sat back, watching her eyebrows scrunch up. Her lips pressed together, holding her breath.

Her response startled me. "AARGH! I'm not going to make partner—*EVER!* Do those misogynistic bastards think they can patronize me with more money? If I wanted more money, I'd find more lucrative clients. I wanted the wall, and now it's never going to happen."

Becca burst into tears, obliging me to bolt from my seat to console her. Setting both our glasses on the glass coffee table, I planted myself next to her with my arm slung around her shoulders tightly. She didn't hesitate to lean into me, and, like a fool, I let her.

"Oh, Becs. I'm so sorry." I reached over and stroked her arm. "You worked your ass off for those jerks. No wonder you're tanked."

We sat like that for several minutes until she placed her small hand in the middle of my chest. That sensation, that one movement, made my heart swell, along with my dick. Being this close to her allowed me to smell the last remnants of coconut shampoo in her long locks. I didn't often get the chance to see her hair down, and my mind went to places it shouldn't.

She fell backward into the cushions with a thump and spun her legs over my thighs, giving me another provocative view of her lace panties and the hidden treasure behind them. Only in my dreams had I dared to think of what was hidden between her thighs. Not a stray hair peaked out of the sides of her hipsters, making my chest ache to put my mouth on her. I forced a look back up to her face, her arm crossed over it, giving me plenty of time to torture myself. Scanning her sultry torso from the curve of a single luscious tit that worked its way out of her blouse, down to her firm belly, to the seductive spot where flesh met lace, sitting over her mound. I wasn't a saint. I was a goddamned man with an erection the size of a horse at this moment, and, thankfully, it didn't attract her attention. *I should stand up and leave. I should pull her blouse back into place and put a fucking blanket over her.* She was drunk, and letting my hands wander another inch would be ungentlemanly. But, no. I was a glutton for punishment, and, since my faith didn't support the idea of hell, I'd have to suffer with unimaginable guilt for the rest of my life.

"Becca. Are you okay? Do you need anything?" *How drunk was she?* She mumbled something. Was it "Touch me," or "Trust me?" I went with the former and gently traced my forefinger down the middle of her abdomen, stopping at the lace of her panties. I redirected my path to run my finger gently over to one hipbone and lazily pulled it across her body to the other, making an infinity sign on her delicate skin. She was breathtaking.

"Spence," she sighed, "That feels so good. Why do you always make me feel so good?" *Did I?*

She lifted her other hand, laying it over mine and pushing it lower. *Fuck me!* She was drunk. Upset and off-kilter. I couldn't take advantage of her. I just couldn't.

"Spence," she moaned, stopping my hand over her mound. I could feel the heat of her pussy permeating through the lace. I was losing my resolve. I had to make a decision. When her voice became husky, and begged, "Make me feel good, Spence," all bets were off.

With all my heart, I wanted to make her feel good. My head was spinning with hope, yet our reality didn't include me fingering her on her couch, drunk. Drunk permission or not, I took a small token of her offering.

I pushed the sexy fabric back enough to gasp at the tiny landing strip of fine, light-red hair resting above the hood of her clit. My moan was painful as my dick swelled in my jeans. *Old ladies, saggy boobs, ice-cold waterfalls.* I needed an image to ward off my desire to take her right now.

"Becca, do you really want me to make you feel good?" I needed her final confirmation right this minute.

She took a long time to answer as my finger dragged down her seam, encouraging her. She whispered, "Yes," as her arm slid from her face.

Her eyes locked onto mine, and the air was sucked out of the room. Every time this happened, I ended up high and dry. I wouldn't go through with this again unless I had her explicit permission.

Her "Yes" wasn't enough for me. I needed to be sure. "Are you sure you want this? Because once I start, I'm not stopping. Tell me, Becca. Do you want me to make you feel good?"

Our chests heaved like we'd run a marathon, and we were just getting started. After eighteen years, we were finally going to fuck, and I was delirious with anticipation.

"Fuck me, Spencer Weiss." Clear as a day without any hangover present, I went to work, sliding my hand farther into the depths of her pussy, eliciting a heartfelt moan from Becca. She arched her back as much as she could with her legs strewn over my thighs. She was gorgeous and expressive, not like she was during the day at work when she kept a lid on her emotions. She sat up forcefully, grasped my shirt, and attacked my mouth. Our teeth gnashed like wild animals unleashed. So many years of repressed longing, and now . . . so many possibilities.

Our kiss turned exploratory as I inserted one, then two fingers into her wet pussy, the palm of my hand pumping her clit. Her fingers combed through my hair, pulling the strands tighter each time I hit that perfect spot deep in her pussy. The idea that we were actually touching each other this way was surreal. I broke the kiss, suddenly needing more.

"I need to taste you," I demanded and slid off the couch to reposition myself between her legs. She looked at me as though she saw me for the first time. Nodding her consent, I almost fainted.

"Fuck, Becca. You're so beautiful."

I should stop saying things like that. I wasn't convinced this was just us fucking to burn off her frustration from work or both our frustration for not doing this sooner. It didn't matter. I wanted her, and she obviously wanted me, too. I slid her panties down her legs and threw them over my shoulder, moaning at how slick and perfect she was. She looked at me with hopeful eyes, and I licked my lips in approval. Had she been wanting this forever, too? I had tongue-fucked enough pussies in my life to know no one was disappointed. Becca wouldn't be either. I just needed to figure out what kind of pressure she liked, how many fingers filled her completely, and how fast she came. I problem-solved for a living, and I would unwrap this woman completely in search of her perfect orgasm.

Shifting her legs closer to her chest, she screamed, "There! Oh my God, Spencer." Becca bit her lip and reached for her tits, still covered in the silky material. That had to feel so good on her skin. My cock pulsed, watching as she squeezed those full globes, her moans making my cock weep. I could feel her clit pulsing under my tongue and knew she was close. I used my hands to push her ass higher off the cushions increasing the sensations. A new, erotic mewl escaped her throat, and all I wanted to do was slam my cock deep into her hot wetness. When she screamed, *"Baruch Hashem!"* I bowed my head and sucked all her delicious juices. Baruch Hashem, indeed. Watching her come undone was a prize I'd waited years to enjoy. Today would mark a whole new chapter in my life with Becca as my muse. I needed more from her—now.

I smiled into her folds, lapping up the last of her essence. I squeezed her ass, thinking God had nothing to do with this. A minute later, I stood assessing her mood. Did she want more? Could I take advantage of her in the state she was in? She smiled seductively and reached her hand toward the bulge in my pants. We both knew what needed to happen.

**Baruch Hashem—Praise be to God*

Chapter 7

Trigger continued to page 60, Line 7

My head was foggy when my head lifted from my pillow. The taste in my mouth was putrid as if I'd licked the bottom of a leather shoe. So gross. As quickly as I could, I went to the bathroom to brush my teeth, then stopped abruptly as I looked at myself in the mirror. I wasn't wearing my pajamas or panties. Where were my panties, or my blouse, for that matter? The realization of what happened last night screeched like a needle yanked from a record. *Spencer.*

Did we . . . ?

Did I . . . ?

Was it any good?

Seriously, if I had sex with Spencer after all these years, I would want to remember it. What happened last night? My last memory was him putting my wine glass down and holding me while I lamented about my horrible job. Well, it wasn't the job, only the stupid board and their deliberate attempt to keep me from making

Then why did my pussy feel tingly and used?

Should I call Spencer? Text? What exactly should I say? "Did you fuck me last night? Because I don't remember it." Or, "If you fucked me, I couldn't tell because your dick was so tiny."

No. That's one thing I remembered clearly. Spencer's cock swelled under me while I had my legs over his. It was an unmistakable feeling as it pressed behind my knees. I felt like an idiot. I whined, cried, and probably all but threw myself at him, and he ran away. *Shit!* I was a thirty-two-year-old acting like a schoolgirl.

I took a deep breath and bit the bullet. I typed a short note on my messaging app, probing for answers.

Me: *Thanks for coming over last night to comfort me. I was a real mess.*

Setting my phone on the counter, I turned on the shower and stepped in. The water felt amazing as it slid over my body, releasing the tension over what might have happened last night. When I reached down to wash between my legs, another memory barreled through my mind—fingers. Spencer's fingers. Oh my God! I came on his fingers. My head hung in shame while my pussy immediately came alive. After all these years, Spencer finally had his fingers where I wanted them, deep inside me. I loved it—didn't I? *God damn it!*

Snapping my head toward the phone, wishing it would ring, I grabbed my towel hanging on the hook and dried off. Moments later, a ping sounded from my phone, putting my nerves on edge.

Spencer: *The pleasure was all mine.*

What did he mean by that? He was still typing.

Spencer: *I hope you didn't mind me carrying you to your bed. You were out cold.*

Out cold? Before or after something happened? Argh! Men and their inability to communicate clearly.

Me: *Given my drunken state, I hate to ask, but did anything happen between us?*

My face twitched as my finger pressed send. Not waiting for a reply, I scurried across the room and got dressed. I checked the screen every few minutes, but no messages arrived. I twisted my hair into my usual tight bun and applied a light coat of mascara, nude lip gloss, and some contour. I didn't have it in me today to put on my best face, though I didn't want my colleagues to see that I had cried my eyes out last night.

I skipped my usual coffee and toast and grabbed my briefcase and papers off the coffee table when I saw two wine glasses. We didn't finish them. More like we never started them by the high line of the liquid in the glasses. Spencer couldn't have been drunk, so what the hell happened?

After stopping at my favorite coffee place for a croissant sandwich and latte, I continued to wait for my response. Emily greeted me at the elevator door, handing me five messages from the date guys returning my calls. I threw my head back in disgust and walked into my office, chucking my things onto one of the chairs across my desk, and Emily slid into the other.

Signal the inquisition.

"What did you find last night? Are you going to sue them? When do you open shop for your own firm?" My eyes went wide at that one.

"Slow your roll, girl. None of the above just yet." I walked behind my desk, pressing the toggle on my lamp. I sat down, eyeing the four hundred and forty-six-page document, and then looked over at Emily.

"Is this it?" My stare bore into hers, knowing what would come of me having this in plain sight.

"Yep." She popped the P, and crossed her legs, staring right back at me.

"And?" I cocked my head down, waiting.

"And, these bylaws haven't been changed in over ten years, and this is the previous copy. Not the one you saw yesterday. I'm going to assume, by your black smudged under eyes, that you've stayed up all night reviewing this document's latest version or got drunk. Which one is it?"

Emily missed her calling as either a litigator or a twelfth-century inquisitioner. Nothing got by her, and she was ruthless about getting what she wanted.

"The latter, but it's your fault. You're the one who sent *two* bottles of my favorite wine, and after I finished the first one the second one popped open of its own accord." I smirked, hanging my head in shame.

"It's a good thing I know you're not a lush or I'd have you admitted to an inpatient program today. Did you really drink all that wine alone?" Her tone smoothed out to admonish me like my favorite aunt.

I rubbed my eyes carefully, not smearing my mascara, and slapped my hands on my polished maple desk. "Mostly. I forgot to return Spencer's text and he got worried and showed up."

My evasive eyes said more than I was willing to share. While Emily could pull the truth out of a stone, I was the queen of redirect and distraction. There was more to this story, but, for the life of me, I couldn't remember all of it and wouldn't incriminate myself.

I waved off her last question and opened the enormous document to where she placed a page marker: LAW FIRM STRUCTURE. I continued reading until I found the turnkey piece of information.

"Emily. How many employees does our firm have? And, how do we rank in size in our field?"

Eyebrows raised, she leaned forward. This woman was an encyclopedia of firm information. If she didn't know these answers, no one would.

Without hesitation, she said, "We have one hundred seven employees, including the executive team. Based on the last Forbes article, we rank eighth among Intellectual Property firms in the Midwest. Why?"

Hmm. I tapped my polished nail on the corner of my desk. "My limited research last night found a current article in The Post describing this very topic. The term 'small firms' suggests that three to ten partners would be appropriate for firms under one hundred employees. However, after you confirmed our employee count, we moved up to the next tier. We are now considered a 'medium firm', allowing our board to have as many as twenty-five partners. Are you following me?"

Emily slammed herself back into her chair. "Are you shitting me? Do you really think they shut you down because they knew we grew too fast? What the hell, Becca? What are you going to do?"

I sighed, not knowing what to do. I'd have to talk to my dad and maybe my brother to see what they thought was the best route to take. For now, I'd lay low and focus on my sad excuse of a love life.

I turned to stare her down. "Not fast, Emily. Only that a woman wanted that position."

Chapter 8

Tonight was the first night of Hanukkah, and I was home alone lighting the first candle on my menorah that I carefully placed by the window. Planning for the inevitable thirty minutes each they had to burn or let them burn out, I spent my time reviewing my mail.

Hanukkah wasn't a major holiday like Rosh Hashanah or Yom Kippur; it was a minor one with a big impact. Growing up, lighting candles didn't hold a candle, excuse the pun, to Christmas trees surrounded by tons of gifts and pretty colored lights that stayed up all month or longer. As Jews, our moniker was the gift of light, harkening back to the days of Judah Maccabee and the destruction of the first temple. The miraculous burning of one night's worth of oil turning into eight was why we celebrated in the first place.

My whole life we were taught that miracles are everywhere if only we knew where to look for them. Some see the birth of a child as a miracle, while others avoid a life of servitude qualified equally. Whatever the miracle, it began with bringing light into the world. For centuries, Jews have brought light into the world through their devotion to education, art, culture, industry, and developing financial systems. You can't watch a movie without it having a Jewish writer, director, or producer leading the charge.

For my parents, Hanukkah meant children. Children were the light of the future and, therefore, "Go forth and multiply." So where were mine? That was their beef with me. My single candle—in my lone apartment—wouldn't bring enough light into their lives, so they pressured me to get with the program. Spencer still hadn't replied to my text, and I filed that back in my "Tardis." *Thank you, Dr. Who.*

After I said the three prayers for the first night of Hanukkah, I went into my closet to change, started a load of laundry, and walked out the door for my first date. Time to invoke a miracle. *Please, God, give me strength.*

Joshua was first up in my Eight Crazy Nights of Dating. Ironically, all my dates are Jewish, making us culturally on the same page. I suppose the irony was more planned than by happenstance via my mother's friends. Regardless, I wanted to begin this insanity with a soft pitch, and Joshua was the guy to make that happen.

There was no avoiding going to a vegan restaurant. Thoughts of lemongrass in my mouth made my stomach churn. I arrived promptly at seven-thirty, spotting him in a corner booth.

"Hey, Joshua. Finally, we get to have that meal. Again, I'm so sorry for the time-lapse." I was out of breath after I spewed all that out. I sounded so annoying to my own ears.

He was a gentleman, stood, and gave me a gentle hug. My hands lingered on his biceps, noting he was more buff than the last time I met him.

"Wow. Becca, it's so great to see you again, too. I love your dress." It wasn't new, only stuffed in the way-back of my closet. It was winter and it's hard to make a sweater dress look sexy, so I opted for the taupe cashmere sheath dress, a black shrug, and tall, black Chanel boots.

I slid into the booth across from Joshua, and our server came over promptly to take our drink orders. Vegan restaurants aren't known for their alcohol menu, though I did find a pinot grigio that tempted me, and he got a lemongrass spritzer. *Shocking.* We relived our first meeting at the organic grocery store and his new venture into alpaca apparel.

"You can't believe how many socks can be made from one shearing. I went to Chile to work on an alpaca farm for three months, learning everything I could about them. They are so smart."

His face lit up with joy and reverence as he described everything he learned in detail. It was like listening to a child coming home from camp and vomiting every moment of their experience. The most intriguing part of his story was the way his sexy mouth moved when he smiled. The corners turned up when he said the word "feed," like a post-orgasmic whisper.

Our server came back with our drinks and took our dinner order. A vegetable ragout would have to do tonight, as there were no *latkes* on this menu.

"That sounds fascinating, Joshua. Do you have partners you're going into business with? Where will you sell your socks?" I feigned interest while pondering how soft those socks might feel. "Are they soft enough to wear every day?"

I took a forkful of my ragout and was pleasantly surprised. The spices made it quite rich and satisfying.

"Soft enough? I'll have to get you a pair. They are amazing!" Joshua's eyes glazed over in what appeared to be love. "Would you like to come over after dinner and try them? It's an experience you won't want to miss." His eyes twinkled brightly, and illicit thoughts of his goatee rubbing against my sensitive skin were provocative. I'm ashamed of myself for thinking this way. My mission was to have a date with this guy, not land in bed with him. Although . . .

"I'd love to, Joshua." My lazy smile had him nodding.

He eventually asked me superficial questions about why I wore leather and what type of skincare Industries I used because I was radiant. While I wouldn't call him out by calling me a cow killer, he did infer that by continuing to buy leather Industries, the methane levels would increase ozone issues. By the time we finished dinner, I was sure I'd find myself on a most-wanted poster titled, "Planet Killer."

We walked through the chilly downtown streets, admiring the Christmas lights and what the holidays meant to him. We entered his five-story walk-up, leaving me out of breath and sweating. A delightful sight in cashmere wool.

"Have a seat. I'll grab those socks for you."

Joshua lived simply but comfortably. He was neat but not organized. The kitchenette seemed functional, especially with his Ninja Juicer front and center.

"Here you go!" he said, holding up a pair of socks. "I hope you like blue. It's the only one I had in your size."

Joshua didn't stop to show them to me but kneeled in front of me, unzipping my knee-length boots instead. I was shocked at his bold actions, and I loved how he kneaded my calf with his strong hands.

"Nice. Do you work out? I love to run. Great cardio," he muttered as he rambled on.

From my perspective, he was less than a foot from my apex, and the way he looked at me suggested he was aware of that also. He finally managed to focus on slipping on the first sock and then slid the second one over my heel, slowly running his eyes from my big toe to the gap between my thighs. *Was hipster Joshua making a pass at me?* Not that I minded, but he was slick in his approach.

"What do you think?" he said as he watched me maneuver myself to the edge of the couch, my dress shifting higher, giving him more of a show.

"Holy shit. These *are* soft, Joshua. You weren't bullshitting me—at all. Where are you selling these? I want a dozen pairs. How much are they?" I walked around his apartment several times, enjoying the silky wool with each step I took.

He rubbed his goatee casually as if deep in thought. He stood and walked over to me, leaning closely. "Expensive. Very expensive." His voice became gravely, making my core clench.

"Is that so," I whispered back. "Would I get a Friends and Family discount?"

"That depends." His wicked smile raked me over from head to toe.

"Depends on what?" I countered, staring into his piercing blue eyes. *A good lawyer needs all the facts.*

He reached up and tugged on one of my long, curly locks. "If I can wrap my hands in this fucking awesome hair while you suck my dick."

My spine tingled, and my eyes bugged out. I shook my head, wondering if I heard him correctly. Did I want to go down on him? For a pair of socks? Fuck, no. But to have those hands in my hair while I pleasured him, maybe. I loved to have my hair pulled. It drove my libido through the roof.

Not letting this opportunity go by, I stepped closer and countered. "Make it a dozen pairs. Various colors and patterns, and you have a deal."

"Damn, woman. You are one hell of a negotiator. You've got yourself a deal. Now strip." *Christ!* I loved how he went from chill to demanding in a split second. Sadly, he wasn't getting a whole show out of me, though I wasn't going to ruin my cashmere dress with his cum. I shrugged out of my jacket, wiggled my dress over my head, and watched it drop soundlessly to the floor.

Joshua watched every move I made as I watched his bulge stretch his pants tighter and tighter. He wasted no time unbuttoning his pants and shoving them to the floor, nearly falling to the ground as he tore off his boxer briefs. I knelt before him, admiring his impressive shaft, deciding how to get it into my mouth. Thick, long, and already seeping pre-cum, I licked my lips in anticipation and made him wait another minute while I blew hot air onto his crown.

"Fuck, Becca. You're a tease." He grabbed two handfuls of my hair and pulled me closer.

He pushed his cock towards my mouth, stopping so I could run the tip of my tongue along the rim. He sighed, muttering words I couldn't comprehend. I grabbed the bottom of his shaft and squeezed hard, loving how he swore with each compression. Between licking him up and down his thick shaft and touching myself, my mind shut off any reason why I shouldn't be doing this to a veritable stranger.

"Yes, Becca. Yes. Take me all the way back. I want to feel the back of your throat." Joshua thrust into my mouth, gagging as I took him all the way in. I hadn't chocked at his size until he did that, and I couldn't decide if I liked it or if it offended me. He did it three more times and blew his load down my throat. Quick and to the point. *I like that in a man.*

"Jesus, woman. You have skills?" He stepped back and offered me his hand to stand up. His eyes roamed all over my body, shaking his head slowly from side to side in amusement.

"I should have promised you your own fucking Alpaca. If you fuck like you suck, I'll have one delivered next week."

I wiped my mouth with the back of my hand and bent to pick up my dress, sliding it on with a little shake of my hips. I bent again and slipped my jacket around my shoulders, looking over his impressive form as he rubbed his cock back to life. I slipped on my boots, remembering how nice his hands felt on my calves, wondering if I should schedule another date so he could finish what we started.

"That's an awfully kind gesture, but I do not need a hairy animal at my apartment. I will, however, be looking for my socks very soon." I reached for his broad shoulder, and he stepped closer. "Thank you, Joshua. This has been fun. Happy Hanukkah. You certainly lit me up." I kissed his pouty lips gently and scooped up my purse, strutting out of his apartment door.

When the door shut, I opened my ride-sharing app and ordered a car. Walking down the five flights of stairs, I discovered I liked being a minx. I felt unleashed and completely in control of my life—the first time in a long time, to be exact. Date number one was a success, and I looked forward to recording the highlights in my database right after I got myself off.

latke —a round, shredded potato pancake made with egg, onion, salt and pepper. Delish!

Chapter 9

It's been two days since I heard from Spencer, and I'm getting annoyed. He was deliberately avoiding me, which led me to believe that something other than his fingers entered me. Does he think I wouldn't figure that out? I'm a freaking lawyer, for God's sake. It's my job to connect the dots, though I don't have to do that part too often these days. I've mostly been writing IP contracts and patents for aspiring inventors and corporations that develop new research and development components and want them patented. My courtroom trips involve fighting a patent infringement or other intellectual property circumstances. I'm a good litigator, but I am not a good sleuth.

"Emily!" I called out, again, skipping the intercom. My door was usually open, and she could hear my breathing through a brick wall. "I'm leaving today at five-thirty. If you need to discuss anything with me, please do it before then."

Sweetly, she replied, "Yes, Ma'am. Whatever you wish, Ma'am." Sometimes, I wanted to berate her for her obnoxious retorts, and other times she made me laugh. Today, it was laughter.

I was buried in busy work that the managing partner thought "only I could do properly," leaving me with filing motions for hours. You would think a paralegal could handle this stuff, and they could, if only I hadn't presented my earlier offer to Mr. Timmins, the second man on the wall of partners.

"Mr. Timmins, I have recently learned that I won't be up for partner until one of them leaves, dies, or retires. I hoped you could offer me some interesting cases to explore to occupy my time otherwise."

Yes. I sounded snarky because I felt snarky. He politely stood up and stared at me intently with a wicked smirk creeping up his long face. "Of course," he said patronizingly. "We have just acquired LeafLorn Industries and Roland Laundry Industries, and their development teams have terrific opportunities for our firm. I'll have those files sent over immediately. Thank you for coming to me personally."

This guy was so creepy. When he extended his bony-fingered hand, I hesitated to shake it. It was like shaking a warm skeleton. So gross that shivers ran down my spine. I turned quickly to leave, keeping the door open in my wake. I wasn't ever coming back to this office again.

As promised, five boxes of R&D for each client appeared via the mailroom courier before lunch.

I reviewed each document, highlighting anything that could be contested, and began thinking about my second date tonight, Larry Swisher.

I received a call from his assistant yesterday asking for my dress size. Reluctantly, I gave it to her, asking what it was for. She giggled and said it was a surprise. *Dear God, what was this guy up to?*

We agreed to an early dinner with a fun, upbeat activity afterward, though he wouldn't specify what that was. Larry only said I should wear comfortable black shoes and arrange my hair into a ponytail. Listen, I'd already blown one guy who tugged my hair. I wasn't doing it again.

I left my office on time as promised and got home shortly afterward to light my second Hanukkah candle. Inserting the second candle right-to-left, I struck a match and lit them left-to-right. Everything in Judaism had a mystical reason for doing them. Some tested my time and patience. Like most Jewish children going through Hebrew school, we forgot most of what we were taught. In retrospect, the Bar/Bat Mitzvah, when boys and girls become adults and accept the Torah as their guiding light, should be postponed for when we are adults. Thirteen-year-olds don't remember squat or care much about being responsible and accepting the 613 commandments of the Torah. Adults usually don't have a choice but to be accountable, and, therefore, they would do many of them anyway. *Yeah, we have a lot to live up to.*

I shucked off my suit and hung it up nicely, just like my *bubbe* taught me. She was an Old World gal who only had control of the interior of her home. The external portion was for the man of the house. I stepped into my ensuite, unfolded my bun into a ponytail, and curled the ends. I touched up my makeup, then dug around my closet for some low, black, strappy heels and threw on a tunic dress with swirls of blues winding around my hips and torso. Upon my final assessment, I concluded that I looked sexy and sophisticated. My watch showed thirty-two minutes had passed, and what was left of my candles pooled in the foiled cup set into the candleholder opening. I blew out the burning wicks and grabbed my things to meet Larry at Rango's, a Tex-Mex joint halfway between his house and mine.

I loved Mexican food, though it didn't always love me back. All those carbs and beans meant that whatever Larry had planned had better be near a restroom. I made the conscious decision to eat light tonight, just in case. Larry was a stylish, good-looking accountant. To be clear, there was no pocket protector, greasy combover, or unfit suit coat. Nope. Larry, by all accounts, was easy on the eyes. He wasted no time pulling me into a hug that lasted slightly longer than appropriate, but we had met before, so maybe he felt a stronger connection than I did.

"My goodness, you look lovely," he crooned, staring at my chest.

I bent my knees slightly, bringing my eyes to where he had been looking, making him snap his eyes back to mine. "You look great, too, Larry. How have you been?"

He pulled out my seat and tucked me under the table set with candles and a small bouquet of colorful fall flowers. He had taken the liberty to order a pitcher of margaritas and appeared to be halfway through his first glass.

"I have so much to tell you." His animated demeanor was fun and gave me hope for a good night. "I secured two tickets to ComicCon at the Renaissance Center tonight And, bonus! We have been chosen to be in a cosplay! Isn't that amazing?"

He sat back in his chair, glowing while waiting for my response. I hated to burst his bubble, but I wouldn't be giving him a reciprocal response. Conversely, my jaw dropped, and my eyes blew wide, imagining myself prancing around in some costume in front of God knows how many people. I closed my eyes, wishing I would pass out and not have to go. I didn't want to hurt his feelings. He obviously went to a lot of trouble and expense in procuring these tickets, so I dug deep and became as interested as possible.

"Larry! Really? Did you get us tickets to the hottest event of the year? I'm impressed." I vigorously nodded my head, trying to sell my gratitude and appreciation. "What a terrific idea. I would never have imagined that I would be doing this tonight." *I meant every word of my enthusiasm. Truly.* While I didn't lie, I disguised my disdain with emphatic joy.

He clapped his hands together and then turned in his seat to pull something off the back of his chair. "Look! I got you your costume, that's why my assistant called you. Only you could pull off Wonder Woman with the properly fitted costume."

I spat the liquid in my mouth onto my plate. "Wonder Woman? What the fuck, Larry. There wasn't any other character that had more clothes?" I grabbed my napkin, hid my face behind it, and spit proverbial nails from my mouth.

"How else could I be Superman if you weren't Wonder Woman?" He was so serious when he said that. I felt like throwing my drink in his face.

I appreciated his remorse at how upset I was. "I guess I overstepped here, didn't I?"

I nodded. "Why not Lois Lane? At least she didn't have to wear a strapless bodice." My thoughts of how I got myself into this mess distracted me from his discomfort until he opened his mouth.

"You're hot, Becca. I thought you'd rock this costume and selfishly wanted every guy at the convention to be jealous of me."

How could a guy who looked like Christian Bale think that women wouldn't flock to him? He almost didn't need the Superman muscle suit to fill it out. Then it struck me—Annie. She told me he had a kink. Something about capes. Yes! That's it. He liked to fuck with a cape on. *Damn it!* Now, I would have to go because it would bruise his ego if I didn't. I wanted a graphic poster of me, fearlessly galloping across a high road while everyone else walked below me. I'm such a people pleaser.

I pressed my lips together and sighed. "Thank you for the compliment. I'll wear it, but I'm done if I feel uncomfortable being ogled or it cuts into me." *These are the things I do for my mother.*

Larry stood up and rounded the table to kiss my lips softly, "You're incredible, just like I remembered." Thankfully, the waitress came and took our dinner order, and we were left to talk about regular things, like tax abatement law. *Yay!*

After shoving my tits down as far as this bustier would allow, I stepped out of the handicapped bathroom stall at the convention center. *Sorry. The others were too small to change in.* I turned myself in several directions in front of the mirror, deciding if the costume Larry supplied was the correct size. I told the woman I was a size ten, but clearly, this outfit was for a size four. Too much tit and tush were showing. Wonder Woman didn't wear a cape. *Shocking, I know.* A man must have originally designed this getup. If I let my hair down, it could act as a cape and cover some skin. Yeah, that was the ticket. My Velcro red boots with gold laces were my pièce de résistance.

Larry waited by the entrance as instructed, fidgeting. His eyes looked like a cartoon character bulging when I approached. All could almost hear the "Awoogah" sound in the distance. From my point of view, I could have blown that horn, too, because Larry filled out that costume almost as well as the real Superman. Flat belly, broad shoulders, with a small tuft of brown hair peeking out of the top of his bodysuit sent my nether regions on high alert. He was delicious. But as my eyes wandered down to his lower half, he became awe-inspiring. Strong, muscular, long legs met at his rather prominent bulge. A girl had to wonder whether that was a codpiece or the real deal. *Hmm?*

"Geezus Christ, Becca. You are ten times more gorgeous in the flesh than my imagination." He stepped forward to plant another delicious kiss on my lips. Mild-mannered Larry may have lived the life of Clark Kent, but with his costume and cape, he embodied a living Superman. Tonight will go down in the annals of dating history.

The blush I felt from his x-ray vision radiated down through my bodice, settling between my legs. Larry may not be my dream guy, but he sure did know how to flatter me.

"I'm happy I exceeded your expectations," I smiled. "Come on. Show me the world of ComicCon."

We stowed our belongings at the coat check and walked hand in hand, receiving catcalls and "You two look hot." We did, and we knew it. There was nothing more freeing than owning your awesomeness. Maybe I would consider another visit next year.

Larry dragged me all over the twenty-five thousand square feet of this convention hall, stopping often to take selfies with other cosplayers and an unexpected opportunity to get a picture with Henry Cavill in his Superman costume. That face! *Oy!*

Four hours later, we fell into a cab, exhausted. The time flew by so quickly, and I'm ashamed to say I enjoyed every bit of it. Especially when we had to improvise a narrated scene and act out what was being said. Everyone laughed so hard that Larry called for a timeout so we could catch our breath.

When it came, I let my head fall on his shoulder, and his right hand settled on my thigh. I was still in my costume, fully aware of how little I wore. Larry had softer hands than Joshua's since he worked in an office. His fingers, however, were long and thick, and they made fast work of moving up and down my thigh and landing on the gap between my crease and my costume.

"I can't thank you enough for indulging me this evening. Not everyone can let themselves go and have a good time. You surprised me." He spoke into my hair softly as his thumb moved gently across my sensitive skin. It was intoxicating.

I wanted to see his face. To see how earnest he was about his appreciation. When his dark, steely eyes met mine, I knew this moment would be transcendent.

"You made it easy. You're like a big kid who makes this world his playground. I don't think I could ever do that." My words sounded seductive, though it could have been an after-effect from yelling to be heard at the venue.

He brushed his thumb over my bottom lip. "Your lips are so rosy and plump." He leaned in, slowly placing a promising kiss on them. His tongue pressed gently between my lips and I opened willingly for him. "I want you, Becca."

Oh, hell. Do I let myself go with the flow or shut down the urge? The little devils on my shoulders were arm wrestling for the win, and time was running out to reply.

"If I say yes, will you promise not to call me every day?" He reared back slightly.

"You don't want me to call within twenty-four hours? Or buy you stuff? Or make promises of love? You only want pure fucking fun?"

His look of shock at the simplicity of the offer was priceless. Yeah, guys ask for this all the time, but women? Now, that was a reversal Larry appreciated.

"Is that okay with you?" I pleaded.

"Hell, yes, it's okay with me. You are Wonder Woman. It's a wonder that I found you and that you gave me everything I wanted from this evening. I might fall in love with you yet." His hands cupped my face, pulling me into a greedy kiss that left me breathless.

Our cab dropped us off in a swanky neighborhood uptown. Larry lived in a beautiful brownstone walk-up on the second floor, and he quickly swooped me into his arms and carried me up those two flights. Like the speed of light, he unlocked the door and unzipped my bodice, and I, in turn, unzipped his bodysuit to find that there hadn't been a codpiece after all. *He wasn't the only one full of wonder.*

He picked me up again and rushed me down the narrow hallway, forcing me to duck my head into his shoulder for fear of getting knocked off. He dropped me onto the bed and ran out of the room, returning with his red cape. *Of course. Can't have sex without a cape.*

"I need to ask you for one more favor tonight, Becca, and please don't think I'm crazy." I pushed up onto my elbows, remembering I had only worn a black lace thong under my costume.

"Don't keep me in suspense, Larry. What is your favor?" Pushing myself off the bed, I walked over to cup his ever-growing cock.

Larry's groan was animalistic and I increased the pressure of my hold.

"Over there," he pointed across the room to what looked to be a salon chair.

I pointed at the same thing, hoping there was something, anything, other than that chair. Annie was right. Larry wanted sex in that chair. The same chair Annie had sex in over a year ago. How many other women got lucky with Larry in that chair he was pointing at? When I connected the dots, whether they did fuck him in that chair or not, none of them wanted a relationship with him in the long run. Interestingly, he did seem excited about not having to commit to seeing me again, so maybe one time was enough. That was all he was getting from me. Making sure we were on the same page, I asked for clarity.

"Do you want to fuck me in that chair, Larry?"

"Geezus, Becca. I want to fuck you every which way in that chair." *Well, God damn.*

"Sounds like you've been utilizing that chair to its fullest potential." I laughed, tracing his firm jawline.

"You have no idea," he said, yanking off his underwear and grabbing a condom out of a glass bowl on his dresser as we walked across the room.

"Pick a position, sweetheart. You're only getting one go at this." I slid my thong down to reveal my almost bare pussy. His cock bobbed up and down in his excitement, and my mouth watered.

"Ride me—hard." He wasted no time sheathing himself and sitting his fine ass in that chair.

I moved between his legs, admiring his length. Not as thick as Joshua's, but longer. This position was going to hit my G-spot, which doesn't usually get hit by an average-sized cock. I may have mocked him as Annie described her experience in the chair, but now I was excited to see what Lucky Larry had to offer.

I mounted him, pausing in awe of his seeping dick. I wanted him to beg me to sink over his straining cock. It didn't take long.

"Put this on me," he croaked out, handing me his red Superman cape. A pleading look begged me to understand his kink, and I wouldn't deny him. I knew it was coming, so acting surprised wouldn't be sincere.

A slow, understanding smile crept across my face that made his dick stretch right up to my hovering, wet pussy. When the cape was tied carefully around his neck, he arranged it over his shoulders and wrapped it around his torso like a shield. How in the hell did this kink come to be was beyond me. But tonight was a night of firsts. And I was feeling adventurous.

I lifted myself higher, lining him up to my aching pussy, pausing as I watched his face contort in anguish. I pressed my ample bosom closer to his face, and he gladly latched on, flicking and twisting my tits expertly as he grabbed my ass tightly. I slowly lowered myself inch by glorious inch until I settled deep onto his shaft. His balls felt so erotic nestled on my backside entrance that I considered asking him for seconds. More shivers ran up my spine, spiking my heart rate beyond healthy.

Larry had big hands, and he used them to his advantage, wrapping them on both fleshy cheeks and pulling me tighter back down each time I raised myself to his tip. I ground myself relentlessly against him as he sucked my tits and squeezed my ass so hard there were sure to be bruises. This was heaven. Why did I think this wouldn't be good? I-I . . .

"Holy shit, Larry. I'm going to come."

He slipped a finger between us and commanded that I hold on one more minute. I could feel him stiffening, and he pressed that glorious finger onto my clit and pressed it perfectly just as he released himself inside me. Tingles began in my lower back, radiating up my spine, shivering in delight as we came together, roaring our pleasure.

Out of breath and satisfied, I released a chuckle that turned into a laugh. Larry joined me, and we sat connected for as long as his erection lasted.

"This was fun," I admitted, dragging my fingernail down his abdomen.

"Best night in a long time. Are you sure you don't want another round? I'll be ready in a few minutes." He waggled his eyebrows and squeezed my ass again.

"Tempting, Larry. Very tempting, but I have an early morning meeting and need to get home." I pulled myself up his chest and kissed him gently, pulling his bottom lip as I finished. I felt pleased with myself getting an offer that most never received—seconds.

"You're trouble," he countered, pulling me back for another long, sultry kiss.

I smiled and tipped my head coyly. "See you around, huh?

He nodded, not moving a muscle. "Yeah. See you around."

I slid from the chair and collected my thong off the floor. I grabbed my hanging bag and stepped into the bathroom to clean up and get dressed. The mirror didn't lie. I was a Wanton Wonder Woman with no shame. "You really are something, Becca," I said to myself and opened the door.

Larry stood in front of me buck-naked. "I ordered you a cab; it should be here shortly. Let's not let time go by so long, okay?" His smile was so endearing and sexy.

His soft croon made my knees wobble. Larry hit top marks in my database categories. I may even add one, "Impossible to Leave."

"Thank you for the cab. Call me sometime. I'll be sure to answer." I sucked on his lower lip one last time and gave him a wink. He moaned, catching my hand as I pulled him toward the door. He looked so fucking good. Tell me why I don't stop this whole bullshit deal with my mother and bring Larry to the party. *Oh! Yeah. Capes.*

bubbe - grandmother

Chapter 10

Spencer: *Sorry for taking so long to return your call. I dropped my phone, and the screen cracked. Black blobs covered the whole thing. It's fixed now.*

Bullshit! That absolutely did not happen. Spencer used one of those ironclad military-grade phone cases.

Me: *That sucks. Glad you're back in business. So???*

Time to rip off the band-aid, Becca. It's been so long since I asked the question that I almost forgot what I asked.

Me: *Did anything happen between us when you came over?*

The bouncing dots went on for a minute, then stopped and started twice more. Was he trying to sugarcoat his answer, or was he actually working and getting interrupted?

Spencer: *Yes, and no. Yes, something happened, but, no, not what you're thinking. And I know what you're thinking. We did not have sex.*

Whew!

Me: *Well, that's good, right? I wouldn't want to make our relationship weird. Please tell me what "yes" means.*

Spencer: *Are you in a quiet place?*

I was sitting at my kitchen counter having coffee before leaving for work.

Me: *Yes.*

Spencer: *I'd like to preface that what happened was consensual and verified four times.*

Me: *I will tear your head off if you don't tell me what happened right now! (Red face, swearing emoji.)*

Spencer: *Settle down. Do you remember laying your legs across my thighs? Do you also remember what you were and weren't wearing that night when I came over?*

What was I...? Oh, no!

Me: *I do. (Said shamefully.) Must have been quite a show.*

Spencer: *Delightful. Memorable. Delicious.*

Me: *What do you mean, delicious?*

Oh, no! I screamed, jumping up from my chair, mortified. I had broken my Friends Code of Conduct—Friends don't eat friends out.

Me: *Did you?*

Spencer: *I did after your pussy enjoyed two of my fingers. (Smirking face emoji and red heart)*

I couldn't breathe. My childhood fantasies of being with Spencer finally happened, and I was too fucking drunk to remember it. I hate myself.

Spencer: *I know what you're thinking, which is why I asked several times to be sure you were conscious of what you were doing.*

Me: *My God, Spencer. You must think I'm a slut.*

Spencer: *On the contrary. I loved you letting your inhibitions down. It was a side of you I hadn't seen before, and I enjoyed it very much.*

Me: *I bet you did. Was that it? Or did we do the full deed?*

Spencer: *No, Red. I protected your virtue reluctantly, and, after we spooned for a few hours on the couch, I carried you into bed and removed your blouse. That view was my prize for not being a cad and fucking you when you were drunk.*

Me: *I've got to go to work. Thanks for the update. I'm going to crawl under a rock now. Have a good day.*

I gently set my phone face down on the marble countertop and drilled the palms of my hands into my eyes. *What had I done?* I'm never going to be able to look at him again without feeling—what? Vulnerable? Embarrassed? Or worse, horny? I indulged my senses in what it would look like having Spencer's full lips pressed to my pussy, sucking on my clit, and cupping my ass cheeks. It was like a fever dream I couldn't press pause on. This was going to haunt me forever!

Another glorious day at work proved to be uneventful. Emily had the day off for some doctor appointments, and I was reading through files on Hump Day. My shoes rested on the floor beside me as I used my couch as my workspace for the day. I dropped my professional pretenses and lounged in my recliner, knowing I didn't have to meet with clients today.

Shortly after I began, I was bored out of my mind and thought about tonight's date, Ravi. This was the first of my mother's choices, and I was going in blind. I reached for my laptop and opened the email detailing each of the five prospects I was to date this week. Everything was there except pictures.

Ravi: Isabelle's nephew. Israeli. Telemarketer. Ambitious. Thirty years old and fluent in five languages.

He sounded interesting, but telemarketing? They were pushy and relentless. This would be an exhausting date. We agreed to meet at the Food Shed in a trendy downtown neighborhood. It was a food court concept with boutique restaurants without any Big Box options. Next door was a posh single-level mall with high-end stores from kitchen to apparel. I'd shopped there a few times a while back and considered this an opportunity to see what had changed. *Maybe something to go with new alpaca socks?*

The bench next to the front entrance was nearly empty, enabling me to relax for a few minutes before Ravi's arrival. Oddly, Ravi didn't spend time uploading pictures to his social media, so I probably wouldn't recognize him out of a line-up, though I'm sure my mother sent every one of her choices a collage of my finest attributes. She's over-the-top that way.

I noticed a handsome man walking by me, hoping it was him. Tall, tight ass, and a sexy swagger. He was built like a rugby player with rock-hard shoulders fitted into a long, knitted cardigan sweater that revealed a six-pack outlined through a white V-neck T-shirt. So yummy. He winked at me as I scoped him out as he walked by. *Busted.*

Sadly, he didn't stop, and my disappointment showed when another man approached me.

"You're Becca? Is everything all right?" He looked more annoyed than interested in my well-being.

Ravi looked almost as good as the other guy, except everything he wore was more finished and streamlined. He reeked of the metrosexual vibe, and I hoped he wasn't a douchebag.

My disappointment abated quickly when I saw his big, chocolate eyes with long, thick lashes. I suppose I shouldn't be so judge-y. Time will tell exactly what this guy was about.

I stood up abruptly, "Uh, yeah. I'm good. You're Ravi?"

"In the flesh." He leaned in for a hug, and I wasn't sure I wanted one yet.

"I'm sure we have much to talk about. Let's find something to eat and get to it."

Did my mother plan for an arranged marriage without my knowing? Ravi seemed so transactional it flustered me, and I'm not easily flustered.

He ushered me forward with his hand on my lower back, directing me to the sushi storefront. "This is my favorite. How about you?"

"Sorry. I have an iodine allergy, so no raw fish for me—unless it's tuna on a bagel with sliced cucumbers. It's worth the heartburn." I smirked sheepishly, rolling my eyes.

Ravi looked crestfallen but ordered for himself. I had my heart set on a burger and fries. It had been a long time since I had one, and it was calling to me.

"I'm going to head over to get a burger. Let's meet over there when our food is ready?" I pointed to a cluster of clean tables in the middle of the food court. He looked annoyed, but I didn't care. This date was already feeling forced and uncomfortable. I'm not putting his comfort before mine.

Five minutes later, we met up, and he wasted no time digging in.

"That looks good." He nodded at my burger, securing his first piece of sushi with chopsticks and shoving it into his mouth.

"Would you like a bite?" Well, not precisely a bite, but a cut-off piece. I'm not a food sharer that way.

"No, thank you. I keep kosher, and I can't go back and forth. This vendor is the only one that has a *hechsher*. Honestly, I shouldn't even be sitting at the same table with that burger while I'm eating fish. Sorry." Now, it was his turn to look sheepish.

Did I mention many Jews, from Reform to Orthodox, keep Kosher? Those six-hundred-and-thirteen laws included what and how you prepared and ate your food. Yeah, it's so fun to be the Chosen People. So many rules. So little time. I admired those who lived an observant lifestyle. It took commitment, dedication, sacrifice, and an unquestioning attitude to what was written in the Torah over fifty-seven hundred-plus years ago. Not unlike every other Christian religion, once the Torah was written, that was it—no changes for progress. No questioning God's word. That's why I'm Reform. We looked at the Torah a little differently. Meaningful stories, structure in our world, and many beautiful points of reflection on how to live a good life, but there had to be room for evolution in its application—and a cheeseburger. Call it a loophole if you must.

Ravi ate his food like a Hoover vacuum, and I wasn't even halfway through my meal when he suggested we get going. *Slow your roll, dude.*

He stood up, grabbing his tray while I rolled my eyes and dabbed my napkin at the corners of my mouth. *I guess I'm done.* Not only did I pay for my meal, but I couldn't eat it. Another check in the "no" box for this guy.

We walked across the busy street to the Ballard Street Boutique Mall. I prepared for a casual stroll through the mall, window shopping, and revealing conversation. I wanted to know enough about these men without getting emotionally involved. Ravi, however, elected for a power walk and a bulleted list of his finer attributes, including his stamina. I swear God wants me to meet the kookiest guys in the world before meeting the right one.

"Hey, Ravi," I called ahead to him. He was always two steps ahead of me. "Can we slow down? Why the hurry?" I stopped in my tracks, wondering if he had noticed. I was out of breath and suddenly distracted myself, eyeing a pair of shoes in a display.

His annoyance at my request was visible when he jammed his hands onto his hips and walked back to where I'd stopped. "Becca," he looked around the area and pointed to a nearby bench, "Sit down. We need to talk." *Yeah, we did. And stop being so bossy.*

I stepped over to where he indicated, sat down, and crossed my legs casually. He could have sat down by me but instead made a point of sitting the equivalent of three people away. *I called it—douchebag.*

He pulled at his stubbled chin and sighed. "Becca, we both know this setup isn't going anywhere. My aunt insisted I meet you, and if I'm right, your mom did the same. So why are we wasting each other's time? We are very different people."

Wow. He made up his mind in less than thirty minutes. His telemarketing skills were on point. He couldn't stop his tendencies when meeting new people. Secure the sale or move on—there was nothing in between. That may have been his M.O., but it wasn't mine. It was time to educate this brat.

I nodded reluctantly, setting my hands in my lap, inferring I was calm and collected when I wasn't. Now, if I could keep my tone of voice sweet, I could save us both some embarrassment.

"You're right, Ravi. Everything you said is true, though I don't think you have sincerely given us a chance to get to know each other. I happen to be an exceptional listener and an aficionado of music and culture. If you'd like to know what specifically, perhaps you could ask me some questions. Would you like to take the time to do that?" I stared at him like a condescending parent.

His darker-tone skin blanched. I called him out and didn't care if it made him feel small. He was an ass who didn't know who he was dealing with.

He pursed his lips, shifting his jaw while staring me down. "Oy! You're good. Really good. Most women would have taken the out and left. Tell me, Ms. Strauss, what is your strong suit, art or music?" He cocked his head, waiting for my reply.

Was this a test? He wanted to see if I could stand up to him. No. I was the professor, and I would school this prick. "Both. I've studied everything from Chihuly glass to the great Masters. Salieri to Shostakovich. Where would you like to begin?"

Take that, asshole!

"Let's start with Warhol," he winked, then offered me his perfectly white teeth.

Modern art wasn't my forte, but I was game. We spent the next forty minutes debating contemporary techniques to political motifs. He knew his stuff, and I was impressed.

He bowed and said, "I was wrong about you, Becca. I apologize." I sat still, absolving him of his shortsighted appraisal of me.

"Thank you, Ravi. I'm not a test to be scored. I'm multifaceted, and it appears you are as well. Isn't it better to set aside your work stance in the hopes you'll find someone who piques your interest?"

I still couldn't shake having to teach him about relationships. I didn't need his approval, but, if I was going to continue dating him, he needed to know that I didn't need to measure up to him at all. God knows he didn't get very high on my Needs & Wants List.

"What do you say we start over and stroll around the mall? Do you see those shoes over there? I'm going to try them on. Why don't you join me?" I gave him my best smile and started walking to the store.

Happily, he followed, and I got a new pair of black booties with fringe around the top. Afterward, we did more window shopping, sharing stories from our youth. His past was different since he was born in Israel and didn't come to the USA until he was fifteen.

Otherwise, we were cut from the same cultural cloth. There was something to be said about not having to explain cultural tapestry.

The mall was closing, and, though our night turned around, I didn't see a future with Ravi or even a one-night stand. I opened my mouth to tell him as much when he took my hand.

"Can I kiss you?" *Really?* There hadn't been chemistry between us all night, at least for me, and a kiss wouldn't change that.

I looked left and then right, wishing someone would pull the fire alarm on the building. It was a kiss, not a commitment, I rationalized. Hesitating, I said, "Sure."

Ravi stepped to my chest, tipping my face upward. Neither of us touched other than our lips, and, though the kiss was perfunctory, it was sweet.

"You are beautiful inside and out. Thank you for a nice evening." He pressed his lips to mine once more, attempting to push his tongue into my mouth, and I broke the kiss—immediately. *Greedy.*

"See you around," I said confidently, walking away.

"You, too," he chuckled.

I kept walking without looking back and caught a cab half a block away, relieved. Ravi and I would only ever be friends, regardless of my mother's wishes otherwise. Our similar backgrounds weren't enough to make a lasting relationship.

"You'll grow to love each other," I could hear her saying. *Sure, Mom.*

I sunk into the backseat of a cab and focused on the green, purple, and red lights strung up and down the street. Our city spared no expense on giant, sparkly snowflakes and massive ornament replicas under a giant tree in Tremont Park. It was the epicenter of our city and, tonight, throngs of people gathered around carolers dressed in period garb, passing around a donation plate for the Salvation Army. It's times like this that I wish I celebrated Christmas, even if most of these people forgot what the holiday was even about. Bigger, more expensive presents drove parents to near bankruptcy. Along with more trendy trips to tiny islands in the Pacific. Or cruising, which promised obscene amounts of food and massages for everyone. *Do these people even know how much a massage on a cruise costs?* Speaking of which, I needed to book my monthly massage.

Climbing the stairs to my apartment, *She's A Bad Mamma Jammer*, my ringtone for my mother, started playing in my purse. Get it? Or ignore it? I wasn't in the mood to talk with her, but, if I didn't, she'd keep pestering me until I answered.

"Hang on, Mom. I'm just getting home." I unlocked my door, went in, and kicked it shut, dropping my new shoes on the floor and kicking the old ones near the wall. "How are you, Mom? Everything okay?"

I've learned if you don't start with the niceties, you end up with a lecture.

"You're out late." Did you hear the recrimination in her voice? Never mind that I catered to her better side. "Were you on a date? Oh! Tell me all about it." *Not a chance.*

"Yes, I was, but your first pick didn't go well, and, before you ask, I'm not talking about it."

"Can't you throw your poor mother a morsel, dear? What's his name, at least?" She knew how to play me. Fine. One name.

"Isabelle's nephew, Ravi," I spat out. The gasp she uttered was hysterical—an Academy Award winning gasp.

"Don't act so surprised, Mother. It's not like you've met these guys and can vouch for their character." My sarcasm was dry. Encouraging her behavior was detrimental to keeping her calm.

"I know, but Isabelle raved about Ravi." We chuckled at the alliteration.

"After being a douchebag, he mellowed out when I gave him a talking-to. He couldn't turn off his work persona and made me feel like he was testing me all night. I don't have to live up to his expectations. I'm good on my own."

The connection was silent, and that concerned me.

"Mom. Are you all right?"

She cleared her throat, "I'm okay. It's just that what if you don't find a life partner? I know giving me grandchildren is low on your priority list, but I'm not getting any younger, and neither are you. This idea of a knight in shining armor swooping you into his arms and riding into the sunset isn't real. Men are . . . imperfect in so many ways. They aren't like us women."

And that's when I burst into laughter. "Do you hear yourself? 'Women are perfect?' Mom, you're delusional. And, if you haven't noticed, I'm not a schoolgirl with stars in my eyes. I'm not looking for perfection in a man, only that he is not an asshole thinking he's better than me. I'm not taking a back seat to my dreams and desires."

Then came the waterworks. "I've failed you!" *Then, deep, painful sighs.* "Where did I go wrong?"

Her histrionics were where I drew the line. "I've got to go, Mom. I'm fine. You're fine. We're all fine. I'll call you again soon. Have fun planning your party. Love you!" And, done.

I pushed the button to end the call and fell back against the couch cushions. A two-minute conversation with my mother was similar to a 5K marathon. Quick out of the gate, and barely enough time to get your stride before you're wiped out from the uphill climb the whole way.

I really did love my mother, but I realized our game wasn't only for her. After getting knocked down at work and feeling despair about my future not being a name partner at Rutherford, Timmins, and Grovner, my world shifted, and the spotlight followed me. Where once work was my true love, it became a false security blanket to my happiness. It wasn't like I hadn't heard being a workaholic would make me a lonely woman. I knew the ramifications of my choices, though it took me seven years to understand the depth of what those words might mean.

It was time to get with "the program" and start thinking clearly about what exactly I wanted my future to look like. I got myself ready for bed, then sat on the floor next to the dresser, crossing my legs and placing my hands on my knees. I settled my mind and breathed deeply, visualizing my life with a husband and kids. I tried to put color and details into the house I'd live in and the yard where the kids would play. The car I would drive, the activities I would participate in, and the kind of work I would do that would keep me challenged.

Most of this process was easy, except for the piece with whom I would share it all. I couldn't place a face just yet, but they were tall, muscled, and even-tempered. I breathed in one more time and exhaled as I stood up. The rest would come, but for now, I was exhausted. Date number four with David Lisner had potential, even if it was my mother's pick. At this point, nothing would surprise me.

hechsher—A hechsher or hekhsher is a rabbinical product certification, qualifying items that conform to the requirements of Jewish religious law. One e*xample: Dairy and meat cannot be eaten on a table simultaneously.*

Chapter 11

Dating was like Groundhog Day. Each new date was a do-over of the previous one. Complete with professional history, family history, and various points of view. All with a happy face pasted in place. It was exhausting.

"Emily," I called into the intercom for a change. "Can you clear my schedule for the next three hours? You and I are having lunch and digging through these bylaws, line-by-line."

I could feel her disgust through the wall, having to make those calls. In hindsight, I should have made her cancel my afternoon yesterday, but I didn't want to catch the partners' attention.

"Yes, Ms. Strauss." *Oh, yeah, she was annoyed.* "But we're having Thai food, and you're ordering it." *Sure. Whatever it took for her to forgive me.*

I picked up my cell and placed our order, then kicked off my shoes and walked to the big, oversized window overlooking a dense, green-space park. Some people coveted a skyline view or the sparkle of water being kissed by sunlight. Not me. The feeling of nature peering in my window calmed me down, and, with any luck, staring at it would heal my pounding headache. As I pulled out the chopsticks that held my hair up, it unrolled down my back, and immediately the strain behind my eyes softened. I bent at the waist into a swan dive, flipping my hair over my head and threading my fingers through the soft, curly hair, when I heard a deep, rich voice.

"Nice ass, Becs." I looked through my legs to see Spencer running his thumb over his bottom lip.

Was this the part where I chuckled and laughed off the comment or returned with a barb? Instead, feeling feisty, I served up an equally sexually-charged retort.

"I know. You want some of this?" *Oh shit!* That came out all wrong. "I mean, what did you want? Something . . . important?"

I needed to stop talking before I made things worse. I flipped my hair back up as I stood and turned around, checking in my periphery that my boobs went back in my blouse. Spencer closed in on my space and cupped my jaw. "I want whatever you're willing to give."

Oh, girl! My panties immediately were soaked with those seven words, and my skin rippled with electricity. He was too close. I felt my lips move, but nothing came out. Why did he have to touch me? There wasn't time to answer those questions as his lips pressed to mine, humming what could only be his approval.

"Hmm. You always taste so good, Red." My brain shut down when he called me that. When we were in high school, Spencer started calling me Red to differentiate between this other girl in his class named Rebecca. Then he added a slow drawl, and I was a goner. Come to think of it, my crush on Spencer was all his fault. If he didn't give me so many pet names, and say them with a southern drawl, I wouldn't have looked his way. *I mean, I could have!*

Now that we made out, and he—he—touched me everywhere, I didn't know what to say or do.

His thumb ran over my cheek, and I pressed into it automatically. Damn it! How do I fix this?

"Don't get too comfortable doing that, Spence. I don't want to disappoint you." My eyes turned downward, a substantial void filling my chest as I stepped away. I could hear the exasperation in his sigh.

Emily burst into the room. Our lunch arrived unexpectedly fast, and neither of us was prepared for her abrupt entrance. Her eyebrows raised as her mouth gaped open. "Oh. Uh. Lunch is here. You two okay?"

I supposed the sheepish looks on our faces may have given her the impression something was going on, but I had to set her straight.

"We're great!" I said a little too emphatically. "Spencer came in when I was flipped over, and . . ." *Nah. She wasn't buying this.*

Spencer walked back to my office door. "I was in the building and thought I'd swing by and say hello to Becca. Unfortunately, she was upside down, shaking her hair out when I came in. It flustered her." *He was so smooth.*

"Yep. That's what happened. Emily, why don't you set us up at the coffee table, and I'll walk Spencer out." I didn't wait for an answer, took Spencer by the elbow, led him to the elevator bank, and pushed the down button.

"We should talk, Becca." His mouth was pouting, and his hazel eyes showed more flecks of gold around his irises. *Why hadn't I ever noticed them before?*

Mesmerized by the changes in his eyes, I didn't realize the elevator doors were opening, and he pulled me in quickly just as they closed. His hands were splayed around my lower back, pressing me tightly into his chest. I could feel his cock imprinting itself on my stomach as he stole a ravaging kiss. I didn't know how badly I wanted one until the doors opened on the main floor, and Spencer bolted from the elevator car.

He spun around, pointing a finger at me. "We still need to talk," he said, grinning ear-to-ear.

I pushed the button for my floor and fell against the wall. Everything happened so fast. I didn't even have my shoes on! My God, that man unnerved me. How could I be mad and turned on at the same time? We did need to talk, but I was still processing last week's interlude. Today was something out of a romance movie synopsis: *Dashing Man Sweeps Beautiful, Unsuspecting Woman off Her Feet into an Elevator.* Yeah. That's exactly what happened. I bit my lip, smiling. That was hot and fun. Somehow, I didn't think Spencer and I could be in the same room, only talking anymore. Our frenetic energy was off the charts, and I didn't know how to explain it, especially to Emily. She would want the dirt on the whole Spencer thing, but I wanted to hold it close to my chest a while longer.

I entered my office and closed the door, trying not to giggle. I flopped down on my comfy couch and picked up a carryout container before looking straight into Emily's staring eyes.

"Dish," she demanded. She didn't resume eating, and I kept shoveling more food in my mouth to buy some time.

"Well, you know, Spencer . . . he's . . . shown more interest in . . . my work."

She jammed her free hand onto her hip and cocked her head, annoyed. "I call bullshit. That man has got it bad for you. Didn't you see the way he kept checking you out?"

He did? Didn't he? "You're delusional. He was concerned I might be lightheaded from hanging upside down for so long." I pushed my hair behind my ear and shoved in more food.

Emily pointed her fork at me, frowning. "You're the delusional one. Whatever. Tell me, don't tell me. I know what's going on. Now, where are we starting?"

We had worked through the bylaw sections related to compensation and advancement for the past ten years, noting nothing significantly changed until this most recent version was three months ago. What was the motivation to make these changes without a full board meeting?

Emily asked, "Can they make those decisions without calling a board meeting?"

Precisely. That was the problem.

"Sure, if there was a compelling reason, but the only way to discern that would be to read through all their meeting notes for the past six months and have access to the firm's financial records.

You know they aren't just going to hand those over without asking questions."

My brain hurt, and, by the look on Emily's face, hers did, too.

"So, where do we go from here?" Emily began cleaning up our mess, trying not to spill the rice box with her breasts as she leaned over the coffee table.

I threw my hands over my head and slid into the couch cushions, staring at the ceiling, helpless.

"I need to sit with this for a while. Let's call it a day. Go home early and stop by Sunny's to get a pretty bouquet and chocolates for yourself. You've earned it."

She made small clapping hands and danced out of my office singing, "Sunny, one so true, I love you-oo-oo-oo." It was just like Emily to extract a one-hit wonder like Bobby Hebb from the 1960s. She couldn't remember a darn word from any song from the 2000s, and she was born then.

"Where would you like to eat dinner?" I queried David's voicemail. He'd been putting off where to meet for dinner, and we were supposed to meet in two hours.

I left work early, looking forward to a bubble bath. Lavender oils infused the hot water, and my favorite vanilla candles were lit on the edge of the tub. Bobby Hebb was singing in the background as I stripped down at the threshold to my bathroom. Giddy at submerging into a cocoon of bubbles peppered with thoughts of

Spencer's tongue deep inside my mouth made my nipples tight and my pussy gush. Damn, that man could kiss.

Thinking of his hands along my sides as he yanked me into the elevator left me speechless. It was reckless, wild, and incredibly sexy. My thoughts evolved into what might have happened last week if he hadn't had a conscience. Those thoughts wound tightly around my core, remembering his eyes on my ass bent over in my office. Once those eyes offered comfort and concern for a little sister, but now he raked them over my body compelling me to look away. The intensity was overwhelming.

Chapter 12

I stared at the bubbles, watching them cave in around themselves. I scooped up a handful of water and drizzled it over my chest, droplets strategically striking my nipples, making them hard. I watched my full globes bobbing over the water line, puckering as the cold air met my warm skin, giving me a tingly feeling. What naughty things would Spencer do if he saw me like this? I slid my hand down between my thighs, needing an immediate release. My phone went off, tearing me away from my fantasy, leaving my pussy ache.

It was David. *Oy.* "Hey, David. What do you think? Where would you like to meet?" I tried not to sound breathy or annoyed since I felt both.

"Hello, Becca," he replied tentatively. "About dinner, how about that tapas place by the courthouse? We could go dancing afterward?"

Why did he seem so unsure of himself?

"Sure. Still on for seven o'clock?" I needed time to finish what I'd started and get myself together.

He cleared his throat. "Ah, how about we meet at six? That place gets so busy. I'm starving."

"Oh." I looked into the mirror. "Go ahead and get a table. I'll get there as close to six as possible." *Or as soon as I get myself off.*

"Terrific. See you soon." David hung up first, and I stared at my phone in disgust. I was having such a good time. Too aggravated to finish what I started, I pulled the plug from the drain and used the shower wand to spray off the sweet-smelling bubbles. Next time, I'm turning my phone off.

I had to give myself credit. I rearranged my curls, reapplied my makeup, and slid into a slinky, emerald dress that split on the side. I looked sexy, sultry, and sophisticated for a night out dancing. Arriving five minutes late, the hostess ushered me personally to the street-side table David had secured. He stood, gallantly pulling out my chair, allowing me to slide in gracefully.

"If your being late gets me the chance to see you in a dress like that, then wow! I'm happy to wait." He skimmed his thumb over his jawline and nodded appreciatively.

Warmth spread over my neck and chest, reveling in the almost forward way he addressed me. David was a paradox. Unsure on the phone, then forward in person. Maybe he was distracted when he called me back. I was perplexed and intrigued.

"Thank you. I did make time to go home and change. Dancing in a suit is awkward and weird." I snickered. "Of course, this dress undoubtedly will have some challenges, too." I lifted the napkin off my plate and laid it across my lap, noticing my breasts pushing out of the flimsy built-in cups. If I guessed correctly, David also enjoyed images of me falling out of my dress on the dance floor; if not, our dinner table.

He pulled his full lips into his mouth, rubbing them together like he had just finished a steak dinner. "I'll be sure to be on the lookout for any improprieties." Dark green eyes hidden by long dark lashes blinked slowly, and a slow smile slid up one corner of his mouth.

Damn, was he hot.

The server took our drink order while pointing out today's specials and dishes that were best to share.

"This place is fun. I've wanted to try it, but I'm always in a hurry after work." Every word out of my mouth was rushed and awkward. What was my problem?

David leaned forward and reached out for my hand, holding my menu. "No need to be in a hurry tonight. If you'd like me to order for the both of us, I'd be happy to oblige."

"That would be wonderful. Just nothing too spicy, please." His grin beckoned to thoughts unsaid.

Our drinks were delivered, and David ordered five dishes that made my mouth water—pulled pork pasties, shrimp garlic toast, a chopped beet salad, mini chicken tacos, and corned beef cabbage eggrolls. It's good that neither David nor I kept kosher because every rule was broken at this meal.

I lifted my glass proudly, "To keeping kosher." He burst out laughing and raised his glass in agreement.

"To keeping kosher."

I liked how he sat back in his chair and spun the stem of his cabernet stem with manicured long fingers. David felt comfortable in his skin, and it was sexy. He didn't shove his sensuality in my face. It just happened. He held my chair for me to sit and ran his hands over my shoulders, asking if I was too cold. Or how he ordered our dinner like he'd written the menu himself. It had been a long time since a man was so tuned into me that it turned my insides into liquid chocolate.

Like we'd done it for years, we fed each other small bites from each plate. The level of intimacy was instant and heady, nothing like I'd ever experienced before. David reached across the table, placing a forkful of beet salad into my mouth as I caught the gleam in his eyes. I wrapped my mouth around his fork like I was going down on him, and the breathtaking moan he let out made my pussy gush. I held the fork a moment longer than necessary, drawing out another satisfying hiss, and feared others around us would hear. I never knew eating could be so erotic.

I cleared my throat, ashamed of how wanton I'd become, and not just this evening.

"So, tell me more about your work. You're a nurse?" I chugged the rest of my wine and almost knocked over the glass when I put it down.

He chuckled. "That's right. A licensed practical nurse. I work in emergency medicine as an ER operating nurse." His lips quirked almost arrogantly, but I suppose he earned it doing such a difficult job.

"That's incredible. You must see some wild cases?"

"I most certainly do. Today, a guy came in with a nail driven through his hand into a two-by-four." He shook his head in disbelief. "Said he was trying to feel closer to Jesus."

My mouth gaped open. "No way! Were you able to save his hand?"

David shifted forward and whispered, "Let's just say he'll need to learn to use his other hand for more than writing for awhile. More importantly, he earned a two-week all-expense trip to the psych ward. Poor fellow."

"Unbelievable. Our country is in desperate need of better clinical mental health resources. I'm happy he'll survive." I let the first part of his comment go. Delusions of grandeur come with a cost.

The server took payment and wrapped up the rest of our dinner while David stood and pulled out my chair. It was refreshing how he took my hand as we exited the restaurant and even sweeter when we stopped in front of an electric blue Ford Mustang.

"Nice wheels. Is this yours?"

He beamed.

"Yeah. I got it earlier this week after my promotion came through. Now I can afford it. Hop in. It's a short drive to the bar."

He opened the door for me and took my hand as I settled into the passenger seat. My dress shifted up my thighs, giving him a good look at not only my legs but my ample tits. Given how David licked his lips, knowing what was under this fabric didn't take much imagination. If I got lucky, tonight would finish far better than my fingers in a bathtub.

David dropped me at the curb of the *Sound Machine Bar* before he parked the car. It was barely seven o'clock, and there was already a line. It's been so long since I'd been to a bar that I forgot how rowdy a Thursday night could be. In college, for some, drinking and dancing was a four-night itinerary. I was lucky to get four nights a month to let my hair down and party. My engineering program was no joke, and law school was worse. I was called a geek, nerd, and a dork, but I didn't care. I knew myself well enough that when I did party, it was with every cell in my body. However, I neglected those cells for weeks on end, making this geeky girl dull.

I looked down the street and saw a very fit, dark-haired hunk jogging down the street with a gorgeous smile on his face and his muscular chest heaving under his stylish, button-down Oxford.

"Hey, baby. Wanna dance?" David arrived, grabbing my hand, turning toward the bar entrance.

"Sure. But can you keep up?" My smile was wide as I threw my head back, happy with my comeback.

He pulled me tightly to his chest, nudging his face to my neck. "Let's find out." *Oh, let's!*

We didn't have to wait since the bouncer was a security guard at the hospital where he worked—the perks of friends in high places. We found a small table to the far right of the DJ stage behind the speakers so we could talk. A waitress in a tight, white, cropped button-down sashayed by. Her straining breasts, pushed out of the too-small red bra hiding beneath her shirt, paired with matching red satin tap pants, were impressive. Even David caught me looking at her.

He pulled his chair closer to mine and leaned into me again. "There's so much more to you than you let on." I gave him a wicked smile, flung my long red locks over my shoulder, and ordered a rum and coke with a lime. David's lips pursed together seductively, then released to order a craft beer.

"So much, David. How about that dance?"

He stood and pulled out my chair while offering his hand. I placed my petite one into his calloused large one, and he unexpectedly maneuvered me into a seductive dip. "Let's stay close to our table for now. Give me one drink, and then we can tear up that floor."

Later, my mind was blown by his ability to move me around the dance floor so easily. It must be his agile nursing skills that made it easy for him. Strong arms wrapped around my waist as he held me tightly to his chest. He kissed my neck and shoulder and damn it if I didn't want to leave and fuck him hard in the backseat of his car. I could hear him humming the song's tune as the vibrations reverberated off his chest. He couldn't have known how that sound rippled down my spine, making me wetter than I already was.

The song was over, and we sat down to enjoy our drinks, but David never took a hand off me. I studied his face from my angle and noticed he had a scar under his jaw and another I couldn't see well before, just above his left eye. I traced my finger along his jaw, and his eyes locked onto mine.

"How did this happen?" I said, treading carefully. I'd seen pictures of dead people with similar scars and didn't want to traumatize him by reliving the situation again.

He pressed his hand over mine, pulled it away, and kissed my palm. That one action sent a flare of desire so deep within me that I gasped.

"I was a Medical Corpsman for four years. You don't get out of the military without a few scars." His half-hearted shrug was dismissive and pulled me out of my thoughts.

I wasn't sure whether to be embarrassed for touching such a delicate wound or deeply appreciative of his sacrifices, so I went with both. "Thank you so much for your service. Your sacrifices must have been great, especially since you have a constant reminder for the rest of your life."

No sooner did I say those words than I wanted to retract them. "I mean, it doesn't detract from your looks. You're—gorgeous."

His hand slid higher on my thigh, pulling me closer—his body leaning closer, filling me with anticipation. "No worries, Becca. I'm over them. I only joined the service to get the GI Bill benefits. Nursing school is costly, and, by working in the Medical Corp, I could transfer hundreds of practical hours to my program, saving me a year's worth of time completing it."

I dropped my hand from my drink and slid it up his thick thigh, appreciating his ambition and wickedly tight body. "You're a clever one, aren't you?"

His Adam's apple bobbed as he smirked. He captured my jaw and held me in place, the anticipation killing me. "Do you want to find out how clever I am?"

Dear Lord, this man knew how to turn me on.

"So badly," I cried.

His mouth crushed onto mine, and his other hand held me still. He pulled my lower lip with his teeth and spoke dirty words into my mouth. My back arched and I could have come from those words alone if he hadn't pulled away so quickly.

"You taste so fucking good, Becca. I want to do so many things with that mouth of yours, but I promised you a dance, and, damn it, you'll get one."

David threw back the rest of his drink and slammed the glass on the table. "Let's go," he growled, pulling me to the dance floor again.

The music pumped through the room, making everything vibrate. The dance floor was packed, and people writhed like a wheat field in a heavy breeze. Back and forth. David and I moved independently yet within inches of each other. His eyes were laser-focused on how my tits bounced, and every chance he got, he slid his hands around my ass cheeks, squeezing my flesh appreciatively. My mind buzzed from the alcohol and the thump of the beat, but it was the grinding David did against my hips that had me out of my mind. I wasn't Becca, the tight-assed patent lawyer. Or the mouthy daughter of an elitist mother. I felt liquid from head to toe. I moved unabashedly, waving my arms above my head, lifting my hemline high up my thighs, and not caring a damn bit who saw it. I couldn't remember the last time I felt so light and unencumbered.

"Fuck, you're beautiful," David moaned, capturing my body to his as the music settled into a sexy R&B groove. My hands spread over his taunt pecs and hissed at how perfectly flat his abs were. Thoughts of what he looked like without that shirt on made my mouth water.

"David?" I angled my head upward and kissed his lips gently.

He bent to snuggle into my neck, squeezing me so tightly he lifted me off the dance floor.

"Yeah, baby." The wetness from his tongue as he traced the shell of my ear was intoxicating.

"I—I want you—now." In all my days, I had never uttered those words to anyone. Not even my boyfriend in high school.

David crushed his mouth to mine again before setting me back on my feet, and he delivered a promise I'd hold him to. "I'm going to fuck you so hard you're going to forget what day it is."

In a flash, he grabbed my hand and, with the other, ushered me out of the loud, thumping bar to the freezing cold air. I left my coat in his car so I wouldn't have to worry about it in the bar, and David wrapped me in a hot embrace as we speed-walked down the sidewalk to his car. He flung my door open and pressed another deep kiss on my lips before sitting me down, buckling my seatbelt, and laying my coat over my lap. He stole another kiss and pulled my bottom lip, promising to use my mouth for good and not evil.

"You're a very naughty girl and deserve a spanking when you get home." My lips curled devilishly, plotting how much fun we would have.

I gave David my address, and, like a good boy, he broke in his new toy in record time. He pulled me from his car into a fireman's carry and took the stairs to my apartment two at a time. Setting me down carefully against the wall, I fumbled in my purse for my key, but David had another idea. He flipped me around to pin me against my door, kissing my shoulders and sliding the spaghetti straps down my arms, exposing my breasts.

"God damn it, woman. Your tits are perfect." David wasted no time pulling out one of my breasts and bending down to suck my puckered nipples.

"Fuck, David. We're in the hallway. Please, open my door."

He looked up at me, realizing where we were. He grabbed the keys without a word and jimmied them into the door lock. We fell into the room as our clothes fell to the floor. David's cock was smaller than Joshua's but longer than Larry's. I couldn't believe I was running a data analysis in the middle of an imminent sexual encounter. *Focus, girl!*

David bent, yanked his wallet from his pants, and found two foil packets holding them high like he'd hit the jackpot.

"Couch or bed?" he demanded.

Good question. The couch reminded me of Spencer and me taking chances with our relationship, but the bed seemed too intimate. Larry had it right. A salon chair was perfect for those precarious moments.

"Spare room, now," I demanded back. I grabbed David's hand and dragged him across my apartment past the hall bathroom and into my spare room slash office. Every room in a big city had dual purposes, mine included.

I pushed David onto the full-sized bed, pushing the decorative pillows to the floor. I grabbed one for my knees, knelt before him, spread his legs, and licked my lips. When he fully realized what I was about to do, he fell backward, yelling, "Thank you, God!"

I may not be very practiced in blow jobs, but I had a few tricks up my sleeve, and David was the recipient of my talents.

"Geezus, fuck, Becca. Yes, baby. Suck me slow." I moaned at his words, licking my lips when his tip released a small pool of white cream.

I took my time giving David a show of how I looked with my mouth sliding down his shaft. He played with my hair and pulled on it when he wanted me to take more, and I gladly did.

"You're so good at this. I don't know whether I want to come in your mouth or your pussy," David croaked out.

That got my attention. We had condoms, and we would use all of them. There would be no bare-backing tonight. David was fun, but spending the rest of my life with him? Too early to tell. I reached for the foil packet to his left and tore it open with my teeth. His cock bobbed as I rolled the condom into place, cupping his balls when I was done.

"Show me what you've got, big guy." My comment might be misleading, but I had surmised that David loves dirty talk, and I was happy to feed his ego to get him harder.

"Yes!" He pulled me up and threw me onto the bed without care. I yelped when he planted his hands next to my head.

"Hair! Your hands are pulling out my hair." My scalp tingled after he smoothed my long tresses alongside my face.

"Oh. Sorry, babe. I love this hair, but there's so much of it." There was nothing to be done about that but push it away.

He grabbed his cock and tugged on it a few times before he lined himself up and slowly slid his shaft into me. I watched his face morph from conquering to determination. His thrusts slowed, and there seemed to be less of him in me. The dip between his brows was concerning, and I pushed my fingers through his dark, wavy hair.

"Are you okay? You look pale." I moved my hands to his back, hoping to use my fingers to soothe him, but my hands slid through a sheet of sweat. *What was happening?*

His final thrust fell short when his flaccid penis fell out of me, and I knew what had happened. He couldn't keep an erection. He must feel awful. I know I felt awful. I wiped my hands on the sheets and brought them both up to rest on his face. David hovered over me, bolstered by his strong arms, but his ego was crushing him. I reached up to kiss his beautifully soft pink lips in consolation.

I tried to get him to look at me, but he wouldn't give me his eyes. "Sometimes that happens. It's okay." I kissed him again, but he snorted and rolled off the bed.

Muttering profanities and hisses, he turned his back on me, scrambling for his underwear. Once he had his briefs on, he whirled on me.

"It's not okay. It's never going to be okay to have a limp dick with a hot woman. Fuck!" He stormed around the room, stuffing each leg into his pants and zipping up his fly.

I wrapped myself in the sheet, left the bed, and approached him carefully.

"David, will you sit with me for a minute?" I placed my hand on his forearm, trying again to get him to look at me. It was as though he was lost in another time and space.

I led him to the bed, and we sat silently for a few minutes. I wondered what had triggered this situation, but nothing came to mind.

He took my hand in both of his, massaging the back of them, making me feel relaxed and safe.

"You can stop wondering about what happened. It started after I left the service. Without going into all the details, just know that a good friend I'd made during my four years as a Marine died during a skirmish, and I couldn't save him. He died in my arms, and I felt incompetent, impotent, and bereft. I went to counseling and seemed to get better. At least I thought I was better. But now I can see this bullshit will continue to haunt me forever." He stood and kissed the top of my head.

"You're an incredible woman, Becca. This was the best date I've had in a very long time. The guy that gets you will have hit the jackpot." Dejected and resigned, David grabbed his shirt and swung his arms into the sleeves, buttoning it slowly.

I moved to his side and stopped his hands from moving with my own. "Listen carefully because you'll only hear this from me once.

You are not broken, and a pill isn't the cure. Circumstances created this feeling, but new circumstances can fix it if you let it. Please keep trying to find the right combination of forgiveness, success, and love. You deserve it, and you certainly have earned it. Maybe we'll try another time. If not, I think you're incredible, too."

He pulled me close and held me tightly. I could hear him sniffle, and my heart broke. Sex was only a part of a meaningful relationship. I'm sure he would find the right woman to help him heal his heart, mind, and spirit. God knows his body was worth the fight.

"Goodbye, Becca. Don't be good." He winked.

"Never," I promised coquettishly.

Date number five ended as a dumpster fire, but before his E.D. wrecked him, this night was smokin'. Tomorrow was another day, and another date was on my calendar to look forward to. Evan Zweig, a financial guru. *Wish me luck!*

Chapter 13

Another text pinged on my phone—the third one today from Spencer. I didn't want to face another conversation about being friends or about how he respected my brother's wishes and needed to keep his distance, but I needed to respond.

Me: *Hey, Spence. Sorry about not getting back to you sooner. Work stuff.*

Spencer: *Cut the bullshit, Becca. We need to talk.*

Me: *I know. I want to, but I'm afraid we won't talk and do other stuff.*

Spencer: *Like fuck each other?*

Holy Shit! Did he say that?

Me: *Probably.*

Spencer: *Are you afraid of me? That's not like you, Becca.*

I had too much to do today without having Spencer on the brain. The truth was that I was afraid of him. I can't keep my hands off him now that we've broken the dam on our sexual feelings for each other. I was worried after all the lust wore off, he'd get bored of me, and then I'd lose my best friend. I was afraid my family would flip out if they knew we were what—dating? We weren't actually dating, though. We were fooling around like teenagers at a Friday night football game. There were so many questions I couldn't wrap my head around, and talking with him now would only cloud my judgment.

Me: *Of course, I'm not afraid of you. You're the one person in the whole world who I trust the most. It's . . . I'm afraid of myself.*

Spencer: *I'm picking you up after work, and we're going to talk this through. I'll grab Chinese.*

Me: *I can't. I have another date at six-thirty. Can this wait until next week?*

Spencer: *You'll still go out on the rest of your stupid dates when you know how off-the-charts our chemistry is? (Angry emoji)*

Me: *(Frowning emoji) I'm so sorry to disappoint you, but I promised my mother, and I don't want her throwing this back in my face for "not trying hard enough."*

Spencer: *Then tell her you found a guy, and you're done with dating.*

Me: *Are you saying you want to be together?*

Those damn three dots bounced on and off for over five minutes. Was he having second thoughts about committing to me? We haven't even discussed that! I guess that's why we need to talk. Sometimes, I'm so slow to pick things up.

Spencer: *We need to talk this out. I won't deny I have feelings for you. I hope you'll reconsider going on those dates.*

Me: *I've got to go. I'll send you some time and dates. We'll talk soon.*

I couldn't make myself add a heart emoji like I usually did. The pain of attaching one when I knew it meant more than the one I sent last week gave me *shpilkes.*

A loud knock on my door pulled me from my lament. I knew it wasn't Emily because she knocked out a soft code. This was someone else. My intercom went off, startling me.

"Becca, it's Timmins," Emily whispered hastily.

"Got it," I whispered back, standing as I called for Mr. Timmins to enter. It was time to face the reaper—God knows he looked like one.

I pressed my skirt down and perused my desk for any papers that might get me into trouble.

"Mr. Timmins, to what do I owe the honor? Please have a seat." I motioned for him to take either of the chairs in front of my desk, but instead, he walked to the wall of windows overlooking my greenspace.

He made a quarter turn, hands behind his back, and spoke with a dry, crackly voice. "Something is amiss, Ms. Strauss, and it appears you are the cause of it."

What? Does he know that I'm scrutinizing the bylaws?

I walked closer to the windows, keeping several feet between us. "Me? I'm not sure of your meaning."

I had to stay cool, calm and collected. I was a lawyer, so there wouldn't be any fidgeting or other telltale signs that would give me away.

Timmins faced me directly, perusing my countenance. What was he thinking?

"Our new client, LeafLorn Industries, is unhappy with your background research for their new building. They specifically stated they needed a list of abatements offered by the city last Friday, and it's been a full week of failure on your part by not submitting that list. Is there a logical reason why that hasn't happened yet?" His breathing was asthmatic and smelled of anchovies. It took all my effort not to heave.

He was right. I dropped the ball, and now I would lose my job over it. Between these stupid dates I'd crammed in this week, my mother's nagging, and the Spencer thing, I didn't have my head in my job. I needed a reasonable excuse, and I think I knew a way out.

"I'll take responsibility for that, Mr. Timmins. I had sent the request over to the Urban Development Department as requested and was told Mr. Weiss would be out of the office most of last week, and I failed to follow up with him earlier this week. I'll reach out to Mr. Gilmore immediately and offer my apologies." I hung my head in regret, trying to show my sincerity for not following through.

He turned toward the door and glided like a ghost across the floor. "Don't lose this account, Ms. Strauss. It's taken us three years to land it. Get a list on Mr. Gilmore's desk by the end of the day tomorrow, or you'll be walking out that door for the last time." He opened the door with his bony hand and glared at me, slamming my door hard enough to shake the picture on the wall.

Emily burst through my door just as I heard the elevator chime in the distance.

"I heard every word. Was that a me-thing or a you-thing? It's not like us to be so flakey." I felt her pout.

I slinked to my desk chair and dropped unceremoniously into the Tempur-Pedic seat.

"Anything to do with my work is a me-thing. It's not your fault. I've been distracted, and, apparently, my follow-through sucks. Please get Spencer on the phone immediately and see if he can squeeze me into his schedule today."

I folded my arms across my desk and lay my head in the cradle. My eyes stung, and there was a nauseous feeling brewing deep in my belly—and it wasn't because I was excited to meet with Spencer. Moments later, Emily responded.

"Mr. Weiss can meet with you in thirty minutes. He said to have you meet him at the bench in front of his building."

Not the bench. The bench was for bad news, while my office was for good news. His office was only for business, but the bench was an omen of disaster.

"Thank you. Did you mention it was regarding the LeafLorn files?" I said sweetly, hoping she had.

"No, I didn't. Sorry, I forgot."

"No problem. Please call back so he knows what our meeting is about and can prepare accordingly." It was a rare moment when I had to chastise Emily, but I wasn't accepting "the bench" as a meeting place.

"Sure thing, sorry again."

I heard her pick up the phone immediately and waited for her reply.

"Hi again, he said to come up to his office to go over the request."

Yes! "Thank you, Emily. Please put those files together for me, including the city ordinances."

"Consider it done." The phone clicked. I let out a massive sigh of relief, letting go of how this day had turned south so quickly. Now, if I could only keep Spencer on track and not get into our personal life.

**shpilkes (shpil-keez)—impatience, restlessness, anxiety*

Chapter 14

"Hi, Gina. Thanks for getting me onto Spencer's schedule last minute. I dropped the ball on this one."

My sheepish demeanor was sincere, and her kindness was paramount to me fixing my problem. The Southfield city offices didn't exactly scream sophistication, so I chose to walk around the lobby, giving the impression I was viewing the intricate drawings of past projects along the wall adjacent to the elevator. Spencer may not have drawn these renderings, but he had a hand designing where and how these buildings would make each city block more vibrant. His attention to detail was like none other than I had seen. Tiny details included planting tall arborvitae as a natural barrier to other surrounding buildings and then putting in hardscapes like fences or walls. He was clever like that.

After time dragged on, I peered over to Gina, who was speaking to someone and looked my way. Was that Spencer on the line, or was she plotting to get rid of me? I turned around, not wanting to make her self-conscious, and finally sat on an overused couch to read a three-month-old copy of *Architectural Digest*.

The elevator dinged, and there was my appointment, looking disheveled, annoyed, and belligerent. His hazel eyes bore into me, putting me on high alert.

"Come on, Becca," he barked, striding across the lobby to his office door. "Gina, please hold my calls. I assume you've rearranged my schedule to accommodate Ms. Strauss?"

"Yes, sir. You're all clear until your three o'clock meeting." She smiled meekly. I wondered if their relationship was strained since she didn't make direct eye contact with him.

"Thanks, Gina." I bowed my head in contrition and quickly followed him into his office.

Spencer pushed the door open and ushered me in unceremoniously, shutting the door with a bang. I wasn't sure what to do next. Sit? Stand? Offer an ice-breaker? It didn't matter. Spencer had other plans.

He threw his satchel on a cushioned visitor's chair, grabbed me by the back of my arms, and pulled me tightly to his chest. His face inches from mine, leaving me momentarily paralyzed.

Spencer hissed, "You're driving me crazy!"

I felt a spark of electricity running from his body to mine. I saw the veins in his neck straining to keep himself in check. I felt the sinew of his muscles straining through his shirt, blasting tingles that ran down my spine. Even after the four dates I just had, Spencer was far more dangerous to me. He could tear me apart and leave me in a weeping mess. My one and only friendship that kept me sane would be gone if I allowed it. The price was too high.

Without notice, Spencer stepped closer and kissed me softly. I could have cried. That kiss. Those lips. And that clever tongue sweeping the inside of my mouth would be the end of me. His hands were in my hair, pulling out my ponytail and holding my head back so he could fully access my face and neck. I had to stop him. This had to stop now. He could never be mine.

I grabbed his wrists and pulled them out of my hair, trying to release myself from his grasp. "Spencer. Please . . ."

"I love it when you beg." He moved forward again, pressing his prominent bulge against my belly.

"Please, stop." He went still. "I know we need to talk, but I'm here on business." I stepped back, the energy dissipating, the void palpable. He took two steps closer, rubbing his forehead and shaking his head.

"I'd like to repeat my first statement. You're driving me crazy. Do you not feel the same things I'm feeling when we kiss? Don't lie. I know you too well." He stared at me openly, pain and hurt all over his face. He was right. He did know me too well, sometimes better than I did.

I looked toward the door, wondering if I could make a run for it instead of telling him how I truly felt. I came here foolishly thinking our situation wouldn't come up. I needed to convince him that the cost of losing our relationship was too much for me to handle. My arms involuntarily wrapped around my waist, and I felt sick to my stomach about how this conversation could ruin us for good.

Tentatively, I walked over to his worktable and sat down.

I stuttered, " Before this, this conversation, please know I only came here for work. I need the LeafLorn tax abatement opportunities I forgot to follow up on earlier in the week."

Spencer whirled on his heels and marched to his desk, rifling through stacks of folders and pulling out the one I needed. He took three strides toward me and slammed it on the table.

"There!" he shouted. "I was hoping we could have met for lunch, and I'd give it to you personally, but you are too busy to give me the time of day. I have to steal every moment with you because I have somehow offended you. What is it, Becca? Why are you pissed off at me?"

Damn! Damn! Damn! He was right. I was as scared about ruining our relationship as I was at having him pissed off at me. Or worse, that I disappointed him. I could take his anger. He'd cool off like he'd always done before, and then we'd figure it out. We'd be cool again shortly afterward. But disappointment meant shame. And shame would be hurtful, and I'd be the cause of it.

He looked like a bull waiting for his toreador, hands jammed onto his hips and huffing out his breath. His stare was resolute. If I didn't answer soon, nothing good would come of this.

"Please sit down, Spence. I don't want to hurt you. You're right. We need to talk. I'm sorry this is happening at your workplace." My body shook as I forced the words out. I needed to get my emotions in check so Spencer could hear my words.

"I'd like to start from the beginning." I nodded, hoping he would give me more time to explain. "My feelings for you go way back. Back to the first time I met you. You were intriguing.

Different from the boys in my elementary school. You may have been two years older than me, but you acted like you were ten years older. I couldn't describe how I felt about you until high school. Do you remember my graduation party? We kissed for the first time."

Spencer's face softened, and he leaned back in his chair. I was making progress, but I had so much farther to go.

"You changed me. All my silly ideas about you and I having a relationship now seemed possible. That was until Nathan threatened you. I knew you kept your distance from me for years because of what he said until my college graduation. You looked at me again. You touched me again, and everything I'd suppressed bubbled up—again. I didn't know whether to be hopeful or feel tricked. That moment was cut short once more, and I didn't hear from you for years. I had to put those feelings under lock and key to survive. Do you understand what I'm saying? I had to move on."

He leaned forward, resting his arms on his knees, looking at the floor, "Me, too."

Me, too?

"What did you just say?" I crumpled in my chair.

He looked up, his jaw ticking as his head swayed back and forth. "I said, 'Me, too.'" Our eyes locked, and in those two words, our reality shifted, and understanding bloomed.

I gripped the arms of my chair and leaned forward, "You liked me? All those years ago—and said nothing? Do you have any idea how anguished I felt thinking this was a one-sided relationship?"

I stood up and walked around the back side of the table, smacking my hands down on the glass top, hoping I wouldn't shatter it. "What the hell have the last seven years been, Spence? Girlfriends that hang out together on a Saturday night? Why didn't you say something?" Steam rose from my head as I spat the words out.

He stood up, shoving his chair back angrily. "For the same goddamned reason, *you* didn't say anything. I didn't want our relationship to suffer by fucking around."

Wow! And there it was. Dumbfounded, I pulled the chair in front of me out from under the table, collapsing onto the seat and digging my fists into my eyes. Spencer's truth sounded so much worse than mine. He was angry about it, while mine was despair. *Where do we go from here?*

I heard the soft shuffle of his footsteps rounding the table and stopping behind me. I felt the tension emanating from his body, then the heat from his hands gently sliding onto my shoulders, pulling me upright. His touch was equal parts home and hell.

"Well—aren't we a pair," his soft chuckle floated into the ether.

I wiped my eyes with the back of my hands, pausing as I reached over to lay mine on his. "We sure are."

Spencer wrapped his arms around my head and neck and whispered, "Do we have a chance, Red?" Warm lips feathered my cheek and neck. *I hoped so.*

"Maybe. There is more to talk about. And there's this deal I have with my mother." I stood up, kissed him on the cheek, and collected my folder.

"What the fuck, Becca? Tell your meddling mother that we are together, and screw your deal." I felt Spencer's venom as he crossed the room. I didn't want to get his hopes up, especially since I had another awkward date tonight.

"I'll talk with her, but I can't promise anything. You know how she can be. You aren't her favorite person after the huge fight your mom and mine had years ago over differing Mahjong rules." I slid the folder into my bag and walked to his door, waiting for the age-old expected reply.

"Why do the children have to suffer for the father's or mother's sins?" The finger pointed at my face was deliberate, like I was the one to control the narrative.

"Don't point that finger at me! I suffer every damn day with my mother; at least you don't have to worry about yours anymore, God rest her soul." *That was low, even for me.* Spencer's mother had passed two years ago, but it still felt fresh for both of us. "I'm sorry, Spencer. That was callous of me."

I hung my head in shame, walked to the door, and turned with a hopeful smile. "I'll try," I whispered. "Okay?"

I didn't wait for an answer and left.

The worst part about fighting with Spencer now was that he left me agitated and wet. One hot, searing kiss was enough to get my juices flowing, and, after that fight, I needed to let off some steam. Date number five better have game.

Like every well-intentioned Jew, we sometimes forget to light our candles each night. We would pray extra hard for more light in the world. This was my penance for missing last night. I didn't want to light my menorah alone, so I called my sister-in-law, Eleanor, for support.

"Hang on one sec, Becca. Daniel is trying to climb out of his highchair." I heard her put the phone down, cooing at her two-year-old to stay seated while she clasped the tray. "There you go, little man. Here's your cup." I heard a clunk, then water running. "Okay. What's up, Becs?" She was out of breath as usual.

"So much and nothing at all." I learned to minimize my issues so she didn't ask too many questions. Eleanor was becoming my second mother, and I had reservations about the first one. "I was hoping we could light our candles together tonight. I miss having people around to light them sometimes." I played it off lightly because I didn't want pity or to pressure her to come over. She lived across town closer to my mother; heaven knows, I didn't want her to join us.

"Uh, sure. Hang on . . ." She put the phone down and screamed across the house for Nathan to come to the kitchen. They needed an intercom system. Or, like the younger generation, text from the other room.

Minutes passed, and we talked about how Daniel chewed the corner of a book and threw up, followed by how she was feeling nauseous again and hoped she wasn't "preggers." Finally, I could hear Nathan's exasperation, "What's up, Honey?" I could hear her mumbling about lighting candles, then promised to call back in fifteen minutes when they were ready to light them.

I knew it was an imposition to request their time at the last minute but, for some reason, I was feeling nostalgic. My dad would drop five pieces of chocolate *gelt* on the table in front of me and Nathan each night and make us choose which of the five hand-painted dreidels to spin. My mom would *yent* about how it was wrong to teach children to gamble, and he'd shoo her away immediately. It was our time to bond with our father, and if it was gambling with chocolate coins and a *dreidel*, then so be it.

gelt—money
yent—to complain
dreidel—A spinning top with one letter on each side. Each letter represented the words: Nes Gadol Haya Sham: A great miracle happened there. Or "po" here.

Chapter 15

Blitz was a swanky rooftop bar to which only the elite or ridiculously rich had access. Evan texted me to wait for him in the lobby, saying he would find me when he arrived. I was unsure how he planned to do that since he only knew about my red hair, and I wasn't sure I'd recognize him from his nearly empty social media pages.

Men in custom-tailored suits paraded by me, offering curious stares, presumably wondering if I was available. Their dates jabbed them in the sides when they checked me out. It was flattering and embarrassing at the same time. Sitting and waiting for court was one thing. Sitting on display at a bar was another. I wished Evan would get here already.

I looked at my cell phone again, hoping there was a message from him explaining why he was running late, or that he had to cancel, or any other bullshit story. It had been a long day, and I didn't want to be here feeling awkward. The time said seven-thirty, and he was thirty minutes late. This wasn't a good first impression. Time was up. I stood to leave when I heard my name called across the room.

Oy. I'd already decided I was going, and now I had to have a chat with myself to get back in the mood.

"Hey, Becca. Damn! You're gorgeous." His eyes raked over my black one-shouldered cocktail dress. It was classy and comfortable, perfect for an overpriced place like Blitz. It was clear Evan was a douchebag. Obnoxious, loud-mouthed, and self-absorbed. Especially since he kept pumping his muscles for me to see through his well-fit suit. It sucked that he was gorgeous. *Maybe he'll keep his mouth shut for the night.*

I extended my hand politely, "You're Evan. Nice to meet you. Did I get the time wrong? I've been here since seven." I wasn't letting go of my irritation until he knew he kept me waiting.

"Yeah, seven. What time is it?" *Time for you to get a watch!*

My feisty attitude couldn't be contained. "Not seven. Are you sure you have time for this?" I gave him some serious side-eye, hoping he would pick up what I put down.

He glanced at his Rolex, unaffected, "You're right. Let's get going then so we can get a table."

This asshole was getting on my last nerve. No "I'm sorry I'm late" or any remorse for holding me up. This night better include a one-eighty, or I'd be home in time to watch *Survivor.*

The hostess at the rooftop lounge directed us to the last high-top table next to the kitchen. This was not a table assignment for someone who said he would secure our view.

We ordered our drinks and appetizers, and when I went to speak he would cut me off.

"I made a killing today. I'm so glad we're celebrating. I've worked on this client for six months, and he finally caved in." Evan punched the air like he sunk the winning hole at a celebrity golf classic. It never ceased to amaze me that men were only big boys in suits. Crass, acting stupid, and making a lot of money gave them an excuse to be idiots.

Since Evan didn't pose a question to me, I only smiled and sipped at my pinot grigio. This should have been when my date would have turned the conversation over to me. However, he would have wanted to learn more about me to do that. Sadly, that was not the case.

His smarmy grin was nauseating. "You should have seen this guy's face when I showed him what a hundred grand would look like if he invested in Bitcoin. I told him in ten years, he could retire, and he couldn't write me a check fast enough. Have you invested in Bitcoin, Becca?"

Oh, hell no! I was not getting involved with this joker.

"No. I haven't and won't be going that route. I'm well diversified in other areas." His face shifted from a fraternity bruh to cheetah-on-the-prowl.

"Seriously, all you need is some patience, Becca. I could show you hundreds of examples of how people turned their futures around. You wouldn't believe it."

Yeah, I would. He'd take their solid investments and hang them out to dry while telling them to be patient until he reached his contract threshold.

Evan waved over our waitress and ordered us another round of drinks. I looked at my phone again. This was the slowest half hour of my life. I wished I wasn't arguing with Spencer; otherwise, I'd text him to bail me out. Instead, I texted my mother as Evan drew on a paper napkin the scintillating facets of crypto banking. *Boring.*

Me: *Hey, Mom. I'm on date #5, and I want to slit my throat. Do I have to keep going on these ludicrous facades? I could bring Spence to the party as my date, and I could go home afterward without making excuses about not wanting to go on another date.*

Ten minutes passed, and our appetizers arrived. I smiled and nodded politely at the waitress and then Evan, who was still going strong on his finance scheme. I enjoyed the tasty bruschetta with goat cheese and the Thai chicken satays when I saw the three bouncing dots on my phone.

Marilyn: *Yes! A deal is a deal, dear. Spencer is a nice boy, but after what his mother put me through, you will never date him, let alone marry him. I forbid it. Now, paste a smile on your face and make your mother proud.*

I hate her. I hate her. I hate her! Emphasizing the last one.

My eyes rolled back, and I slumped in my chair, annoyed at my predicament. Evan kept yammering on, and I kept eating. Another twenty minutes passed, and I grabbed my purse and stood up.

"Excuse me. I'm going to the ladies' room." I didn't wait for an answer, and he looked offended that I was leaving his riveting speech. This was not a conversation. Conversations were an exchange of thoughts, and I hadn't put two words into this evening.

The bathroom was swarming with shallow conversations of who would "bag" whom tonight and if their boob job, butt lift, or fill-in-the-blank looked good. It seemed I started a habit of using this room as a haven when I felt trapped. It was childish, I know. There had to be a better way to excuse myself without hiding. Texting Spencer was out. Texting my mother was a hard no. Emily was out on a date, so she was out. That left Annie.

Me: *Hello there, long-lost friend.*

I gently leaned my head against the glass tiles that covered the wall behind the tufted bench I perched on. Thoughts of how to spin this evening were few and far between. *Should I call Evan out, like I did to Ravi when he was trying to blow me off without trying to get to know me? Or I could go with the standard, "I don't feel well?" That was so cliché. Am I interested enough in forcing him to get to know me? Not really.*

My phone pinged.

Annie: *Becca! Yeah, it's been a while—at least a couple days. What are you up to? We should put a date on our calendars for an in-person gathering.*

We should. I would. Just as soon as she could get me out of this pickle.

Me: *Not much. Only dealing with my meddling mother, who hooked me up with a crypto-currency finance guy that won't shut the f*ck up.*

Annie: *You're hiding in the bathroom, right?*

Me: *You really know me. Do I have to stay? He was late getting here and didn't apologize, and now he's trying to get me to convert my whole retirement plan to Bitcoin or Dogecoin. Do you understand that stuff?*

I got up and walked over to the now vacant vanity mirror. My eyes were smudged with dark circles from lack of sleep, and my posture was that of a petulant child without crossed arms. I looked good in my dress, and my hair was dangling in sexy curls, which some of the other women commented on when they walked past me. It's nice to know the female crowd gave me attention. Everyone but the dude who was supposed to be giving me his attention. I was fed up.

Annie: *I'm sure you've run all the data on this situation, so I'll skip to the point. Go out there and tell that asshole to shut the f*ck up and leave.*

I could do that. It wasn't like me, but I could do it. I was a people pleaser, not a steamroller. Perhaps this was why I didn't fight to get my promotion. I didn't owe this guy anything, so why was I considering his feelings over mine?

Me: *You are brilliant, friend. I knew I could count on you to get me out of this jam.*

Annie: *When you've dated over a hundred guys, you have to get creative with your responses. Take care of yourself, sweetheart, and put me on your calendar for Saturday, December 20. Shopping, lunch, and massages. I'll book it all.*

Me: *You're incredible. Thanks again. (smiley face with hearts emoji)*

I looked at myself again in the mirror and shone Annie's light on where to put my focus. I fluffed my locks and did a one-eighty, marching out of the ladies' room and back to my table.

Evan had finished the appetizers and was looking at his phone when I reappeared.

"Hey, where did you go? I've been waiting here for like fifteen minutes." His hands splayed outward with his phone in hand, baffled by my abrupt departure.

I didn't sit at the high-top table but crossed my arms, ready to fight this loser.

"Shut up, Evan." His eyes blinked rapidly. "Do I need to remind you that you deliberately kept me waiting for a half hour downstairs? And that you didn't bother to apologize?" His head cocked to the right like a dog, not understanding the command.

"For over an hour, you haven't stopped yammering about your fucking job or trying to pressure me into buy a highly volatile, unstable, possibly illegal currency just because you said so. Do you know anything about me, other than my name, since we met? NO! You haven't because you're a narcissistic asshole!"

I grabbed at my half-filled wine glass, chugged the rest of it in one gulp, adjusted my purse on my shoulder, and spun on my heels. I was so out of here. I took one step, and a large, firm hand pulled at my elbow, forcibly stopping me in my tracks.

"Wait!" Evan hissed.

I turned slowly, fortifying myself that I'd made my decision to leave and I wouldn't be coaxed to do anything else.

"What do you wa—?"

Before I knew it, Evan had landed a demanding kiss on my lips. The abrupt motion threw me off guard, and I grabbed hold of his shoulders so I wouldn't hit the ground. I'm sure he misinterpreted my grip as passion because he pulled me in tighter, locking my hair in his fist. *I needed to get my hair cut.* I pushed back hard, and he broke his hold, forcing me to grab the bar stool to keep myself standing.

"What the fuck are you doing? What did I say that gave you the idea I wanted your slimy lips on my mouth?" I wiped my lips with the back of my hand, making spitting noises of disgust.

"It's not what you said, but how you said it. I love your sass. You're one fiery bitch. Let's find a place to fuck."

To what!?

I shook my head violently, rolling my shoulders back, hoping to shake the heebie-jeebies off. This guy was such a creep. "I wouldn't fuck you with her pussy, or her pussy, or even her pussy!" I pointed to two pleasant, average women and the third, someone's grandma.

He laughed manically. "So, you want me to beg, huh? I'll beg for you." He took two steps forward, and I moved the stool I was leaning on between us.

I looked around to see a crowd forming. *Great!* "Fuck off, Evan. Lose my number, and if you even think of following me, I'll rip your balls off and feed them to my cat!" I fired every word with as much venom as possible, which got me a round of applause. *Now I need a cat.*

Dumb-shit Evan waved his outstretched arms like he just won *American Gladiator* instead of being fed to the lions. If my mother saw this asshole in action, she'd be mortified and apologetic.

I didn't stay for the aftermath and bolted toward the elevator, putting as much distance from Evan as possible. The doors slid open, and, unbelievably, there stood Spencer with a beautiful blonde looking at him adoringly hanging onto his arm. *Fuck my life!*

They walked off the elevator, Spencer not registering me until he spun around to hold the door.

"Are you okay?" He knew me too well.

"I'm fine," I said miserably, and he let the door go as I panted, waiting for them to close completely before I cried into my hands. The elevator dinged again, and I pushed through the onboarding crowd and finally made it to the sidewalk. The cool air woke me up from what I hoped was a bad dream until Spencer showed up at my side. He stood there—waiting off to the side for a few minutes—and then signaled for a cab. He said nothing, and I did the same. A yellow cab arrived, and he opened the door. I stepped off the curb, trying not to falter and feeling worse than I already did. Our only communication was his warm hand covering mine over the car window. I couldn't look him in the face, devastated that not only did he have to see me this way, but because it confirmed how much he felt for me, and I wouldn't let myself give in to it. *What was my problem?*

I cried as the cab crept through traffic for blocks. My phone pinged, and I didn't have the energy to lift it to see who texted.

I didn't care. I was feeling equal parts pathetic and idiotic. Both unflattering and not becoming of a thirty-two-year-old professional woman. I had to be better than this. I stood up to Evan tonight. I gave him a piece of my mind and walked away with dignity, only to negate all of those proud actions with those of a pitiful child seeing Spencer on a date. Who the hell was I? Where did that strong, independent woman go? Why couldn't I live peacefully and say no to everything else?

I only had one answer—Jewish guilt. It was a powerful motherfucker.

Chapter 16

Finally, it was Friday—Shabbat. By sundown tonight, I could go to temple, light the Hanukkah candles with my community, and enjoy the Kabbalat Shabbat service with prayers and songs. The best part was that my little nephew, Daniel, would sing "In the Window" with his preschool class while miming the Hanukkah song. I remember looking through a scrapbook several weeks ago, reminiscing about doing this myself all those years ago. I'm sure Daniel will do a much better job than I did. I was a terrible singer.

It was a good thing I listened to Emily and synced my social calendar with my personal work calendar since I completely forgot that I scheduled another date for tonight. Nathan and Gina would be pissed if I begged off for a date, missing my nephew's big stage debut. Instead, I told Joseph, the obstetrician, I could only meet for drinks after Shabbat services and asked if it would be all right with him. To my dismay, he invited himself to join me. While that sounded encouraging, I was having *shpilkes* at him meeting my whole family at the same time I met with them. This would either be a great night or one I'd never live down.

The hours leading up to my date were fraught with deadlines and partners following up on all my cases. One mishap in seven years, and I needed a babysitter for all my accounts. It didn't help that I got a questionable text from Spencer regarding last night. My logical brain told me that he put me in a cab and wanted to ensure I was safe and did what any good friend would do and check on me later. However, my panic-stricken teenage brain said, "Please, please, please, check on me!" I sounded neurotic. God forbid I voiced those feelings out loud. I'd not only sound neurotic—but be labeled that as well.

My intercom sounded, yanking me from my sordid thoughts. "Ms. Strauss, you have a delivery. Should I bring it in?" Emily feigned propriety when I knew she was actually taunting me, knowing who it was from.

"Of course, Ms. Stanley. By all means, please come forth." We loved playing this game.

A moment later, Emily shouldered her way into my office with a giant vase filled with fragrant stardust lilies, birds of paradise, fronds of whatever tropical tree it was pulled from, and dozens of tiny purple blooms. Goodness, this was extravagant. Surely it wasn't from Spencer.

Emily placed the arrangement on my round worktable, plucking the card from the plastic floral pick. "Let me guess." She waved the card over her head, landing on her brow and incanting something ridiculous. "It's from date number one. He misses your mouth." Her eyebrows shot up, hoping she was right. That would have been funny if I had actually told her the details of my dates, but I had not. Maybe she was a witch?

"Uncanny, Emily. How right you are." I said, keeping with the British formality we started.

She dropped her arms to her sides and cocked her head to the right, annoyed. "Was I right, or was I right?" All formality was gone, and her stare was locked onto my face.

I gingerly walked over to where she stood, snapped the card from her red talons, turned my back on her, and opened the card. Rough, block-style, untidy letters spelled out an apology, if you could call it that: *Sorry, I didn't say sorry. Let's meet up for that fuck. The Crypto King.*

A surge of disgust and wrath bubbled up, and I ran for a couch pillow, screaming into it so loudly. Unfortunately, the pillow hardly stifled my shrieks, frightening my assistant. "What in the holy, fucking hell? Does this guy think I would get anywhere near him? He is as dense as concrete."

I threw the pillow back on the couch, marched over to the table to grab the massive floral arrangement, and walked out of my office, arms as far out in front of me as I could physically manage. Using my elbow to call the elevator, I waited until the doors opened, set the flowers down in the middle of the car, and pressed the down button. They were gone, and I could see straight again, though a headache was brewing after my uncontrolled screaming. At times like this, I wished I had smoked pot. I needed to space out and relax.

Emily timidly walked out of my office, catching up with me. Her eyebrows knitted tightly, "Should I ask?"

I closed my eyes and swiveled my head. I eventually gave her the Cliffs Notes version of last night, and she stood aghast. *Yeah, me too.*

Time passed and we got back to work. I was still looking into loopholes in the new bylaws, but last night's epiphany nagged at me. If I had fought more, would I have gotten further? Recommitted to finding my answers, I had to reluctantly thank Evan for his obnoxiousness and Annie for her insights helping me overcome my people-pleasing nature.

Temple Kol Shira was halfway between my home and Joseph's, so we met twenty minutes before Friday night services. Something about him called out to me, identifying himself without my having to ask. *Was this beshert?*

Date number six, Joseph, was a tall, striking man with a smoldering swagger that got my juices flowing. When he turned to shake hands with my brother, I couldn't help but notice his tight ass and broad back. His smile was captivating, but I'd fallen for that trick too many times this week. If it weren't for his white, straight teeth, high cheekbones, and square jaw that exuded confidence, I would have kicked him to the curb already. I felt shallow, but I was tired of this game. Still, I liked his casual, confident demeanor, but more so his strong shoulders and cut abs tucked behind his knitted cardigan. Yeah, my mom would like him a lot. And, if God has anything to do with it, what comes out of his mouth will complement his exterior.

"It's a pleasure to meet you finally, Mrs. Strauss. My grandmother speaks highly of you." Joseph ingratiated himself to my mother shortly after giving me a satisfying close hug, where his hands lingered longer than a new introduction hug should last.

My mother blushed, offering Joseph her bejeweled, not-so-youthful hand. "Her picture of you doesn't do you justice."

He dipped his head appreciatively. "You're too kind."

Joseph was charming. Anyone who could get my mother to blush deserves an award.

"Why don't we find our seats?" I told everyone, but Joseph winked at me, delaying me another moment. His eyes were too damn sexy. Long lashes outlying his vivid blue eyes captured mine whenever he looked my way. It was like he knew me, but I'm positive he didn't.

His eyes weren't the only thing that captured me. A strong hand laid flat on my lower back, sending tingles up my spine as we followed other congregants into the pews. Attraction threw all reason out the window—especially for me. I looked up to see him smiling down at me, presumably because I allowed him to do it. There was an invisible pull that ricocheted between us, similar to the one I had with Spencer. Knowing that could happen with another man was refreshing, especially given our situation.

Any given service in Judaism has the same components, much like other religions. Every week of every year had the same passages.

My religion was like clockwork. However, at my temple, on Friday nights, we meditated. Books down, eyes closed, hands and feet still. I loved this part of the week when I could just breathe and relax and let every ounce of tension fall off my body. In the process, my hands fell to my sides and slid next to Joseph's. I had been focused purely on letting my thoughts go when my palm fell into his upturned one. I don't know if he was looking at me. It didn't matter. I felt him. His pulse, the smoothness of his skin, the feather-light thumb he used to press circles gently into my palm, and the heat that rose through my body and deep into my core. Having erotic thoughts at temple couldn't be good; nonetheless, they were there. And when the meditation ended, neither of us let go of each other. We stared at each other, smiling bashfully. I couldn't help chuckling about a phrase I'd heard a million times before but never so literally as, "Let go. Let God." *Are you there, God? It's me, Becca. Please make this work out.*

Our hands fell apart when we were asked to hold our prayer books, and later, when Daniel and his preschool class came out to sing, my whole family—as well as Joseph—*kvelled*. We witnessed my nephew bouncing around and singing while every other toddler sat still. Boy, was Nathan headed for a future of trouble with that kid.

After what seemed like nonstop clapping, the congregation said their final prayers, and everyone exited the sanctuary.

"How did you like our services?" I said demurely to Joseph as we exited the pew.

His devilish smile quirked at the corner of his mouth. "Far better than I'd planned. They were—pleasurable even." *Yeah, so pleasurable.*

It was time to get out of there. I took Joseph by the elbow and led him to the coat closet before saying goodbye to my family.

"Allow me." He held open my coat so I could slide my arms in. I turned my back so he could pull it over my shoulders, enjoying his warm breath on my neck. *Hmm.* When he nuzzled his lips to my neck, I wondered what the rest of the night might look like. If only Mr. Weinstein hadn't shuffled into the tight space, searching for his coat, I could have kissed him without an audience.

Joseph stilled, waiting for him to leave, then said, "Can't have you getting caught doing unspeakable things in the Temple Coat Room, can I?" *If everyone would get the hell out of here, then, yeah, you could.*

My forehead fell into his shoulder, chuckling, "Probably not. Let's go."

Joseph stayed one step behind me as we said goodbye, nabbing a brownie on the way out. I looked forward to the after-service *Oneg,* but tonight, dessert wouldn't include a hundred other people.

Just like every other Michigan day in winter, one moment, the weather was clear, and the next, it was as if you were in a snow globe. Tonight was no different. I opted to drive since my Subaru

SUV was more practical than his Porsche. My all-wheel-drive car puts his fancy car to shame.

"If you don't mind driving a little way, I made us a reservation at Salieri's for Italian. Have you been there?"

Joseph pressed the button on his seat, pushing it back to allow his long, muscular legs a place to stretch out. He didn't bother fastening his camel-colored overcoat, which let me enjoy the contours of his abdomen when stopped at every light. There wasn't an angle that his face didn't look strong and sexy, and, truth be told, it was hard to keep my eyes on the road when he flashed me his perfect smile.

"I don't mind," I said, pushing my hair behind my ear that kept falling into my face. "It's been several years since I've been there. Good choice." I chanced a glance at his pleased smile, but, when I turned away quickly, my damn hair fell again on my face.

"Here, let me help you with that."

Joseph shifted in his seat, reaching out to catch two long curls, and twisted them together before tucking them into my coat. The gentle pull on my scalp was exciting, and his care in making the locks become one was kind. Those sensual fingers that brushed the tender skin behind my ear were very intimate, adding more difficulty in focusing on the road. He continued brushing his knuckles down my neck until he pulled his fingers from my collar, ensuring that my hair was safely secured. I was breathless, and my panties were drenched. If I hadn't forced myself to watch the road carefully, we'd be finishing this date in a ditch.

He tipped his head to the side pensively. His arm remained on my headrest as his eyes studied my profile. I couldn't help but blush under his scrutiny.

"Is that better?" he crooned.

I smiled and bit my lip. "Much better." He continued playing with my hair by selecting another bunch of curls to twist through his fingers until we arrived at the restaurant.

He unbuckled his seatbelt and stared unapologetically at my face. "Your hair is such a turn-on." Neither of us moved. "I want to kiss you, Becca."

I reached down and pushed the button to release my seatbelt, allowing me to shift to as I scanned his perfect face. I leaned forward, giving him my consent, and waited for his lips to touch mine.

"Please," I whispered as his soft, full lips pressed to mine. His hands went back into my hair; gone were the sweet twists as he pulled more assertively, feeling it to my roots. Joseph's magnetism radiated through me when he tipped my face upward, pulling me deeper into the kiss. I loved how he varied the strength of his pulls and the skill of his tongue as it glided over my top lip and then the lower, pulling on that one, too.

"God, I love a first kiss." Joseph sat back, out of breath, gazing at my face. I couldn't help noticing how his eyes dropped to focus on my breasts and legs. I knew this guy was charming from the moment I met him, but now I could see it was just a ruse for his dominant side. Being with a doctor who knew women's bodies amped up my expectations, coupled with his strong alpha side was intoxicating..

I looked down where he aimed his stare to see that my dress had ridden to the top of my thighs, giving him enough of a peek to see the lace of my black panties.

"Damn, Becca. Dinner is going to be a bitch knowing what you are wearing under that dress." He licked his lips, and a small moan slid from my throat.

I swiveled around to grab my purse next to my seat and looked up again. "Well, let's get inside. I know what I'm having for dessert. . .cannoli."

We both laughed at my double entendre. Joseph opened his door first, telling me to stay still while he walked around the car to open my door. "Careful, it's slippery."

Such a mensch.

The server sat us at a quiet table back by the woodburning fireplace, placing our menus in front of us. Joseph seemed to have other seating arrangements in mind, and moved to the seat adjacent to mine, squeezing my knee for approval.

I licked my lips appreciatively and decided to behave myself in the restaurant, and prepared to cross-examine him.

"So, you're a gynecologist. That must be fascinating work with all those women parts to inspect. How do you do it?

His smirk had me smiling. "The trick is to have your assistant drape the patient before you examine her. It helps to separate the body parts from the person. You get used to it over the years. However, a new older patient of mine decided that the paper gown was 'abrasive' and wore her silk negligée instead. And it wasn't just the garment. She wore kitten-healed house shoes with a white puff on the toes to top it off." He burst into laughter, and I was aghast.

"You're kidding, right? She really did that?" My mouth hung open, waiting for his reply.

He nodded his head multiple times, trying to regain his composure. "Yep. And when my assistant came in, she did an immediate about-face, grabbed me by the elbow, slamming the door behind us. Boy, did she give me a talking-to. Since that day, I've sent my staff to drape my patients *before* I enter the room."

I brought my hand to my chest, speechless. "Unbelievable."

Joseph slid his hand down my thigh, humming. "I could tell you stories for months. I could also tell you about the heart-wrenching moments, too. I'll save those for another time."

Our dinner was delicious, and, as promised, I ordered a cannoli.

"She'll have that to go. We have to get going. Need to beat the heavy snow, you know."

The server bowed slightly and went off to get our bill and package my dessert while I probed further into Joseph's life.

I rolled my lips together, trying to phrase my next question carefully. "How did a good-looking man like yourself miss getting married?" He had to be at least ten years older than me. And while

I loved a hot, older man, he had to have attracted dozens of women over the years.

He lifted his water glass and took a long drink, keeping his eyes on me the whole time. When he was finished, he leaned back in his chair, pursing his pillowy lips.

"I'd be lying if I said I hadn't been married before, but I was. I have two kids in high school and a dog that keeps me up at night. I thought it was forever, yet, alas, it was not." His shoulders slumped, and he broke eye contact for the first time all night.

I reached out and placed my hand on his forearm. "Life happens, Joseph. I hope the breakup wasn't ugly, for the kid's sake."

Judging by his sad smile, it seemed like things didn't go well. "Let's just say it's a work in progress. The kids were devastated, but we went to family therapy to make the transition easier for them." He hummed, deep in his thoughts.

My heart broke for him. I still didn't know exactly what happened, but his integrity shone through as he cared for his children during such a difficult time.

The server placed a white carryout bag and our bill on the table. Joseph stopped him from leaving and dug out two, hundred-dollar bills and placed them into the black folder.

"You're all set. Keep the change."

Wide eyes shot out from the guy's face, knowing he got a ridiculous tip. I wasn't sure if Joseph looked at the bill or didn't care. He stood quickly—pulling my chair out—and grabbed the bag as we headed for the coat room.

Being the consummate gentleman, Joseph stood behind me, slipping my arms into my coat and then putting on his as the valet brought up our car. His strong fingers slid behind my neck and rubbed as he whispered into the shell of my ear.

"I hope you're still as hungry as I am because I can't wait to eat your pussy." I gasped, astonished at his bravado with other people within hearing distance. I was no prude, but my privacy was imperative. Regardless, my panties were soaked, and we needed to get out of there fast.

"Starving!" I growled. "Where do you live?" I begged, hoping it was close to his home.

He kissed my neck, licking between each small peck. "Too far away. Yours?"

"Same," I hummed.

"Is a hotel okay?" He dropped a smoldering kiss on my lips. How could I say no?

The snow was coming down hard, and neither of us lived nearby. I hadn't had a hotel shag since college spring break in Ft. Lauderdale. *Now, that was a night to remember.*

Joseph tucked me into my seat, shooing the valet aside and buckling my seatbelt as he kissed me deeply. "We passed The Rosebud Inn two miles away. Let's go." He braced himself on the car as he rounded the bumper and slid into the passenger seat. We were like two kids who stole their parents' car doing things they wouldn't approve of.

I couldn't see more than twenty feet ahead of me and was grateful we only had a short distance to travel. I pulled into the covered entry drive and handed the keys to the valet when he opened my door. Joseph took my arm and walked me safely into the opulent lobby.

"Have a seat, and I'll get us a room."

I found a deep purple velour settee by the bay window and enjoyed the beautiful lobby. A dark oak, Victorian-styled hutch sat behind the front desk with mirrored mercury glass inset into the arched cutouts. It matched several side tables, including the one next to me, which offered hotel-branded mints. I watched as he pulled out his wallet and laid down three more hundred-dollar bills. I was shocked. Who carries that much cash around nowadays? Maybe his divorce had his assets tied up? I wondered how long he'd been divorced anyway. These were questions for another night. Tonight held great promise. Hopefully, the kind that could erase a life-long yearning for someone I couldn't have.

I pushed back thoughts of Spencer in exchange for focusing on Joseph's swagger as he walked back across the lobby, jangling an old-style keychain in his hand and waggling his eyebrows. This pussy doctor better know how to make a woman scream, or I might cry.

"Hey, pretty lady, wanna get a room?" He waggled his eyebrows and cocked his head toward the staircase. "This old Victorian has been here for over a century and has been newly renovated." He sounded like a tour guide. "How do you feel about dirty sex in a four-poster bed?" *Duh.*

My imagination ran wild with that thought. I hustled up the stairs, praying that he had a coil of soft rope hidden in his pocket.

Joseph opened the door to our room, escorting me in. The balance of old and new was perfect. Tiny rosebud wallpaper hung along the wall behind the promised four-poster bed covered in an ivory crepe duvet and plump feather pillows. An ivory porcelain bowl and pitcher sat atop a mercury glass chest with glass nobs. It was stunning.

Strong arms wrapped around my waist as he breathed in my hair. "Do you like it?"

I spun around and grabbed his face in my hands, searing his lips with my own. I let my kiss do the talking. All I wanted to do was get these damn clothes off. I wanted his hands and mouth everywhere and dropped to my knees to help him untie his shoes.

Joseph grabbed his belt buckle and quickly unhooked it, never taking his eyes off me. The ratcheting sound of his zipper was slow and taunting, making my body grow feverish. But when he dropped trou, I almost passed out. I'd never seen anything like it in my life. My jaw gaped, not knowing whether to laugh, scream, or drool over what I saw. I'd read of—even seen—large, thick dicks, but this one was special—very special.

"Fuck, Becca. Suck me." Those were two of my favorite words both in and out of the bedroom. However, how would I get a whole bent dick in my mouth? Not a slight bend, but a large curve upward. I loved sucking cock, but it would take a lot of effort and care to satisfy him and not choke me. My hands reached for his thighs, pulling him closer. I didn't touch him, only breathed hot, moist air over his throbbing head. My efforts were rewarded when he leaked pre-cum perfectly perched, just for me.

"That's for you, baby. Lick it off with those gorgeous lips." I moaned as I leaned in, slowly swiping away his cream. His hands dove into my hair, pulling me forward to claim his cock, and I was thrilled by the level of desire he felt to plunge his cock into my mouth. Slow pulls brought me halfway down his impressive shaft, and I did my best to relax my throat and jaw. If he thought I could take all of him back, he would be disappointed. Six inches was one thing. Eight curved inches was an entirely different animal. And Joseph . . . was an animal.

He rubbed my hair along his thighs and belly, creating a blanket over my head as he moaned my name over and over again.

"I need more, Becca. Take me all the way back." He gently pressed my head down with the palm of his hand until I gagged. "God, yes! I love that sound. Again."

I took perverted pride in getting those extra inches into my mouth, but the next time he pushed down, he didn't release me for a few seconds, threatening to choke me out. I pushed off his thighs, gasping for air, saliva dripping from the corners of my mouth and my makeup dripping down my face. I knew my limits, but damn if Joseph didn't test me. His bent dick wouldn't straighten out, so I had to improvise, forcing it up to hit the roof of my mouth. *I hoped it had the same effect as the back of the throat.*

He wiped my teary eyes and tipped my chin up, forcing me to look at his dark, glazed eyes. "I'm going to come down your throat, and you're going to suck me dry. Understand?"

I wasn't a twenty-something who obeyed when told to suck off her lover. I was a highly-paid lawyer with two degrees who obeyed when she was told to suck off her lover.

"You better come fast or I'll throw up all over your loafers." I grabbed his cock and clamped down hard.

"Jesus, fuck, woman!" Sweat poured off his brow as he grabbed my hair tightly and bucked his thick dick into my mouth and down my throat. I gagged each time and felt more tears streaming down my face, but I wasn't going to give up. I asked for a challenge and got one with Joseph. Three strokes later, hot cords of cum shot down my throat, forcing me to swallow hard—and quick!

"Fuck. Fuck. Fuck, Becca. Your mouth is perfect. You're perfect." I sucked the end of his crown, milking every drop until he pulled me to my feet and lifted me off the floor. His strong, sinewed arms lifted me higher onto his chest, and I wrapped my legs tightly around his waist, letting him kiss me so hard our teeth gnashed.

I was so out of breath I was lightheaded. "Joseph, you're a beast." I pressed my hands to the sides of his face, wiping his exertion into his hair. "Let me know when you're ready to go again."

I unwrapped my legs and stood proudly in front of him. Somewhere in all the kissing, he unzipped my dress, and my tits spilled out of my bra. His hands slid down my arms, effectively shoving it off to the floor. His hands slid back to my waist and set me onto that gloriously cloud-like bed.

"I'm going to make you scream my name," he growled between kisses. Climbing on the bed himself, he pushed me upward toward the heavenly down pillows as he feathered soft, gentle kisses down my abdomen right to my panty line. "God, you smell so good, Becca."

He nudged his nose into the lace material that pressed into the hood of my clit, generating a jolt of electricity, making my body quake.

"Ah," I moaned, wanting more. "Joseph, I want you." My hands grabbed hold of his short hair and pulled.

He immediately slipped his fingers into the dainty material, yanked them down, and stepped back. He slid off the bed and put his hands on his hips, assessing me for several moments, not saying a word. My breath was out of control as his eyes went dark, devouring me. The anticipation was driving me wild. I knew I was a good-looking woman, but he looked at me like I was the last of womankind and would defile every inch of me.

"Is this what you want, baby? Prepare yourself for the fuck of a lifetime." *He wasn't kidding.* Joseph checked all the must-haves in the cock department and one extra box for bent. Yeah, this man's shaft took a hard U-turn up, even at full mast. This *was* going to be a fuck of a lifetime.

Shit! Was I ready for that? Would he ruin me for all other men?

"Bring it on!" I barked.

He didn't waste time unbuttoning his shirt. Instead, he unbuttoned two buttons at his broad chest and yanked off the rest, including his T-shirt, in one pull. His muscled abs and bulging shoulders indicated he worked his body hard, and I planned on rewarding him by kissing and licking every inch of it

"I've been looking at your tits all night. Remember me when I leave marks on them. I may be a gentleman outside the bedroom, but, baby, inside, I'm an animal." *No shit!*

He climbed my body and latched onto my tits like a dog with a bone. He wasn't kidding about roughing them up. I loved nipple play, but this guy wasn't about sensual arousal. He was direct and to the point. Large hands squeezed my D cups, and his mouth sucked hard on my tender nipples, nipping each bud harder and harder until I yelped. Pleasure turned to pain, and that's when I called a time-out.

"Joseph, I can't," I whined. He must have known to move to my other breast because I was squirming under his ruthless touch. *God!* What had I gotten myself into?

I endured his onslaught for several more minutes until I reached down to grab his cock.

"This, Joseph. I want this." My breaths were shallow, and my pussy needed relief. I wasn't here for just his pleasure but my own. If his bent dick gave me the orgasm of a lifetime, I wanted it now.

"Yeah, baby. You want my serpent. You got it." *Serpent? Didn't teenagers say that shit?* He was killing my mood. That was until he lined up his head to my opening and slid into my wetness. *Jesus, fuck!* He wasn't kidding.

Joseph filled me like no other man had. Each thrust hit places that never had been touched, and, wow, did it turn me on. It felt like there were two cocks in me, but damn—I was so full, I couldn't think straight.

"Dear Lord, Joseph. Don't stop. This feels too good." I was breathless, mind blown. Everything in me tingled and zinged with electricity. I couldn't hold my orgasm back any longer. "I'm going to come. Are you ready?"

His hands gripped my hips, and he squeezed hard, thrusting as if his life depended on it. Perspiration glistened over his brow, and strangely, his eyes were locked where our bodies met. Hell, I think it's hot, too, but his non-stop laser focus was creepy. It seemed like he was more interested in his dick pounding me than the person he pounded.

"So close. Almost—ahh. Fuck, yeah." He finally looked up to my face and stopped pumping. *Could he read my mind?*

"Don't you dare fucking stop! I waited for you." *Selfish fucker.*

It was as though he snapped out of a trance, and he began thrusting several more times until I came.

"Yes! Yes! That's what I needed." I panted until my breath smoothed out, but Joseph had already slipped out of me and rolled to my side. His fingers circled my belly button, begging for forgiveness.

"Becca, I'm so sorry. I thought you said you were coming. I must not have heard you correctly. You felt so good, and I was lost in the moment. Please forgive me." His ragged breath brushed my neck, squeezing me tight as if that would make things better. I tried to be gracious, allowing him to soothe me as I turned onto my side to face him. I brushed a bead of sweat from his eyebrow and looked closely at his deep, blue eyes. "I could see how that could happen. How long has it been, Joseph?"

He rolled to his back, draping an arm over his forehead, thinking. "Six months." His chest heaved, and I took pity on him.

The dark hair on his chest was damp from his exertion, but I traced an infinity sign around the edges of his nipples, seeing if I could get him excited for round two. He rolled to his side and pulled down the duvet and sheets from under me and tucked me under the covers.

"I'm going to take a quick shower," he called over his shoulder, not waiting for me to reply.

"I could take one with you?" I called after him.

"I'll only be a few minutes. Rest and I'll be back before you know it." He closed the door, though not completely.

Wow. Did I just get blown off? This guy was truly a puzzle and one I'm not sure I could solve.

There was a buzzing sound from the floor and I jumped up to find it. A light from Joseph's pants lit up and I slipped the phone from his pocket to bring it to him when I noticed the screen name, 'Love of my Life.' *What the fuck?*

My lawyer instincts went into overdrive, and I debated if I should invade his privacy for answers or let him tell me his version of reality. Decision made—I tapped the green button only to hear a woman's sultry voice.

"Hey, baby. Is your meeting over? When are you going to be home?" *Fuck. Me! I've been played.*

The bathroom door opened wider. Joseph was damp and wrapped in a towel around his waist looking fine. I held his phone out so he could see who was on the line and watched his face fall. I stared him down, pulled the phone to my ear, and answered her question.

"He'll be home soon after he puts his clothes back on. I didn't know. Sorry," and hung up.

Nothing in my life prepared me for the hurt this man caused me. Not because I had any feelings for the fucker, but having been duped. That was despicable and premeditated. That asshole met my family! He *schmoozed* with my rabbi, for God's sake. What was I supposed to tell them? That I—we— broke several commandments in one night? And, beyond sex, this bastard destroyed his wife to get his rocks off.

I should have seen it coming. Cash for dinner. Cash for the hotel. Leaving his car at the temple. He probably had a GPS tracker his wife could follow. *Argh!!* So many levels of deception. I'm so pissed at myself. Of course, he wasn't into me. I mean, he was in me but not into me for the right reasons. The way he was fixated by his fucked-up, bent dick sliding into me was more important than making eye contact with the vessel he was pounding. It all became clear that he was only in it for himself. I am one stupid, sad case of a woman. A real fool. *Spencer would never have done that to me. Damn it!*

I chucked his phone onto the bed and got dressed. He tried to tell me I was mistaken—*blah, blah, blah*. I grabbed my keys, purse, and coat and walked to the door. Joseph was no *mensch*.

"Becca. I'm really sorry." His pained face was fake. His only regret was that he was caught.

"Save it, Joseph. I guess you should prepare for the divorce you claimed to have already. I'm sure one is coming your way soon." I made to slam the door, but he grabbed it before it shut.

"Can't you take me to my car?" *What the fuck, dude?*

I threw my head back, laughing. "Ask your wife for a ride."

The valet had my car pulled up before Joseph could make it downstairs, and I wished I would never see this guy again. The nerve of some people playing on other people's feelings. Is this what Spencer thought I was doing? Not even close. Unfortunately, I hadn't considered my feelings in this stupid game. *So much for having the upper hand.*

beshert —inevitable or preordained
kvelled —express joy or delight
schmooze—talk with someone in a lively and friendly way, typically in order to impress or manipulate them
mensch – a person of integrity and honor

Chapter 17

After Friday night's fiasco with Joseph, I desperately wanted to cancel my next two dates. What was the point? A few fun moments with a nice guy wasn't going to deliver me a worthy date for the Hanukkah party, let alone a boyfriend. Ironically, even with all the sex I was having, I felt more like a psychologist offering therapy to most of these guys. I think Annie had the right idea—Rent-A-Date.

I skipped my shower and dressed in yoga pants, a thermal liner, another thicker liner, and a sweatshirt to power-walk my anger off. It may have been winter in Southfield, but the sun was out, and the ground was dry. More importantly, I needed to vent, and I had my sights on my mother, Marilyn.

"Hi, Mom. I just wanted to call and let you know your dear friend, Pauline, screwed me over," I spat out bitterly as I stretched out my hamstrings.

"Slow down, Becca. What are you talking about?" My mother's unflappable demeanor was my least favorite characteristic about her. Didn't she ask any questions about these guys so as not to create more problems for me?

"The doctor you met on Friday, Joseph, is *still married!* And do you know how I found out about that little tidbit? His wife called him, and I answered because he was indisposed. Now, *she* has a huge problem to deal with. Why didn't you ask your friends if their sacrificial lamb was legitimately available to date?" My blistering diatribe didn't help me feel better. However, the complete silence on the other side begged the question, "Are you still there?" I picked up my pace and began to run. I don't run. I hate running. But I sprint when I'm angry and need an outlet to burn off my vitriol.

"I – I don't know what to say, sweetheart. I just assumed my friends weren't that vicious to put you through that experience. I suppose I have to call Pauline now." She said this like it was a chore and not a means to vindicate her daughter's honor. My mother had become so entrenched in her social status over the years that she forgot how to be a thoughtful, protective mother. Let's be honest. Since I flew the coop ten years ago, she threw off her mother's mantle and became a vapid bitch. But I still loved her. There's that Jewish guilt again. It forced me to forgive her.

"Were any of the men I sent you good candidates?" she simpered.

I slowed my pace and stopped at a streetlight to catch my breath. To my horror, I spotted Spencer arm in arm with a petite blonde, who was hanging on him like a teenager, across the street. Spencer hated clingy women. He liked sophisticated, confident women, like . . . me. What was happening to me?

"Becca," my mother barked through the phone.

I shook my head, forgetting she was still on the line. "Uh, yeah. A couple were nice. We had fun, but none that I'd want to get to know better. I have two more this weekend, but I still might come to your party alone. I don't want to have to babysit anyone."

My mother let out a screech. One that resembled fingernails on a chalkboard. "You will not come to another one of my parties alone. It's humiliating! I don't give a shit if you have to yank someone off the street, but you will have a respectable-looking man on your arm, or don't come at all."

Her biting remarks stopped me in my tracks. After all that bullshit of meeting her friend's spawn, now she's threatening me? I'm calling my dad. Marilyn was out of control, and he needed to do something about it.

This day had gone to shit and it wasn't even ten o'clock. First, my mother disrespected me, then Spencer appeared with a bouncy blonde ten years younger than himself across the street, and now I have to call my father, who most likely will do nothing because he doesn't want to get involved in my mother's shenanigans. Who in my life stood behind me one hundred percent without judgment? *No one, I say, stuffing down my guilt over Spencer.*

I turned the corner and went the long way back to my apartment, walking sluggishly. Even my run was out of control. I stopped and leaned on a lamp post, and called my dad. I played with the end of my ponytail, realizing the ends were broken. It needed to be cut and styled for the charity event. Just in case, I did go to the party.

My Dad, Albert, picked up my call on the third ring.

"Hey, Sweetpea. How are you today?" His voice was deep and rich and made me feel safe. He read to me lawyer briefs when I was young instead of fairytales, and even those sounded fascinating. I trusted that voice. After telling him my deal with Mom, I hoped he would still use that voice to support me. The alternative response was, "Quit your crying and get over it." Definitely not soothing or trusting.

"Hi, Daddy. I hope I'm not interrupting," I said sweetly, waiting for his permission to proceed. This was another of those behavioral modifications that my brother and I had to learn at a very young age. If you wanted his attention, you had to ask first and wait patiently for him to finish what he was doing to proceed. Otherwise, you'd stand there forever being ignored.

He cleared his throat. "Just finishing a handball game. What's up?" I could hear him saying a muffled goodbye to his buddy who he had a regular weekly game with.

Speaking of games, I had one shot to get this right. Here goes.

"You know how Mom feels about me attending her annual Hanukkah charity event without a date, right? And, you know how that frustrates me. So she and I made a deal for me to do some speed dating with several men to find a suitable one, if not a love connection, for me to bring this year."

Stop. Wait for his response.

There was a big sigh. *Yeah, I felt that, too.* "I'm aware."

"Great. Then, you may also know that she chose several of her friends' grandsons, nephews, and cousins?" I held my breath, hoping he knew this.

"Unfortunately, yes." *So far, so good.*

"Well, you met one of those men on Friday at temple. You know, Joseph? The gynecologist?" *Patience, Becca. You're almost there.*

I heard his locker slam. "Yeah. Seemed nice. You two looked pretty chummy."

"Remember when you studied law, and your professors made a big stink about appearances not always being what they seemed? In this case, that topic applies. Mom didn't vet this guy out at all, and it created a horrible situation ending with his wife calling to find out when he'd be home."

A locker slammed three more times. I could picture him now with his white headband tightly circling his balding head and his jaw clenching with restrained anger. A growl emanated from the phone. "Are you doing okay, Sweetpea?"

My shoulders slumped and my head folded forward in relief. He was listening to me. The realization of my predicament would have a lasting impact on my life. I was made an adulterer without my knowledge. I had been mortified, and my dad understood that clearly.

"I'm fine. Disgusted, but fine. I tried to call Mom out on it, but she didn't apologize, ask how I was doing, or own her involvement in the situation. Her final words were that if I didn't find a suitable person to attend her damn party, not to come at all. I'm seriously considering not coming."

I pushed off the post and continued my slow journey home. Several people were walking their dogs and enjoying a sunny Saturday afternoon while I dealt with an insufferable mother. Farther along, I waved at a neighbor exiting my building as I continued to wait out my dad. Minutes went by before he responded sternly. *Uh oh.*

He cleared his throat again. "Listen carefully, Becca. I will deal with your mother, but you *will* attend that party with your head held high. I don't give a shit about her friends or your mother keeping up with appearances. Bring whomever you want or come alone. You'll still be the prettiest, smartest, most accomplished woman in the room. Your mother included. Oh . . . and no more conversations with her until the party is over. You know how she is before an event."

I swooned over my dad's words. The man I wanted would be his equal, and, if it took another decade to find him, I'd wait it out. "Thank you, Daddy. I knew calling you would be the right thing to do. I love you so much."

I walked up the stairs to my apartment and saw Spencer standing at my door. My eyebrows raised, and my head swiveled slightly, but my eyes did not leave his.

"Uh, I have to go, Dad. Spencer dropped by." I moved past him, unlocking my door.

"I love you, too, Sweetpea. Have a great day and tell Spence I said hello and that he owes me a handball game soon." Dad had all but adopted Spencer into our family, even though my mother resented his presence. That stupid Mahjong game she accused his mother of cheating on ten years ago was running my life.

Spencer walked through behind me and closed the door quietly. I kept my back to him, trying to pull myself together. "Bye, Daddy."

I dropped my keys in the bowl on the end table and walked to the refrigerator to collect my water pitcher. Why was Spencer here? Wasn't he just with some teenager? The frequency of him dropping in didn't go unnoticed.

"Water?" I called to him, still not turning around.

I heard his soft footsteps move across the light brown, engineered hardwoods. His energy arced from where he stood to me a few feet away, and my hand shook as I poured the water. I'd been out with six men this week, and not one of them made my heart flutter like Spencer's did. He wasn't mine. It would never work with us. My family had too many people to overcome, specifically my mother, and I couldn't lose his friendship. That point had not changed these past weeks.

A gentle hand came down over mine and slid the pitcher from my hand, setting it on the counter. I pressed both of my hands on the cold granite, trying to catch my breath. Warm air whispered over my neck as his other hand found the small of my back.

"Breathe," he whispered. My legs felt like jelly, especially when he leaned closer to keep me from falling.

"I think my blood sugar is low. I-I haven't eaten yet today." That was a good excuse, right? I mean, I hadn't eaten because I was so upset at my mom. Fighting with myself, I decided to turn around and face my fears. Spencer needed to hear from me one last time how important our friendship was and that he should continue to date flighty, childish blondes. I was boring. I worked too much. I was emotionally unavailable. *That was a lie.* All of it was a lie I told myself to survive around him.

I turned, ready to lay it all out for him, when he bent his head within an inch from my lips. "Stop fighting yourself, Becca." He pressed those sexy lips to mine, not waiting for a reply. His tongue pressed between mine, probing my mouth, and I couldn't get enough of him. Cinnamon swirled on his tongue from his favorite frosted pastry. One that tasted better from his mouth than from the plate. His hands crept up behind my shoulders, pulling me off the floor high enough to slide my ass onto the countertop. He stood there, looking down at me, a glint in his eye that told me he wouldn't stop until he got what he wanted.

"You want this, Becca. Don't you?" Spencer was a fucking magician the way he turned me inside out. All of my willpower and self-talk was gibberish when he spoke to me from behind my ear.

I needed to be honest with him. My mind was a ping-pong game that wouldn't end.

"I can't help myself," I hissed. He was pushing my limits and this was not how I wanted this conversation to go.

Spencer's lips left my mouth, leaving a trace of small, wet kisses down my neck to a spot on my clavicle that opened a floodgate of wetness between my thighs. I moaned and gripped his shoulders tightly.

I tried my hardest to remember why we couldn't be together when the image of a small blonde popped into my mind. I pushed him back.

"I saw you earlier—the blonde. You were on a date. You should be dating her." I sounded so pathetic. I even heard a glimpse of my martyred mother in my voice and I cringed.

He stopped abruptly. See. I knew he was dating someone. Spencer just needed to be reminded of her. If he would only stay away from me, he would forget about me and move on. Why won't he move on?

The grimace on his face was menacing. "Are you jealous, Becca?"

I pushed farther back off his chest, frustrated. "No!" I said too vehemently, crossing my arms under my voluminous chest.

His eyebrows raised. "Really? Then why did you react like that?"

Ugh! He was so annoying. "Like what? I'm not jealous. You should be dating anyone you want. Look at me. I'm not sitting around pining for you, Spencer. I'm dating the whole fucking city this week. I'm not thinking about you." Okay, that was harsh, but he didn't have to know how I compared every one of those guys to him. My database of pros and cons was almost complete and he wasn't even on it. *Should I add Spencer to it?* Bad idea.

He stepped back, assessing me, a cocky look on his face. What was he thinking? Did he think this—I—was a joke?

"What?" I demanded.

He moved several steps closer to the door, turned and jammed his hands onto his trim hips. "Tell yourself whatever you want, Becca. But your body language says differently. I'm not going to wait around for you forever, sweetheart. Figure your shit out, but don't lie to me or yourself. You know what you need to do."

He gave me a wink and walked out the door like he owned me. *Fuck!* He did. No! He can't. *Shit!* I still didn't know why he came over. I was such a mess. I slid off the countertop and covered my mouth with my hand feeling like I would vomit. My lips were deliciously puffy and tingly. No one kissed like Spencer.

I had to stop this nonsense. He was just testing me. I drank my water, ate some yogurt, and ran for the shower. I focused on my next two dates and decided that I would find Mr. Right on one of them. Today's date was at the Natural History Museum with Alan, my sexy science nerd associated with Warrington Industries. I'd learn about dinosaurs and shit and have the best fucking day of my life.

Chapter 18

Lester's was a classic Jewish deli with walls lined in celebrity headshots and delicious-looking posters of corned beef sandwiches and all-beef hotdogs. Little League photos donned the bathroom hallway of all the teams Lester's supported over the past fifty years. Everyone knew the menu. It never changed. The name of each stacked sandwich came from someone in his family, and, if you were a notable human, once a year he would create a special one with your name on it.

Lunch crowds were popular, but Saturdays and Sundays attracted shoppers for miles around. There were no reservations; it was first come, first served. I arrived fifteen minutes before my dinner with Alan, people-watching while I waited. I didn't have to wait long for a table and was escorted by a tiny, grandma-type person named Estelle, Lester's mom.

"Good to see you, Estelle. Are you doing well?" I was genuinely concerned since she had diabetes.

"Yeah, yeah," she pooh-poohed me with her Yiddish accent. "If you live long enough, you get everything." She continued to shuffle me to the far side of the restaurant by the window, and I smiled, loving her attitude of acceptance over regret. Her eyes lifted to me, "Two for you?" I nodded.

She placed the two oversized menus on the table, and a young girl came by with two glasses of water. The worn, red banquette was remarkably comfortable, though I felt like a kid at a too-high table. The longer you sat there, the deeper into the cushion you sunk. I looked up at the cat clock hanging across the room. Eyes swiveled left and right as each second went by. That clock made me laugh my whole life. Not much time passed when I heard the jingle from the door and saw Alan walk in. At least I thought it was Alan. He wasn't wearing those tortoise-rimmed glasses anymore. And his shaggy blond hair was shorn down into a professional, and, damn it, sexy chopped cut that looked like an edible Ryan Gosling to my lusty mind. *No more boring, Alan.*

I waved my hand to get his attention, and he smiled, waving off Estelle. I stood to hug him. *Because that's what you do when you want to get your hands on a hot guy.*

"Alan, wow, it's great to see you." I forced myself not to make a comparison of his physique to Spencer's. They were two totally different bodies. *Stay in the present, Becca.*

He hugged me tightly, which I didn't expect, and pushed his hand through his hair while he sat down. "You still look amazing, Becca. Your hair is longer." Trying not to feel self-conscious, I touched my hair and took my seat.

"Yeah, about four inches or so. It makes it easier to put up when I'm working," I said too professionally. *Settle down, girl.* "You've made some changes, too. No more glasses and a new hairdo. Very nice."

He preened. He knew he looked good, which was refreshing since the last time he was so bashful. The question was, when did he make these changes? For our date or a while ago? Either way, I got to enjoy the benefits.

He smiled sheepishly, "Thanks. My work is getting more attention and the director of my department suggested, recommended, uh, strongly recommended that I look into a stylist," he said, bobbing his head.

"Well, they did right by you. Should we order?" I picked up my menu, already knowing what I was having. Alan waved down the young girl; she arrived looking annoyed. *An annoyed server is part of the charm of a Jewish deli.*

I tucked my hair behind my ear, my face still in the menu, and ordered a lean corned beef on rye with Russian dressing and an old dill on the side.

"Full or half," she snarked like I forgot to mention my preference, forcing her to ask yet another question.

"Half, please. I always forget to mention that. Thanks." I graciously smiled and handed her my menu.

"And you?" Little Miss Sunshine had better watch it, or her tip would be zilch.

"Burger and Fries. Medium rare, grilled onions, Thousand Island, and a new dill." He returned his menu with a grimace. He definitely stuck the landing on his ordering skills. Shifting my attention back to Alan, I remembered how beautifully shaped his hands were. Lightly calloused, strong, and bronzed. Unusual for a guy who typically works indoors. He had powerful forearms dusted with blond hair and clean, manicured nails. I loved hands. They said a lot about a person's life. Alan said he worked hard but cared enough about himself to look professional even if his hands got dirty. *Dirty.* I giggled to myself. Was this nerdy professor a dirty guy, or was he like his personality, unsure of himself? And, more importantly, would I find out?

Our conversation was stilted as he described his new project both in and out of the museum. Apparently, there was a worldwide convention he was preparing a paper for, and that's why he didn't have much time to meet. I liked his drive and commitment to his field. He was making a difference in the world, and I respected that.

"What about you, Becca? What have you been working on?" He put down his water glass and looked me straight in the eye. I froze. I'd never seen him look at me straight in the eye before. He was always hidden behind glasses, and—because he was shy—he never caught my attention. But there was something more. His shoulders were bigger, one slouching slightly lower than the other, making him look hungry and inviting. He licked his lips slowly, light catching on his lower lip. If I were a greedy woman, I'd be sucking on that lip right now, but I behaved, weighing what his body said today versus his personality from before. The duality confused me.

"Um. When last you saw me, I was fast-tracking to , but that fizzled out a couple of weeks ago when the partners decided they had enough partners representing their firm. Currently, I'm writing Intellectual Property briefs for three clients and deciding what my next life move would be. You know, the usual." I gave a pathetic laugh, feeling like a failure.

He leaned forward, pressing his forearms closer to the middle of the table, securing my hands in his own. "I'm really sorry to hear that. I knew you'd been working like a dog when last we met. I didn't know you were making a run for partner. That sucks having it from under your feet. I get it. For me, it's like someone else in the world publishes new findings before mine and two years of research goes down the tubes. So frustrating."

His thumb continued to rub the inside of my wrist, and a tremor shot through my body. "Thank you for understanding. That means a lot." I nodded, biting the inside of my cheek.

"Hang in there. Opportunities are everywhere, even if you have to create them yourself," he said encouragingly.

I looked at him, closely turning my head to take in all his angles. "That has to be the most profound thing anyone has ever said to me, Alan. Thank you for that wonderful piece of encouragement." Even my goddamned mother couldn't squeak out an ounce of encouragement, and this total stranger had life-changing words for me.

We looked at each other intently, staring, absorbing each other's energy. It was kinetic and inspiring until the waitress broke our connection dropping our food onto the table.

"Need anything else?" Her attitude really sucked.

We both shook our heads, and she whirled on her heel, running to fetch her next order. During dinner, I brought Alan up to speed on my professional life, and he apologized again for being weird two years ago when we worked on the Warrington Industry patent. Finished with our meals, there was a lull in our conversation that could be detrimental to continuing this date. Fortunately, Alan took the lead.

"Ready to meet my latest find?" He looked like he won a ticket to a seat to the moon. Come on."

He gallantly held out his hand and pulled me out of my seat. Admittedly, my ass was numb from sinking into it for an hour, needing desperately to do a bend forward to stretch my back.

"Meet? Is it alive?" What kind of prehistoric *Jurassic Park* craziness was I going to see?

He laughed and paid the bill. "Her name is Lila, and she's one hundred and fifty million years old. She's a real looker," he chuckled to himself.

We walked through the chilly December air, puffs of smoke billowing in front of our faces, enjoying each other's company. Huddled together, we rounded the backside of the natural history museum, where he took out his key card and swiped us into a breezeway separated by a thick plastic curtain.

"Right through here," he gestured, pressing his hand to my lower back. If I had any doubt that he was a creeper, I'd have left after dinner because this was a perfect setup for a slasher movie. "Let me grab the lights."

Thank goodness.

Looking around the vast room, there were several long tables of bones that looked like someone was assembling a jigsaw puzzle. Small paintbrushes littered the tops with small bowls of water, with some other acrid solution permeating the air. On the far wall were rolls and rolls of parchment similar to architectural plans that were labeled for the Triassic, Jurassic, Cretaceous Periods, and Mesozoic Era. If I were a gambling girl, I would say they were assembly directions for other dinosaur erections throughout the museum.

"Here she is. Well, on these three tables, anyway. Isn't she a beauty?" Alan's eyes went big and glassy when he stared at Lila. It was comical watching him fawn over fossilized, green bones. I suppose if I were a dinosaur geek, I would feel the same.

"She sure is something. Tell me about her," I encouraged. Better he does most of the talking tonight. I didn't have any interest or need to impress him with my childhood recollections of prehistoric animals.

"Oh my gosh, where to start?" He began pacing. "As I said before, she's one hundred and fifty million years old. Not the oldest of dinosaurs, but she falls into a new genre because we have never seen anything like her before."

Alan looked at me as if I wasn't exuding enough awe over this new finding. I had to raise my game, if not to keep this date on track, but to show my respect after I blew him off two years ago.

"That's incredible. I haven't a clue how that could happen." My animated actions made his chest puff out, and he clapped his hands together describing the whole process. I feigned fascination for ten minutes and then chimed in with a question that a five-year-old would have asked.

"How many teeth does it have? Are all dinosaur bones green?" *Seriously. These were base questions.*

Relieved, he answered excitedly, "Great questions!" *Even I knew how to capture the attention of the professor.*

"Lila has five hundred teeth, the most teeth recorded for a dinosaur. She's green due to an oxidation process that happens after fossilization. It's way too long to spell." *#Interesting #not interesting*

He finished his monologue with his hands outstretched, his eyes open wide, and doing a slight back bend. "...And, incredibly, she's the biggest dinosaur ever discovered."

Alan was out of breath and beaming with delight at this new discovery. One didn't have to love dinosaurs to love his enthusiasm. It was adorable and contagious. Every word he spoke was rich and seductive, making all the details that much more interesting.

Instantly, he fell out of his dino-trance, remembering I was in the room. His movement toward me was sensual and apologetic. Strong hands gripped my upper arms, squeezing me softly.

"You must think I'm the biggest nerd in the world. Once I start talking dinosaur, I'm a lost cause. Thank you for indulging me."

My eyeballs rolled slightly back and I laughed. "Maybe a little, but I like your passion for your work. It's refreshing."

His eyes locked onto mine, moving one step closer. "You're so beautiful, Becca. I wish I weren't so clumsy with my words so I could express how I felt about you back then—now."

When Alan decides to be a man instead of an intellectual, he becomes very charismatic. Dirty blond locks dusted over his serious brow, making my insides tremble. As his hands slid to my back and down to my hips, my hands slipped around his neck.

I was surprised at that moment by how easily attracted I was to very different-looking men. I knew I didn't have a "type," though I preferred a man who took care of his body. Each man I dated this week was like a tray of intoxicating sweets, none better than the rest, but delicious in their own way. Coming to this realization, the stigma of being a woman-whore—*Is that even a word? How about wo-ho?*—*I* didn't feel so bad. Realistically speaking, I would have preferred to have all this fun over a few months, not eight days, but there you go. *Thanks again, Mom.*

"Alan, you are a complex man, but I like how you are balancing your strengths." I smiled into his eyes, liking how they crinkled at the corners.

He hummed. "I'd like to balance out even more if you're game." His mouth lowered to mine, stopping briefly over my mouth before landing gently on my lips. It was a promise and a plea at the same time, asking me silently to open to him. He hummed again.

"You taste so good, Becca." Small puffs of warm air feathered over my face as he continued to probe my mouth. "Do you taste this good everywhere?"

Did I? Alan would have to tell me himself.

"Maybe you should find out," I said hoarsely, smiling at his vivid blue eyes.

No time was lost as he picked me up by my ass and walked me over to an empty stainless-steel worktable. Setting me down on the top, he kissed my nose and stepped back to unbutton his dress shirt. Alan's defined pecs were evident, while not as ripped as David's or Joseph's. A dusting of blond hair spread between his erect nipples, and I loved how excited he seemed. By the time he was finished with his buttons, I had stripped off my blouse, sharing my lacy, black bra that strategically had black satin rose appliqués over each nipple. My nipples were so puckered from the anticipation of what was to come, plus the cold, sterile room, that they felt painful. Alan's eyes flashed as he drank me in. I loved my view, too. Wanting to move this moment forward, I pushed his hands away from his shirt, which allowed me to finish unbuttoning it for him.

He stepped between my thighs, pushing my knees farther apart and running his large, calloused hands—and my skirt—up to my waist. I loved seeing Alan lick his lips, preparing to devour me. He was finally unleashed.

Forehead to forehead, he hissed, "I've been waiting too long for this, Becca. You'll find that when it comes to fucking, I'm not awkward at all. I love all forms of fucking and I plan to do dirty things to you that will blow your mind.

God damn! Where the hell had this guy been two years ago? I loved his dirty talk. Was the awkward professor just a ruse to lure me into his lair? If it was, it sure as hell worked.

"For the love of God, do all of them!" I'd been cockblocked by a nurse with PTSD, an asshole finance bro, a hippie I traded the softest socks in the world for a blowjob, and a guy with a bent dick. I reveled in three men, another with a wicked kink and the other with a wicked bent appendage. Even Annie would lose her mind when I told her what happened this week.

"Lean back, baby. I want to know which is sweeter, your mouth or your wet pussy." He knelt on the floor, hooked his toned arms around my thighs, and jerked me down to the edge of the cold, clinical table.

My back arched at the first swipe of his tongue, my moans echoing off the walls. His hot breath blew in wisps over my tight bundle of nerves as his pointed tongue edged each of my folds. He was deliberate, precise, and calculated in his examination of my pussy. I felt like he set off a rocket sequence headed for Mars, engaging all thrusters. No one had ever teased and taunted my sex like he had.

"Alan, please, you're killing me," I whined, hoping he would stop his torturous ministrations. I was out of breath and near to passing out when he flattened his tongue and pulled a long lick from my pink hole to my hood.

I shuddered as he did it again. He looked up, stopping to make sure I was watching him.

"Is that what you were looking for, Becca? Is my tongue what will make you mine?" I was speechless, nodding my consent. Gone was the unsure, awkward scientist. Alan became the masterful lover that I couldn't have ever dreamed he could be. I wanted this dirty man, and if telling him I was his to get it, I would. In the end,

I said nothing. "Prop yourself up and watch me as I bring you your first orgasm." *First? Of how many?*

I watched in amazement as he latched onto my clit, sucking and nibbling on me with the most perfect pressure, inching me to my climax. He watched me over my belly, seeing me writhe each time he changed his technique. He was incredible. A bundle of electricity formed at the base of my spine and I knew I was close.

"Alan, I'm going to come. Don't stop. Please." I'd never been so desperate to come in my life, and he seemed happy to draw it out for as long as he could. He inserted two fingers, ratcheting up my climax so that my back was completely arched off the table. If he hadn't locked down my hips, I would have rolled off the other way.

"Come now, Becca. Come on my tongue." He jammed those two fingers inside me, pumping steadily as I chased my climax. I came hard and long, barely able to keep consciousness. My thighs trembled. My core became convex, and I fell back to earth, exhausted. Alan was a fucking genius between my legs, and I was more than happy to reciprocate.

As he licked his fingers clean, his devilish grin shone with my essence, and my pussy began to pulse again. He looked like the cat that ate the canary, and he didn't hide the fact that he was pleased with himself.

"Are you ready for your second orgasm?" *Of course, I was!*

I fought the urge to unzip my skirt, liking the way it made me feel even dirtier, having it scrunched around my waist. I was a naughty girl, and I knew it. Who fucks around with so many men in a week? *Don't answer that.*

Alan wasted no time stepping back, pulling out his wallet to secure a condom, unbuckling his belt like it was a striptease, and shoving his pants and briefs to the floor. He shuffled back between my legs and ran his hands down the tender flesh of my inner thighs before slipping the latex onto his twitching, red cock. He reached under my ass and pulled me tight against his impressive length, murmuring under his breath. He lined his tip to my folds, bucking his hard length once, driving into me until his balls hit my ass.

"Your pussy is almost as beautiful as you are. Relax. Let me introduce you to my dinosaur."

I tried not to laugh as he impaled me with his thick cock. I guess you'd call it a Brontosaurus due to its girth, but the length was a whole other animal.

I moaned, letting my inner muscles relax, and then flexed around his massive cock. He felt amazing. I felt full in a very different way than Joseph, but equally satisfying.

"Damn, Alan. That feels so good—so good." I said, drawing out the "oo."

His left hand held tightly to my left hip while the right shifted from my breast to my right hip. I wrapped my feet around his back and hooked my ankles, changing my angle to feel more of him.

"Fuck! Squeeze me again. Yes! Just like that. Perfect," he commanded, and I obeyed. His eyes roamed from my face to my chest and down— to where we connected. Slick noises, slapping together as his speed increased, sounded like a symphony of harmonic flesh. I needed to come badly, and I could tell he was so close, too.

"Touch me, Alan," I begged, his eyes darkening to sapphire. His thumb slipped between us, massaging my clit, forcing my back to arch off the table as I screamed his name. I felt so sated and happy until I saw Alan still slamming into me.

"God, I could do this forever," he said as he slammed into me. His prayers were answered since he didn't reach his climax for another ten minutes. This dude could have been a porn star with his endurance. It was hot to watch all those muscles bulging and working hard over me. His eyes bore into mine while his core tore me a new pussy. It was sexy as hell. I'm not sure how happy I would be to have him going this long so often, but tonight, I reveled in the fact that I fulfilled his fantasy, and I glowed knowing I had two glorious orgasms with a giant one-hundred-and-fifty-million-year-old dinosaur watching over me.

We stayed pressed together, Alan's cock twitching inside me for minutes as we caught our breath. I couldn't imagine what he was thinking, but it had to be good from the ebullient smile gracing his face.

"This was better than any dream I ever had about you." His words flattered me, and I pushed his back into his preferred style, back with my fingers, trying to come up with the perfect rejoinder.

I pulled his face down for a tender kiss, knowing that this date was coming to a close. Expecting another date would be out of the question. Sex wasn't enough for a long-term relationship and Alan's social skills were rough.

"Never in my wildest dreams did I think I would be having sex in a natural history museum, on a stainless-steel table, with a prominent professor of paleontology. Alan, you have exceeded every expectation I ever had of you, and I already thought very highly of you. But now . . ."

He pulled me off the table awkwardly, setting me carefully back on the floor. To my dismay, he morphed into a Jekyll and Hyde-like persona, switching from red hot lover to his previously nerdy self. He stepped away from me quickly, pulled up his pants, tucked himself in, yanked up the zipper, buckled his belt, and shoved a hand through his hair. Realizing I was staring at him confused, he reached forward and pulled down my skirt, buttoned up my blouse, and pressed down my disheveled locks, arranging it like a child would do with their doll.

"Alan, are you okay?" I asked, concerned.

He scrambled to find his shirt, locating it in Lila's jaws.

"I'm—it's just, I don't know what came over me. I mean—you and me—we—don't want to get caught by the night watchman. We need to get out of here." Swiveling his head left and right, trying to decide what to do first, was quite comical, but I was more concerned about him having a heart attack.

I stepped forward, placing my hands on his shoulders, his shirt buttoned askew and began to fix the alignment.

"Shh. Alan. Breathe." He stopped short, watching me intently. "There." I patted his chest as his hand covered mine.

"Thank you, Becca. You were amazing and so understanding. I don't—it's been—thank you."

He touched his brow to mine appreciatively. I took another moment to enjoy our time together, running my hands over his chest again.

"Are you happy we did this?" I hoped he was.

He let out a deep sigh and wrapped me tightly in his arms. "Best night ever."

"Better than finding Lila?" I winked seductively.

He laughed, rubbing his thumb lightly over my bottom lip. "Equally." He kissed my forehead, leaving his lips in place. We stayed like that for several more minutes before he turned away, heading toward the door.

"Let me get the lights and we'll go." He smiled a sideways grin like a teenager after his first lay. Cute for a teenager. A little sad for an adult.

He helped me with my coat, and we left after he had set the alarm and secured the door. We walked hand in hand the short distance back to the diner parking lot. He spun me around for one more sensual kiss goodbye, returning his persona to Dr. Jekyll, not Hyde. This man was still an enigma inside an enigma.

"Becca. I know you probably wouldn't go for a guy like me. You're too sophisticated . . . and beautiful . . ."

I stopped him with a soft kiss of my own. "I went on this date because I wanted to keep my word and go out with you. You surprised me, and that alone makes you very attractive. Your passion for your work and ability to make science seem simple was refreshing and fun. I had a great time. Know your value, Alan. You're going to make some lucky woman very happy."

He smiled genuinely and stood up straighter, knowing this wasn't a pity date. Would I have actually gone out with him if I hadn't brokered a deal with my mother? Doubtful, but who knows?

"I hope to see you around. Drive safely." Alan opened my car door and shut it after I was settled in. I'll think fondly of this night the next time I'm in the museum. But if I see Lila hovering overhead, my body will remember Alan's adorable smile, rich, deep voice, and remarkable sex skills, setting me on fire. I waved to him through the window and pulled out of the parking space. Looking in my rearview mirror, I saw him standing there, blissed out from our evening and smiling. He was a good man. I hope he finds his person soon. *Me, too.*

Chapter 19

It's been two nights since I lit my Hanukkah candles. Ironically, this thought sounded like the opening line in a confessional. I hadn't been home much this week, and leaving my candles burning without me being present wasn't an option. Please, God, forgive me.

I opened the cardboard box to pull out eight candles, organizing them in alternating colors. That was always a fun thing to do when I was young. Some days it was all one color. On others, they alternated between two or three colors. On this day, I had enough for four orange, and three blues and used a white one for my *Shamash* to help light the other candles. It was the second to the last night of Hanukkah, and I paused, remembering why we lit them—Bring light into the world.

I couldn't tell if I was bringing more light into the world, but after these past seven dates, I could proudly say that my parting words were always positive and uplifting—except for Evan. *What a loser.* I concluded with the required two prayers, thanking God for their wondrous deeds and making us holy with their commandments to light the candles. I sat back against the bay window, watching the glow they made, wondering if anyone ever looked up to see my menorah. I was supposed to be a beacon to the world to bring more light into it, but nowadays, everyone is too busy watching out for themselves to care about anyone else. It was a sad state of affairs. I took refuge in the fact that my trying was more than others did, and that alone brought more light. *Amen.*

My phone buzzed. It was Annie.

Me: *Checking up on me?*

Annie: *You bet. I need some new spank-bank material. What do you have?*

Me: *Spank-bank? You're too hip for your own good.*

Annie: *I'm young—well, youngish, and I'm not dead yet. So, spill.*

Me: *I'm calling you. Too much to tell in a text.*

I pressed her face icon on the screen as I walked down the hall to my bedroom. Annie could keep me company while I got ready for bed. Goodness knows this call could last for hours.

It's finally happening. My week-long experiment of power dating was ending, and I'm pretty sure I was no farther along than when I started. What I could confirm was that there are some pretty freaky people out there, and while they may be great for someone else, they weren't right for me.

Each of the seven men I dated had one if not multiple, wonderful qualities. Alan was sweet and refreshing. Evan—douchebag. Larry was fun and sexy, but his kink would not be appreciated for the long haul. Joshua, also sexy, was relaxed and had some appreciable assets that made bartering for those silky socks very worthwhile. The telemarketer, Ravi, was too pushy and made me feel less-than. I loved David, though. Strong, masculine, with the right amount of alpha that made me feel alive. Too bad his past haunted him at the most inopportune times. I felt for the guy. PTSD was nothing to be ashamed of. I hope he finds the right people to help him move through it. Then, there was Joseph. *Damn!* I thought he'd be the perfect guy. He did everything right, except he *lied* to me. Seriously, did he think I was so stupid I wouldn't find out? In retrospect, I liked how I found out. The look on his face when he saw his wife's name, "Love of My Life," in big, bright letters on his phone screen, was priceless. He deserved everything that woman could extract from him.

Today was Max's day. The travel influencer was five years younger than me. At this point, unless he were a complete creeper, I would take him to the party. Everyone else had too many issues to overcome and I promised myself—and Spencer—I wouldn't lead anyone along. This process had been grueling and quite ridiculous. Why did I think I'd find Mr. Right this way? I should have listened to my gut and told my mother to go to hell. My pride and integrity are much more important than trying to please her or make her look good to her friends. My happiness was more importatnt. And, for that, I'm ashamed.

Our date was scheduled earlier than the rest. Sunday was tough since we both had work early the next day, and Max was leaving town for a job in Peru. He suggested having an early dinner in

Mexican Town, which tracked with his traveling persona. *Who didn't love a taco?*

Finding parking was challenging enough, but construction kept me from arriving on time. I found a spot three blocks away and parallel-parked between a tow truck and an earthmover. Welcome to Michigan, where construction cones are our state animal.

Me: *Just parked but have a few blocks to walk. See you soon.*

Max: *I had the same problem. I'll get us a table.*

I finally arrived intact, if not disheveled. The formula of hat plus hair never equaled a finished look. Nevertheless, I finger-combed my locks back into place, catching my image in the entryway mirror, and gave myself a thumbs up. Passable and cute. *I'll take it.*

Thanks to social media, I stalked Max to discover what he looked like and what he did for a living. You wouldn't be wrong if you asked me if I was trying to see if he was scary, you'd be right. Thank goodness he wasn't. A nice-looking man stood, waving me over, and I began to relax after the trek down to the restaurant. He greeted me with an incredibly enticing smile and a gentle hug.

"Wow, Becca. It's great to meet you finally. You, uh, look even better than your social media profile." *So he scoped me out, too? Nice.* Stepping back, I nodded. "Seems like we both had the same idea." I blushed, smiling into my cream, cowl-necked sweater. "You look great, too." That got me a sexy grin as he pulled out my chair for me. So far, we were batting a thousand.

His face changed quickly to what looked like remorse. "I have to apologize for how we're meeting. My grandmother was so insistent that I met a 'nice Jewish girl' that she refused to keep me in her will if I didn't agree to at least one date."

I burst into laughter, slapping a hand over my mouth to muffle my boisterous outburst. "My mother, too! It's like there is this cultural trauma that every Jewish mother inflicts on her children. It's horrifying!" I wiped at my lower eyelids, pushing the tears away with my middle finger.

Max sipped his water and leaned back casually in his chair. "I guess we can check that off our To-Do List. Now, we can speak candidly for the remainder of our date. What do you say?"

I stared at his light brown eyes trained on mine, aching to touch his silky, long black hair tucked behind his ears. *Would it be as soft as mine?* Our server took our drink order, followed by a quick negotiation to share a few dishes. We both agreed Mexican was the best. I leaned on the table with my elbows and rested my chin on the tops of my hands.

"So, Peru? What's that all about? I inquired.

His mirrored actions felt intimate and conspiratorial. "Companies hire me to travel around the world to either do recon for incentive trips or to build their product brands. It's basically an all-expense paid trip to make sensational, breathtaking images and videos to stimulate their audience to want to book a personalized trip, buy their hiking gear, or merely promote an area of the world that the company resides in. Either way, someone is trying to sell the people something, and I get to spin it attractively." If leaning back in a chair had swag, Max personified it. Legs spread, arms crossed casually, and nodding his head assuredly.

I bit my lip and nodded along with him. "You certainly have the attractive part down." I hadn't planned to be so forward, but he set that up so nicely.

He stroked his chin as he raised it. "There are a few perks I don't often take advantage of, but I would make an exception if you were interested."

My interest was piqued. "Like what?"

Shifting his position back to leaning over the table, "Sometimes, I can bring a guest." His eyebrows waggled.

Was he kidding? "You'd want to take me on one of your trips? Stop. You must say that to all the girls." He barely knew me. Why would he say that?

Reading my mind, he reached for my hands. "I know we just met, but I have good intuition, and it's telling me you'd be game for an adventure."

His eyes locked on mine, luring me into his web. He wasn't wrong. I'd love to drop everything and go on an adventure. Only not with a complete stranger. Shared culture wasn't enough to make me feel comfortable with that idea.

"That certainly sounds exciting, Max. Let's wait and see how things go before we get too far ahead of ourselves."

Our margaritas and chicken nachos arrived, followed by a plate of steaming hot enchiladas and rice. Max entertained me with several of his escapades, with nary an opportunity for me to chime in. An opportunity came as he stuffed a loaded tortilla chip into his mouth, and I told him about my trip to Hawaii and the volcano my family visited a few years back. Remembering that day sparked one of the most hysterical, memorable moments of my brother's life. Signs were posted everywhere about staying back from the fence line. Our docent repeatedly asked Nathan to keep to the marked path, but Nathan decided none of those warnings applied to him and peered over the side of the volcano, slipping down several feet as he screamed at the top of his lungs for help. I giggled. We still razz him about it.

I barely got the words out of my mouth before he one-upped me.

"Oh, that's nothing. I took a helicopter ride, and the pilot dared me to swing from a rescue rope ladder over the top of an active volcano on the island of Stromboli in northern Sicily. Steam nearly baked my bottom as I swung across the opening, moments before it spewed out volcanic ash."

Really? He seemed so proud of himself. Smug didn't look good on anyone.

"That sounds too incredible to believe." I leaned back, feeling annoyed and unheard.

"Oh! Believe it, Becca. I've done some crazy shit in my life. I have the video clips to prove it, too." His hard expression and finger-pointing told me to back off. And I did. *Geez, buddy, relax.*

I changed the subject to his family, hoping to get him to settle down. If I hadn't already promised myself I would give each of these guys a chance, I would have left at my earliest convenience. I believed people genuinely wanted to make a good first impression, but Max missed the mark, intent on one-upping me. Wasn't that a sign of narcissism? Maybe he should date my mother.

I took another stab at leveling the field. "Our families seem pretty similar. Do you light Hanukkah candles as a family or by yourselves?" It was an innocuous question, but it revealed much about how he saw his family.

"Holidays in my family can best be described as a minefield. Enter at your own risk." He smirked.

"Wow," I recoiled. "Tell me more." I crossed my arms and leaned back in my chair, looking around for the server. It was time to get the bill.

His eyes rolled backward in his head. "Apparently, being a travel influencer isn't a real job and shames the family. That makes every holiday I miss a direct assault to my family values and failure as a Jew. I make six figures and get to see the world for free. You'd think they'd be proud that I found a gig that provided all that. Listen, I know you followed in your father's footsteps and became a lawyer like he is, but I'm not following my father into the death business. Funerals are creepy, and I'm not helping those poor souls decide whether to pay a fortune for a pine box or an even bigger fortune for a luxury casket. Both sit in the deep, cold, hard earth."

His outrage was palpable. First, why did he think following in my father's footsteps was less than doing something different? Secondly, funeral directors are an essential part of life. You don't get in the ground without one. Lastly, who does he think he was, making his chosen profession more worthy than anyone else's? *Hey buddy, you don't need to be a travel influencer to book a plane anywhere in the world.*

This guy disgusted me and yet would be the perfect person to take to my mother's party. He'll razzle-dazzle her into thinking he's the perfect man who can swoop me off my feet and take me to exotic places. Marilyn would have lots of stories to tell her friends to increase her status. *Fine.* I was done with this guy, and, hopefully, he'll go with me to this party without too much coercion.

Our check arrived and, when I reached out to grab it to pay my share, Max gently set his warm hand on mine, trapping it against the table. "I've got this. You've been a lovely date." Again, *really?* My insides were roiling and my head felt whiplashed.

I pushed my hair behind my ears and looked down at my empty plate. "That's kind of you to say. It was interesting hearing about your adventures, to be sure." *What the hell else was I going to say? Of course, you had a good time. You got to listen to yourself for over an hour.*

We stood, and Max took my coat from me and helped me put it on. At least he was a narcissistic gentleman. His palm firmly planted at the base of my spine was presumptuous, but I allowed it. His wallet was stuffed with cash and he paid the cashier up front, returning a large tip back at the table, before walking me out of the restaurant. I was at a loss as to how to end this date. I needed to ask him to the party but hesitated for fear that he might think I liked him more than I did.

As we walked side-by-side back to my car, I took a leap of faith and blurted out, "I have a charity Hanukkah party to go to this Wednesday. I need to bring a date. Would you want to join me?" I kept my face neutral, wishing he would answer quickly so I could exhale. His reply wasn't what I expected.

Max stepped closer, cupped my face with both his hands, and kissed me before I could stop him. *One Mississippi. Two Mississippi.* I wasn't feeling it. He was too much of a douchebag to give him anything back. His puffery tried to make me look small, and I put an end to this lame kiss immediately.

"Call me if you want to go. It's at my parents' house. Wednesday at seven o'clock. It's a formal affair. No worries if you can't or don't want to come. Talk to you soon."

He said nothing as I walked away. I'd traveled several steps before he called out. "I'll be there if you promise me more of that." I turned to see his devilish smile and cocky attitude. This guy was full of himself. He had no idea what I could do for him and to him.

"We'll see." I gave him a wink, knowing full well that he was getting nothing more from me.

I held my breath until I reached my car, exhaling deeply when my butt hit the seat. Exhaustion coursed through my body as I buckled my seatbelt, willing myself to keep it together until I got home. It was the last night of Hanukkah and I wanted to spend it in my traditional way—alone.

Shamash—Literally, "helper" candle that lights all others. The location can vary from menorah to menorah

Chapter 20

My father sent me a text, which was way out of his comfort zone, to remind me that not showing up tonight wasn't an option. I sighed, resigned to a night of running from my mother, pushing Max off to whoever would listen to him, and avoiding Spencer. He always came to this event. Honestly, he brought over one hundred thousand dollars of support with him, too. Marilyn may not like him, but she did like his zeal for making her look good. This year's cause was to support juvenile mental health. A hot topic in the news and at her country club made this choice conspicuously obvious. I was all for it. If funds from the party could get kids the support and services they needed to become healthy, stable adults, I would stand behind my mother all year long. Reducing mental health issues meant a reduction in school killings, gun abuse, suicides, and more, making for a healthier coexistence for everyone.

Earlier last month, Mr. Rutherford emailed the entire company asking for donations for my mother's charity, making it a point to have me collect, in person, from anyone who didn't make the deadline. Everyone had to give, which made me want to cower in the bathroom. *Again.* It was embarrassing to beg for money.

"Hi, Lisa. It seems like you forgot to send in your donation to the Brighter Future Charity. Could you cough up fifty bucks—right now?"

Yeah. It was a friend-killer task, but, in reality, each person could write it off and meet their yearly donations quota on their taxes. Oh, and help the kids. Thankfully, I only had to make two stops this year, and I was one of them.

Dressed and ready to go, I opened my computer, clicked on the donation link, and made a two-thousand-dollar donation. Since my mom started doing this four years ago, I've increased my generosity by five hundred dollars each year. It felt good helping the kids and, begrudgingly, my mother.

The buzz on my intercom signaled Max's arrival. We agreed that riding together would make for better optics, and he said it would be more fun. *Sure.* I looked at myself one more time in my beveled entryway mirror, feeling good about my look. I wore a winter white, tea-length high-low dress embellished with a delicate, contemporary lace edging. The bodice crisscrossed over my breasts, accentuating their already voluptuous size, and clasped behind my neck. The salesperson gasped when she saw me exit the changing room.

"Wow! You're a stunner, Ms. Strauss. No man or woman will let you walk by unnoticed." I blushed and stepped onto the platform with a three-way mirror, checking out all my assets. She was right. This dress hit on every curve. Even I was impressed. Choosing this style was easy, though it wasn't the kind that I had ever chosen before. Those dresses were far more demure. I was feeling feisty, and this choice served as my vindication for having to answer to my meddling mother.

I spent three hours at the spa getting my hair coiffed in a loose chignon that clung to the nape of my neck. My stylist pressed finger waves along the sides to give my curls a Victorian flair when combined with the dress, made me look like a 1920's movie star. My red hair popped, and the cherry red lip the makeup artist used was picture-perfect. Small, black, catlike wisps at the corners of my eyes gave me a hint of naughtiness I would enjoy this evening. If I couldn't find Mr. Right, maybe he'd find me.

I grabbed my matching beaded evening bag and the long mink coat my grandmother willed to me and locked the door. I didn't need Max in my apartment, and I didn't plan on having him up on the return trip either. We saw each other through the beveled windows, and he stepped closer to the door when I pushed it open. His eyes shone as he raked his gaze over me. I guess all that time and money paid off.

"Geez, Becca!" he bellowed. "You sure do clean up well. That dress is spectacular on you. And your hair! I'm afraid to touch it. It's so perfectly made." I blushed at his over-the-top accounting of my appearance. I knew I looked good, but he'd never seen me dressed up to know what a full coat of paint and a can of hairspray could produce.

I took his hand as I stepped down onto the damp sidewalk. Sparkly snowflakes fell from the sky effortlessly onto my head and sidewalk. "Thank you, Jos—Max." *Oops! Almost messed that up.* Keeping all these guys' names straight was no easy task.

"Come on. Let's get you into the car." A black Mercedes was parked at the curb, and he tucked me into the backseat, pushing my coat under my tush so it wouldn't fall out when he shut the door. The gesture didn't go unnoticed. He walked around the back of the car and, once seated, realized we had a chauffeur. Eyeing him as he slid closer, I realized why.

Max reached over, setting his hand on my knee. "Becca, I'm sorry if I came on too strong the other day. I forget other people travel and have their own experiences that are meaningful to them, too. I hope you can forgive me." *Well, I was going to before he laid his hand on my knee.*

I fought to tell him off but decided to slide my hand under his, forcing him to hold my hand instead. "I appreciate that, Max. You have an exciting life, but the rest of us cherish our hard-earned trips even more." That should have shut him up, but I was wrong.

I kept my eyes forward, looking out the front windshield while he blabbered on about how "Everyone can take these trips, and they aren't so expensive if only people would plan properly." I would have punched him in the balls if I didn't need him to walk through my parents' front door. *Where was his off switch?*

At this time of night, during the middle of the week, we blessedly traveled across town in twenty-five minutes. My focus this evening was surviving my mother. Everything else was gravy. My dad supported me. My brother would run interference as best he could. And, maybe even Spencer would intercede on my behalf if needed. I'd do my duty, smile, and wave, be charming and effusive; then I was out of there by ten.

I snapped back from my planning when Max snapped his fingers in front of my face.

"Hey, Becca. Are you listening to me?" His sharp tone pissed me off.

"Actually, no. I'm not." My snide remark was intended to cut.

"What's your problem tonight? You're so uptight." His accusation was correct. I was uptight. It was time to come clean about why he was escorting me to this party.

I shifted in my seat, staring at his high cheekbones and full lips. "I may not have mentioned that this charity event is my mother's pet project. Looking good to her friends, extended family, and dignitaries is a top priority for her. Our family gives her full reign to be obnoxious tonight, and tomorrow, we'll rein the Kraken, known as Marilyn, back into its cave until next year. My reality has been that she never goes in quietly and never stays there long. She loves a good 'show,' and with your help, we'll give her one. Understand?" I batted my eyelashes and grimaced.

Max grunted, nodding his head. "Hmm. I get it. So, what's my role in all this? Keep you from being eaten alive? Perhaps steal you away so I can have the honors?" He waggled his eyebrows for effect. *Not a chance, buddy.*

"Something like that. When I introduce you, be charming and complimentary. Dazzle her with your outrageous travel stories. She'll be eating out of your hand in no time, and I will blend into the woodwork out of her line of fire. Sound good?"

He wrapped his arm around my shoulder and squeezed me tightly. If he weren't so self-absorbed, I would have sunken into his firm, warm chest and enjoyed the smell of his woodsy cologne. I didn't know Max well enough to know if his need to share his over-the-top stories was due to low self-esteem or if he really did think his life was so much better than anyone else's, but I wasn't going to stick around long enough to find out. There would be tons of other women he could impress tonight, so I could make myself scarce.

"I've got you, Becca. Stick with me. I've never met a mother I couldn't win over." He winked, owning his bullshit.

"Thanks, Max," I gave him a snarky reply, pulling away from his warmth. "We're here. It's showtime."

An army of valets ushered luxury cars and limousines around my parents' circular driveway to their estate. Five acres of property tucked behind large oaks and maple trees covered in a glistening sheen of snow made the property a perfect winter wonderland for guests to get in the party mood. A red carpet protected expensive shoes and elevated the importance of this event. The Strauss Family Charity Hanukkah Event was like any Miracle Network party nationwide. Over one hundred illustrious guests, dignitaries, and local celebrities contributed their philanthropic pocketbooks to the cause my parents supported each year—all children-related themes.

Max offered his arm to steady me up the grand stairway into a bustling foyer filled with sparkling lights and a champagne fountain. Tasteful, sophisticated blue and silver Stars of David hung like pendants at the bottom of long, crystal strings. It was stunning and vibrant, just like my mother—a decade ago. Festive Hanukkah and Klezmer music wafted throughout the house as we made our way through the rooms on a mission to present ourselves to my mother, ending this long, weary week.

I smiled and nodded to various guests with whom I'd made acquaintance over the years, not introducing Max since he'd never meet these people again, at least with me. To my shock, Evan Zweig, that horrible crypto-dude, bumped into me, sending me into shock. *Why the hell was he here?*

He looked at me closely as if he was trying to figure out how he knew me. "Whoa. Watch where you're going." *Me? You watch where you're going.* "Hey, do I know you?" *Incredible.*

"Yeah, Evan. You do. I'm the woman who met you at the rooftop bar and you tried to sell me Bitcoin the whole time. This is my parents' home. What are you doing here?" I was incredulous, sputtering out my words. Before he could answer, someone tapped me on my shoulder, and I spun around to see who it was.

To my horror, Ravi, looking sexy in a tux, was staring at me. *What the actual fuck was happening?*

"Becca, you look incredible," he shouted over the music. I looked up at Max, feeling him stiffening at my back.

Max bent to my ear, whispering, "Who are these guys?" His tone was not so sweet.

I needed to get out of there. My head spun, looking for possible escape routes, when I saw Spencer walk out of my parents' den. I took two steps, only to stop in my tracks. That , who I chastised him about last week, followed him like a puppy. Why was he still dating her? She wasn't right for him—I was!

Max grabbed my elbow, spinning me back around, demanding an answer to his question.

I looked at these three men, each beautiful specimen of manhood, and yet each lacking what I desperately wanted and needed. I began to apologize when my mother stepped into the fray.

With great aplomb, she greeted our quartet. "Hello, gentlemen. Thank you all so much for coming. I hope you all had a wonderful date with my lovely daughter. Have a wonderful night and don't forget to drop your donations off in the dove-cage in our den. Your contributions will help so many children improve their mental health for the future."

Frozen in place, my eyes fluttered, and I began to hyperventilate. The room began to swim and, if not for the large hands that wrapped around my waist, I would have surely hit the floor. I didn't know who caught me or where they were leading me, only that I was moving in another direction. The music became a whisper, and a cold glass of water was thrust into my hand.

"Drink," a strong voice commanded. I took the glass and gulped down all its contents, realizing through the bottom of the glass that Spencer was standing in front of me. He glared at me, and I felt like throwing up. Where was his date? I felt set up, embarrassed that my mother thought she could invade my personal life by inviting these men, who I told her emphatically were not for me. I could see the hurt in Spencer's eyes and, for that alone, I was miserable. I did this to him, and he didn't deserve this trouble.

"Do you feel better?" Spencer's voice soothed me, but there was a hint of disdain I couldn't disregard.

I couldn't look at him. My eyes were glued to the floor as I answered. "Yes. I, uh . . ."

"Don't," he hissed. "I don't want to know. You're better than this, Becca. Pull yourself together, find your mother, and tell her to fuck off. If you want to be with any of those other douchebags, then pick one, and send the others on their way. They are making your life a circus." I slowly lifted my gaze, trying to find the courage to meet his eyes. His jaw was set, and his brow furrowed. I was disgusted with myself for putting either of us through these gyrations. Where did everything go wrong?

I bit my inner cheek and nodded. "You're right. You've always been right. Thank you for helping me. You can go back to your date." I stood up carefully making sure my weight was distributed evenly on my heels before stepping away from him. He touched my elbow and I turned to see his eyes softening.

"You've got this, Red." His smile brightened, and I turned, quickly exiting the room before I burst into tears.

Like the grown-up woman I was, I hid upstairs in my old bedroom. Not much had changed in seven years, save for the new paint job, duvet cover, and window treatments. No woman wanted to hide in her childhood bedroom with posters of boy bands and piles of stuffed animals.

I felt like an imposter. A disgrace to womankind. This was what comes of trying to please others before pleasing yourself. I thought I'd figured that out when I went to college, and again when I graduated. I most definitely ironed out that boundary when I turned thirty years old, at least it felt that way. Now, here I was again, fighting my desire to be my own woman before being my mother's perfect daughter.

Something had to give. I knew what needed to be done. It was now or never, and her party be damned. I stood in front of my mirror taking a long, hard look at myself. I wiped the smudges from under my eyes and patted my hair into place. Shoulders back and fortified with a new confidence I'd never felt before, I spun on my heels and marched down the grand staircase like a . Head held high and focused on the single most aggravating person I loved and despised, my mother.

My foot struck granite as I strode across the foyer toward the shrill laughter in the dining room. Nothing would deter me from my goal. Nothing.

"There's my little girl." *Except my father.* "I've been looking for you everywhere. You look sensational, darling." My father fawned over me, kissing my cheek and holding my hands so he could get a good look at me. "Just stunning. I like this new look on you."

I smiled and stepped forward to give him a hug. "You have no idea what my new look can do, Daddy. I love you so much. Please forgive me," and I walked past him, finding my prey.

I slid alongside Marilyn as she raved about her friend's latest facelift. This was her second, and I could barely recognize her. I waited approximately two minutes for my mom to stop and recognize my existence before stopping to acknowledge me.

With an affected smile and smooth delivery, I put my plan into place.

"Hello, Mrs. Gendelman. So sorry to interrupt; I need my mother for a few minutes."

She tried to smile, but her face wouldn't move. "Becca. So good to see you, too. Joseph spoke very highly of you."

What the hell?

My mouth gaped open. "He did? Did he also tell you he was still married and was cheating on his wife?" *Oops! Did I say that out loud?*

Now she gaped, and I didn't feel one ounce of remorse. There was no way she didn't know her son was still married. Not a chance. *Disgusting woman.* She stood there speechless, and I took my leave, dragging my mother in tow toward the butler's pantry next to the kitchen.

Marilyn yanked her arm out of my hand and whirled on me. "Who do you think you are speaking to her that way? You can't speak to my friend like that? You humiliated me!"

"Humiliated you? You humiliated me first by sending me out with a married man! And invited half of the men you set me up with to your freaking party! Why?! Do you get your jollies putting me in impossible situations? Or is it because you are so shallow that you would rather see your child suffer to make yourself feel bigger than you are? You're a Mother. A fucking narcissist—I'm done with you. Don't call me again. Don't invite me to your stupid parties or holiday gatherings. I'm *persona non grata* to you. You created this. *YOU!*"

My tirade concluded, and I didn't wait for her reply. There wasn't one I'd accept anyway. I didn't need that kind of love, and I had just enough self-worth to see how she tried to steal my integrity. I wasn't a puppet to her anymore. I would live my life on my terms, family or not.

Disgusted with the whole evening, I walked to the makeshift coatroom and collected my things. A hired valet asked for my parking ticket, but I couldn't produce one. *Damn it!* I threw my head back in surrender, pleading to God for mercy. I stepped into an alcove and ordered a rideshare, then pulled on my coat, enjoying the heaviness of the fur; it matched my mood. The valet opened the front door, and I descended the stairs to wait in peace.

The crisp night air cooled my lungs and my emotions. I did my duty for my father's sake and immediately made a clean break with my mother. I hadn't seen my brother to tell him I was leaving or said goodbye to Spencer. My father would figure out soon enough why I left, and I was safe in the knowledge that he understood things had to be this way.

In one week, I would be on vacation, where I planned to turn off my phone, eat my weight in ice cream, and drive into the sunset as I had planned. I had one final goal for this year: finding the turnkey clause in my company's bylaws that would either make me a partner or push me to find other employment. Next year would be my new start. A clean slate to creating a future that had me at the center and not subject to the control of others. I'm driving my bus from now on, and I'm not letting anyone on unless they understand that.

Chapter 21

I hung my barely-worn dress back on the padded hanger, hooking it over my closet door to air out. It was glamorous and deserved to be worn on a happy occasion, and I looked forward to wearing it again soon. Carrying a glass of wine I poured the moment I entered my apartment, I sat at my vanity and began plucking out dozens of bobby pins, releasing my hair down my back. The act reminded me of saying goodbye to a good friend. It was great while it lasted, but the relationship was over. I slurped another mouthful of the fruity wine, then soaked a cotton ball with eye makeup remover. Gone were the catlike eyes and glittery champagne eyeshadow, revealing dark circles under my eyes that even make-up could barely cover. Blindly, I continued to strip my face of every vestige of the façade I'd let the makeup artist apply until there was only the stark version of myself. How ironic to see myself naked of paint, my body stripped of fabric that created an illusion of beauty, and my heart barren of hope that I would find a bridge to my mother ever again. If a person could feel the way a forest fire looked after being scorched to the earth, then that's what I felt like.

My dramatic thoughts followed me alone to bed. I turned off my nightstand light and looked at the clock, feeling the last stab at my pathetic situation—it was only nine o'clock. The journey to sleep was swift, and when I woke with a start, I couldn't remember where I was. Someone was banging on my door. The midnight, but it felt like much later. I rubbed my eyes and swung my legs off the bed, trying to reorient myself.

"Come on, Becca! Open the door!" I knew that voice and gasped. I fumbled around in my closet for my robe, swinging it on as I stumbled half asleep down the hallway.

"Hang on!" Not caring what I looked like, I peered through the peephole, double-checking that it was who I thought it was. Except it wasn't.

I swung the door open to find Nathan stuffed into a topcoat and looking somewhere between pissed and relieved when he saw me.

"Thank God you're all right." He stepped inside to hug me.

I hugged him back. "Why wouldn't I be?"

He growled. "Because no one knew where you were when you left or why you left. That dipshit, Max, said you were looking for your mom, and that was the last he'd heard from you. I wanted to punch him in the face for being such an asshole date leaving you to fend for yourself."

I laughed. "You should have. Come on in. I'll get you a drink." Nathan walked back into the hallway, stopping abruptly.

"Nah, but I think this guy could use one." He pointed to his left, turned to wink at me, and walked down the hall.

Spencer stepped into view, and my hands flew to my mouth. Why was he here? He was so mad at me before. And why was he with Nathan? I needed answers—now.

I waved Spencer in and locked the door behind him. He moved over to the counter, taking a seat on the barstool. He looked at me carefully as I poured him some wine.

"Becca, we need to talk," he said softly.

I pushed the goblet across the granite and walked around the counter, pulling a barstool in front of him.

"I suppose we do," I said, looking at how he held the glass between his fingers. I wanted to be wrapped in those fingers. I wanted to run my fingers through the crop of wavy brown hair on top of his head. I wanted his arms wrapped around me and to never let go. I needed his legs on either side of me, with the promise of him pressing deep inside me. I had known I'd loved Spencer since the moment I'd met him, and if I didn't give myself to him tonight, I would regret it for the rest of my life.

"Spence—."

"Becca . . ." we said together. "You go first," we said together again.

He put his glass down and clasped his hands tightly together.

"Why are we doing this to each other? I'm in so much pain watching you traipse around with other men. And worse, me dating a dimwit just to have a beautiful woman at my beck and call. I can't take it anymore." He picked up his glass and drank down the whole thing.

I picked at my manicure, wondering the same thing. Every word that came next out of my mouth would either bring us together or tear us apart forever, and I couldn't let that happen. Spencer needed my honesty, my commitment, and my trust. And I needed his.

"Before this stupid dating deal with my mother, I only wanted to be with you." His eyes shot up to mine. "After dating these men, it became evident that none of them came anywhere close to the man you are, and I felt ashamed for having put myself through all of this misery." I reached for his hands, and he gave them to me.

I couldn't look at at first, but needed to get everything I'm feeling off my chest. All the stupid notions I had about him, me, and my family. "I remembered your words about not hurting any of these guys and found that I was the one who hurt most after each date. I was the loser after each ridiculous date I promised my mother I'd go on. That was wrong in so many ways." I hurriedly kept talking.

"When I saw you with that blonde woman, I wanted to kill you." His smile shrouded by his hand. "I was jealous, petty, and stupid for not stopping what I was doing and making you mine. Hell, I don't even know if you want that anymore, the way I treated you. Seriously, Spence. Do you even want me anymore? After all I put you through?"

He rubbed a circle with his thumbs on the inside of my wrists like he'd done before, setting my body on fire. Our eyes lifted and locked into place, searching for the person we knew was waiting for each other. He lifted one hand and kissed the back of it, sucking slightly as he lowered it. Desire pooled between my legs as he stole my breath away. He did the same to my other hand, and another pang of desire flooded my panties. His talented hands kneaded my nipples, sending jolts of desire throughout my body and more when he traced them down to my thighs.

"I couldn't want you more if I tried," he growled.

He leaned forward, pressing a sweet kiss to my nose and then a decadent kiss to my parted lips. Greedily, his hands pressed higher up my thighs, his thumbs digging into my soft flesh. His tongue traced my lower lip pulling it into his mouth, sucking it like it belonged to him. He claimed me with this mouth, our tongues dueled, forcing a moan from his mouth that was the sexiest sound I had ever heard.

I pulled his head back by his hair and smiled teasingly into his face, "Are you ready to dump the blonde?"

He laughed. "I only took her out twice, and both times a disaster. She only came with me tonight because I knew she'd make you jealous."

I gasped. "You did not! You're a mean man, Spencer Weiss."

He grasped his chest, "You cut me deeply, Rebecca Strauss. But, yeah, I did, and it worked. And now, I'm not ever letting you go." He jumped off the stool and pressed my legs open wider. My pulse picked up—hoping and praying that tonight we would finally consummate this relationship.

My mouth was assaulted by his tongue and I welcomed every nip and lick he offered. His hands slid under my ass and kneaded it roughly. "Fuck, Becca. I want you so badly. I need you—but I can't."

My heart sank. *Can't? Or won't?*

Panicked, I asked. "Why can't we? I want it, too, Spencer. We've waited so long. Why not now?" I sounded desperate because I was. My body was on fire and there was only one logical ending to this night, and I'd be damned if it didn't end with his dick in me.

He pulled my hair back, trying to keep himself in control. "We have so much more to discuss and now isn't the time. If we want this relationship to progress, we need—I need—to work through every obstacle so they don't come up again. Does that make sense?" I could tell how earnest his request was, and I respected it. But why did he have to be so rational at a time like this?

Our breaths were short as we forced ourselves to settle down. His fingers threaded through my hair from scalp to tips, leaving me frustrated and languid at the same time. Everything about Spencer felt so good. I told myself I would be a good girl and control myself, though I didn't know for how long.

"When Spencer? When can we get that conversation out of the way?" I sounded whiney but didn't care.

He kissed me again like a truce offering. "Soon, Red. I have to go out of town tomorrow for a few days. We have to have this conversation in person, and I think we both need that time to fully appreciate what we have and are willing to sacrifice to have it." He took my hands again laying them on his chest. "Don't doubt how much I want this Becs, I really do."

The void of him leaving my side was palpable. I wanted to throw myself at his feet, desperate to have him stay and make love to me. I knew how ridiculous that sounded and, thankfully, prevented me from doing so, but my heart ached more and more with each step he took toward the door.

"Wait!" I've wanted to ask him a question ever since he got here. "Why was Nathan with you tonight?"

He chuckled. "He saw how upset I was about your whereabouts and chased me from room to room looking for you. He threw me against a wall and forced me to tell him why I was so crazed about finding you. I had to tell him, Red. He needed to know our truth. Then he dragged me by the lapels, threw me into his Escalade, flicked me in the head with his fingers, and told me, 'Thank fuck, you finally manned up, Spencer. It only took you ten years.'"

I could picture Nathan wrestling with Spencer. Those two were tight. I threw myself at Spencer's chest and hugged him as hard as I could. "Yeah, Spencer. Thank fuck!"

Chapter 22

"It's time, Emily. Grab everything you can and let's get out of here."

There was an executive board meeting today at three o'clock, and that's when I made my move to move my things from Rutherford, Timmins, and Grovner. Messenger bags stuffed with relevant documents, one banker box of my personal effects, and one of case law filled our arms as we entered the elevators at three-ten. If anyone had asked what was in the boxes, I'd have opened the one with my personal stuff and we'd be golden. As it happened, no one gave us a single look. The elevator doors shut as we looked over our shoulders at one another. Mission accomplished.

"Right in front of their faces," Emily exclaimed.

"I guess that sums up my existence here—invisible."

We exited the building via the lower-level garage and loaded my trunk. I knew there were cameras everywhere and decided to make a big show of opening one of the boxes to hand over my prized coffee cup to Emily. She gushed and took the cup from my hands, then threw her arms around my shoulders in appreciation. We hugged it out, whispering smack-talk to each other about how smart we were and how ignorant the partners were. Emily walked to her car holding her cup close to her heart, then placed it in the backseat of her car. We waved at each other as she returned to the elevator while I got in my car and buckled up. I may be an intellectual property attorney, but I'd watched enough cold case law shows just like everyone else. Rule number one: don't be conspicuous. Anyone looking at those tapes would see a boss giving her friend and assistant a parting gift. I was prepared to leave Rutherford, Timmins, and Grovner at any moment, so I didn't care if I got fired?

I imposed on my doorman to help me *schlep* everything upstairs to my apartment. Everything secured safely inside, I kicked off my shoes and plopped down in my bay window to listen to my messages. Spencer had been leaving some sweet and not-so-sweet messages for me every day. And, every day, they got filthier and filthier.

Call from Spencer: *Good morning, Red. I know you won't hear this message until later, but I wanted you to know you are the first thing I think about when I wake up and the last thing when I go to sleep. I love you. Have a great day.*

Call from Spencer: *It's two o'clock, and I can't do a fucking thing because I keep remembering how goddamned sexy you are in your jammies. You are my personal siren! Excuse me while I relieve my gigantic hard-on. Oh yeah, you've seen it, haven't you? Now imagine all of me pulsing inside you. Gotta go!*

Great! Now I have a lady-boner and no time to rub it out. I'm going to get him for that before bed. Two can play that game.

I changed into a sweatsuit and poured a glass of ice water, staring at the mound of paperwork Emily and I had to get through tonight. The paperwork I brought home was a drop in the bucket compared to what Emily and I had tackled over the past three weeks. We had already found that the bylaws had been changed as recently as three months ago, but the question was: why then? What prompted this specific change after ten years of nothing being changed? We'd find that answer tonight, and I would be vindicated. I wouldn't stay at a firm that didn't respect me or my work. Especially since they went out of their way to be sure I didn't see my name on that wall until someone keeled over. And, even then, who is to say they wouldn't find another ridiculous excuse to give me my due? I wanted to see the look on their faces when I pinned them to their own damn wall. I wanted redemption. I wanted millions in potential wages lost due to discrimination. I wanted closure. Wherever I landed, Emily pledged to follow. She deserved my loyalty after all the hoops I made her go through to earn partner. She was almost as devastated as I was when I was shot down. We started as a team, and we ended up as a team.

There were several good points that would make our case, but Emily had her network of executive assistants who could confirm the series of events that predicated the most recent changes. The most compelling point was that there hadn't ever been a female partner in the firm's fifty years, and there were three other female lawyers who had as much experience, wins, and client books as mine. And, they had never been offered partner either. It sickened me that, in today's age, misogyny was still so prevalent in the workplace. There had to be a more compelling reason than that. We would find it. I was sure of it.

My phone dinged, and a close-up picture of Spencer's lips puckered at me. My thighs clenched at the memory of what those lips could do. His desire to please me was intoxicating, so much so, that I didn't hear the knock at the door.

"Coming!" *I wish I was.*

I fired off a quick response to Spencer, hopefully making him feel the same way I did. "I love that mouth, especially when you . . ." *That would drive him crazy.*

Laden with bags of food and work tote bags, Emily nearly tripped into my apartment. "Here, let me grab some of these."

Kung pao chicken, beef fried rice, and egg rolls lined one side of the center island, and three versions of the bylaws, discrimination case law, and a list of possible negligence laid within our reach on the other. With drinks poured and plates piled high, we started with Emily's new intel.

"How did things go with the other assistants? Any dirt we can use?"

Emily nodded her head, her mouth full of fried rice. She held up her finger and chewed quickly.

"Yes." She held up the same finger and took a swig of her water. "Remember Mona Richardson? Word on the street is she was bringing in huge clients and big settlements, but the partners decided she didn't use her voice loud enough during meetings."

I bristled. "Who the hell cares, so long as she's raking in the dough for them? How long has she been a junior partner?"

Emily held up six fingers. "Daisy, her assistant, said she gave up trying to make partner six times. The only way she could make more money was to negotiate higher commissions from each case."

I slouched back in my seat, disgusted. "That's what they tried on me."

"Yeah, I know." Chewing on eggrolls was our new standard for a time-out.

After swallowing, I pressed on. "What else?" Emily picked up the same piece of paper, studying something.

"Danielle Milton had the same problem as Mona, with the added tick of being Black. She pushed back, though, and they reassigned her to a different division so they didn't have to deal with her on a daily basis. And Francesca Suarez got short-stopped because she had too many family problems, which they claimed got in the way of her communicating with her clients in a timely fashion. I know for a fact that never happened because I was her assistant for three years before coming to you." Emily's eyes bugged out, and she slid her mouth to the side, looking cocky. "That is not how I roll. You know me. Have I ever not communicated clearly and in a timely fashion? They had the gall to tell her that her skills duplicated Fred Butler's and that she was redundant. I wanted to pop someone in the face."

Even if I didn't agree with her, I wouldn't mention it because, frankly, I think she'd kick my ass. No. Emily was as professional as they came. "Not once that I can recall."

She nodded her head, owning her greatness. I wish I could say the same. Listening to these women's stories fortified me to step up my game. These assholes wanted a more powerful voice at the table. No problem. They would get an earful next Monday morning. My best line of defense was that no one else at this firm had a mechanical engineering degree. That was critical to designing intellectual property that would stand up to scrutiny. Not one of those bastards would last a week without my credentials.

"Emily, we can stop looking at these bylaws. We can't prove why they changed them three months ago, and it's a waste of time trying to conjure up plausible ideas that would hold up in court. Our first line of defense has to be discrimination. The second is my undergraduate degree. There aren't any other junior partners who have a mechanical engineering degree. The last three out of ten cases I've won are specifically linked to those credentials. If we can secure a discrimination judgment, I can leverage my history at the firm and my degree to get a substantial settlement. What do you think?" I was breathless from my monologue but satisfied with its logic.

Her eyebrows raised—her lips vibrating like a motorboat. "Now we're talking. If we could get Mona, Danielle, and Francesca to corroborate their stories and be witnesses in court, not only would you come out ahead, but these women could also be compensated. We don't have enough people to create a proper class action lawsuit, but now we have strength in numbers. We have the law on our side."

I stood up and rounded the counter. It was wine time. I grabbed two goblets from behind me and reached into the wine fridge under the counter I had installed two years ago. The battery-powered corkscrew whirred as it expertly uncorked the bottle, and I poured us two very full glasses.

I declared raising my glass high, "I'd like to make a toast." Emily sat up straight, holding out her glass, preparing herself for my monologue.

"Your Honor, today I would like to demonstrate how the excruciatingly misogynistic partners at Rutherford, Timmins, and Grovner have deliberately held back qualified women due only to their gender. In addition, the women listed in this suit have suffered emotional, professional, and financial damages for not being promoted into their well-earned position of senior partner at this firm. We are asking for a judgment to include both past and future monetary losses, collectively, in the amount of twenty-five million dollars."

I stood tall, laughing and saluting my glass forward as if honoring the judge. With a small bow, Emily put her glass down and giddily clapped in appreciation. "Brava! Brava! Brava! Now, do that thing you do when you win. I love that part."

I paused, trying to figure out what she was referring to when it hit me. I popped my hip to my client and blustered, "Now that's how it's done."

"Yeah. Girl power, all the way."

We drank in silence, letting the magnitude of the situation settle in. I could lose my job—or my motion—or, worse, they could blackball me, keeping me from working at any law firm in Michigan forever.

This had to be done soon because I didn't think I could stomach working there much longer. Most importantly, my motion had to include that I got to keep the clients I brought to the firm. I did all the work, even if the firm paid for my office, assistant, and supplies. You know what, screw them. Without me, over fifty cases, including Warrington Industries, LeafLorn Industries, and Roland Laundry Industries, would never have happened. They were some of my bread and butter; without me representing them, there would be no reason for them to stay.

Confident in our path, Emily and I spent the next two hours preparing my motion and building our case point by point. I'd contact the other women lawyers passed over for promotion tomorrow and persuade them to join forces in my quest of vindication. Tomorrow would be a new day in Becca Strauss' life. *Tomorrow—I'll be unemployed—definitely.*

schlep—to lug or carry laboriously

Chapter 23

It was three days before New Year's Eve, and I was chomping at the bit for many reasons. Spencer would be home in two days, and I wanted this office bullshit to be over so I could focus on him—all of him. My plans to shut down my phone and drive away for a week were now on hold. Again, man plans, God laughs.

All three women agreed to make a statement attesting to being discriminated against by gender only and attached a financial sum they would settle for in our lawsuit. While I couldn't take the board to court for lost wages at this time, I would as soon as I left my position.

In other news, my mother hadn't bothered to call me after her beloved party. Nathan informed me that Max, the travel influencer, monopolized their conversation for a long while, making her feel uncomfortable. *Welcome to my world, Mother.* Her devotion to good manners prohibited her from telling him to shut up, but, from what my father said, Nathan took pity on her an hour later, escorting her to the kitchen. I, on the other hand, didn't pity her a bit. She brought this on herself and deserved to be subjected to the assholes she sent me to date. *Yasher Koach.*

My shoes were off, and I strolled through my office preparing my confrontation speech when my phone rang. I bolted toward my phone, hoping it was Spencer, and tripped over my discarded heels, throwing me into the corner of my desk. *Ouch.* It wasn't him, but a happy second choice.

"Annie!" We hadn't spoken since a couple days after my date with Larry, and we all know how exciting that was. "I miss you. When are we getting together? We missed our annual tequila and tea holiday lunch."

I pulled out the pins in my bun and let my hair fall down my back, finger-combing the strands out.

"I know! That's why I'm calling. I had to visit my mom in Nevada. You know about her gout, but now she has blood clots. I won't be home until after the New Year. You can't see me, but I'm crying hysterically, and my mascara is dripping down my face." *I'm sure that wasn't happening.*

Annie spoke a mile a minute, and I had to wait her out. "I'm so sorry to hear about your mom. Please give her my best, and let me remind you that you only use waterproof mascara and have never had a smudge in your life. Props for trying to win sympathy points."

We both laughed. "I'll take my mother's gout over your mother's meddling any day of the week. Did she let you off the hook after her party?"

"Ha! I didn't stick around to find out. It's been a week, and still no sign of Marilyn. I'll take that as a win." I cackled.

Annie cleared her voice. "Seriously, Becca. Did you pick one of those guys to take you to the party? Or did you go solo again?" Her tone was patronizing, but I held strong.

Sighing, I replied, "Yes, I picked a guy, the travel influencer. I picked him more for my mother—or in revenge to my mother, as the case was. I was out of there by nine. What a waste of five hundred dollars for a Hollywood-level hairdo and makeup. I'm not even divulging the price of my dress. It's scandalous. I had better find another opportunity to wear it. It's too beautiful to trap in the back of my closet."

"So where are my pictures? Was Spence there? Oh! Did he bring a date? You owe me so many answers." Screams of "Give me a minute" blasted through the phone. "What, Ma?" She bellowed too close to the phone. I've met her mom once, and that was plenty enough for me. At least my mom could afford a nurse if she was ill. Neither Nathan nor myself would have lasted a day at her bedside. "Hey, gotta go. Pictures—and a date to hash through all the details. Love you, girl."

In total Annie style, she blew into a conversation and blew out of one just as quickly. It was like whiplash. She didn't even wait for my reply.

There was only one more thing to do today before I left my office, which made me nauseous—deliver our motion to Rutherford. I'd already been squirreling away more of my personal effects this week, and it was a good thing everyone had started clearing out for the New Year, but still, no one noticed me emptying my office tote by tote. The partners who worked the week between Christmas and New Year's rotated each year, and, just my luck, Rutherford was sitting behind his desk sipping cognac and smoking a stogie.

I arrived and took a long, deep breath, then knocked confidently on his open door. He jutted out his chin to come in since his mouth was full of tobacco.

"Hello, Mr. Rutherford. Do you have a few minutes?" I tried to keep my voice steady and unemotional. In the courtroom, it was paramount to own the floor. Demand that the judge hear each point without distraction. Any twitch or hand wringing would indicate weakness, and that was the kiss of death. That wouldn't happen today. He was my courtroom and judge, but I was the jury and had the last word. I took solace in knowing I was in the right, and tomorrow, four women would be filing a formal motion. Today was only a courtesy.

I strode toward his desk and sat at the edge of the heavy leather chair typical of every pompous old-world mob boss. "There has been discussion about the change of bylaws beyond our last conversation, and I thought I would bring it to your attention." *Opening statement completed.*

He pulled his feet off his desk and tilted himself back again with a smug smile.

"Interesting. Tell me more," he said snidely. I couldn't wait to wipe the floor with this guy.

I continued. "Ironically, those bylaws hadn't been changed for ten years and then mysteriously had been updated to reflect specific verbiage regarding limiting partnership invitations only three months ago." I kept going. "Industry standards for the size of our firm warrant up to twenty-five partners, and yet ours caps it at ten. Additionally, there are now provisions that state unless one of the partners dies, concedes, or is found breaking the law, no other invitations will be offered. I found it interesting that this change happened right when I came up for partnership. What are your thoughts about this?"

He had the facts. Now, all I had to do was watch him put his foot in his big, fat mouth. I sat back, straining to keep a smile from forming on my mouth.

Rutherford put out his disgusting cigar and sipped at his drink. All stalling tactics to make the other party nervous. I wasn't a greenhorn in this business. I knew exactly how to maneuver him.

"Miss Strauss. It seems you've been doing a lot of digging around. Are you implying that we changed the bylaws to specifically prohibit you from achieving partner status?" His melodramatic delivery reminded me of the character Mr. Trotter in *My Cousin Vinnie*, as he deposes Ms. Vito, his girlfriend. Sanctimonious and patronizing. I've seen that movie a thousand times, and, in the end, Ms. Vito proves her case, not the other way around.

"I am. And so are three other women who have been up for partner in the past five years, though those women don't have my engineering credentials. As a matter of fact, no one else at this firm carries them. Neither of those junior partners has a client book as large as mine, and none of them could afford to get fired like I can. Pick your poison, Mr. Rutherford. You and the other partners deliberately kept us from claiming a spot on that wall, and we will be filing a motion tomorrow morning for gender discrimination."

I slapped the motion on his desk and turned to walk out when he barked out his disgust. "You think this stupid motion will hold up in court? After all I've done for you over the years, this is how you repay me? You were a little girl when you started here, and I gave you everything you have today." I spun in my high heels and jammed my hands on my hips. He would not get the last word here.

"Gave me? Hardly. I worked my ass off for every client, day and night, most of whom *I* brought to this firm. You gave me a desk, a view, which I earned, too, and an assistant. Everything else I fought for. Your hypocrisy is laughable. You consistently dismissed my ideas, and yet I kept my mouth shut out of respect for my father's professional association with you. I bit my tongue harder when you rolled your eyes at my attempts to affect change in this company. You didn't back me up unless there was something in it for you personally. But when you did back me up, it only made me the fall guy if something went sideways. You didn't think I saw what you did time and time again? You have no idea what I'm capable of." My words hemorrhaged from my mouth and then stopped abruptly. I was done with this guy and turned around to walk out. "See you in court," I hissed.

I didn't wait for the elevator. Instead, I took the stairs and held the rail tightly as adrenaline coursed through my veins, making me wobbly. I felt happy, yet livid, for having to defend my position and my value. It felt electric knowing that we would have our day in court and be vindicated. When that motion was read and approved, I'd file a wrongful discrimination suit and collect my millions and several more for Mona, Danielle, and Francesca. *If only I had done that with my mother earlier, I could have saved myself a lot of tsuris.*

I pushed through the stairwell door, three floors down, and beelined to Emily's desk. She had packed up all her belongings this afternoon and pushed the stuffed box behind a large plant for safekeeping. It was go-time, and I gave her the nod. She ejected herself from her seat, switched off her computer, grabbed her coat, purse, and belongings, and headed for the elevator. I was right behind her, swinging my coat on as I entered the elevator car. I heard a ding from the other elevator car landing on our floor, Rutherford barking my name. The door slid shut just as he looked at me, and Emily and I waved goodbye. We stared at each other and broke into peals of laughter like two hyenas after they caught their prey. The ball was in motion, and I had no regrets. Next year was my year, and Emily was my faithful steed.

tsuris—trouble or aggravation
Yasher Koach—more power to you or great job. In this case, said sarcastically.

Chapter 24

There was a need in every daughter's life to set boundaries with their mother, regardless of their well-meaning advice. Marilyn called and wasted no time launching a well-rehearsed rant. Today was the dawn of a new era in my life. It would be a day in infamy—Becca's Boundary Day.

". . . you have no idea how your ac. . ." I put my phone on the table and walked to my laundry room to flip the load. Walking back three minutes later, I stopped in my kitchen for a glass of water and returned to hear another vein of rants about not listening to her.

I took a long swig from my glass, carefully set it down on the granite, and slid onto a barstool, pressing the speaker button.

"Mother—mother!" The halt in her diatribe gave me a chance to get a word in. "You can save your breath. As of today, unless you have a specific request or need to update me on all things family, then don't call me. I'm not discussing my personal life with you anymore. I'm not dating another loser you send my way. And I most definitely will never listen to you chastising me ever again. So, unless you would like to compliment me on how fabulous I looked at your party or show appreciation that I came to support you, then please hang up."

You could hear the growling as she grumbled her indignation. "Did you even hear what I had to say?" The whine in her voice was pathetic, and I held my ground.

"No." I deadpanned.

"No?"

"Yes. No. Was there something specific you needed to tell me?" *This tough love thing was hard.*

Several moments of silence gave me pure pleasure knowing she had not only heard me but was trying to reformulate her thoughts with my demands in mind. She cleared her throat and plied a smooth, bell-like tone to her voice. "Becca, you—you looked radiant at the party." Bellows of air could be heard through the receiver as if she exercising.

"Thank you for noticing, Mother. It was a new look for me, and I'm glad it caught your eye." *See, a pleasant conversation between a mother and daughter.* She sucked in another audible breath of air.

"That man, Max, was, how shall I say . . ."

"Annoying? Long-winded? Self-absorbed?" My voice dripped with sarcasm.

She hummed, "Yes, all those things. So why did you choose him for the party?" she said, bereft.

I chuckled. "Because he looked the part of the man you wanted me to have and seemed to match your endless narcissism."

She gasped. "Were you punishing me, Becca? Am I that horrible that you would inflict that obnoxious man onto your mother?" *Ah, the guilt.*

I held nothing back. It was time to end this call. "I'm going to let you stew on that one, Mother. Thank you for calling. I'll try you back after the New Year."

I went to hang up the phone, desperately needing to pee.

"But, aren't you coming. . ." she wailed again. I ended the call and dashed to my bathroom. I hated it when people took my call in the toilet. It was so gross and unrefined. This was the only elite mannerism I clung to, and I had no regrets for calling someone out when I heard a flush. Ironically, that's when Spencer called. Manners be damned, I was answering.

I used my accessibility feature and told my phone to answer the call. "Spencer! Hang on a minute. I'm washing my hands."

"Are you in the bathroom? You never answer your phone in the bathroom. Are you okay?" I could hear the sarcasm in his voice and imagined the smirk stretching across his handsome face.

"Ha. Ha. Laugh all you want, but it was either that or miss talking with you for three more days." My theatrical delivery was straight from my mother's playbook. *Gah! Am I turning into my mother?*

"Are you on your way home? How was your trip?" Though I wanted to hear his answer, I mostly wanted to hear his deep, melodic voice. There was a slight gritty quality that was so sexy to my ears that I could listen to him read the encyclopedia and get wet.

"The trip to Chicago was illuminating. We toured several heavily populated areas and discovered that their urban plan was far superior to ours, especially for electric car charging stations, parking, and public transportation. I don't think Southfield wants to invest that much; urbanites in this area don't commute enough to the city daily. The EV stations, though, are a must for us to stay competitive in the Motor City. The question is where and in what intervals do we place them."

"I'm glad you're thinking about this stuff. I barely use my car, but I would like more suburban public transportation if you can swing it." I chuckled.

He laughed, too. "I'll get right on that. Are you home for the night?"

I flipped off the bathroom light and began to strip off my clothes. I considered turning on the video feature so he could watch me, but if he was driving, I didn't want him to wrap himself around a tree—*death by Vixen Video.*

"Yeah. It's been a long day, starting with filing our motion and then dodging calls from the firm's partners and their lawyers. I'm not afraid to lose my job, Spencer. I have plenty of money to last me a few years, but I don't want these other women to suffer financially. I was thinking we could open our women-only law firm. Our own chick fort."

The idea just popped into my mind, making me squeal. We'd have talent and support staff. My name would be on the wall first, and we would set a new standard in office etiquette and upward mobility. This would be great!

"Sounds like you're already onto your next big goal. Can I help?" The way he dragged out the *I* would be considered entrapment. How could I say no to him?

There was a knock at my door and I needed to get my shirt back on to answer it.

"Hang on, Spence. There's someone at my door." I put the phone down on the kitchen counter, flipped my camisole over my head and hoped I didn't need to open the door completely.

"Hang on! I'm coming," I yelled at the idle door. "How can I—"

"Help you?" Spencer stood at my door looking delicious in low-riding sweats and a ragged Harvard sweatshirt. He pulled his hand through his wet hair as he wet his lips. Damn, was he pretty—and home early!

"Spence! You are such a stinker! Why didn't you tell me you came home early? I would have made you dinner." I jumped into his arms, wrapping my legs around his waist, feeling excited when I pressed into his hard cock. His lips crashed into mine, tangling his tongue around mine and moaning into my mouth. Several moments passed before he carefully set me down with lust in his eyes.

"Cook for me? That sounds so domestic, Red. Are you sure you wouldn't rather heat *me* up?"

Our eyes locked. There were so many things I wanted to say. There are so many comebacks that could get me into trouble. Deep, sexy, naughty trouble.

"You're always hot, Spence. No preheating for you." I pulled at his bottom lip, eliciting a moan that made me clench my thighs.

"Damn, Becca. If anything is in that oven, you'd better take it out now because where I'm taking you, it will burn to a crisp. Without another word, he swept me off my feet, and I grabbed his neck tightly as he walked me down the hallway to my bedroom.

Kicking the door shut, he laid me out on the bed, hovering over me, kissing me senseless. His tongue was among the best things I knew I would love about Spencer. So talented. The other thing I knew I would love equally was his thick, long cock. I remembered through a drunken haze, staring directly at his engorged shaft, glistening with his pre-cum, begging to be inside me. My insides wept when Spencer tucked himself back in his pants during my delirium that night; being the fucking gentleman that he was, we were both deprived of history-making sex. I was tired of sweet, wonderful, thoughtful Spencer. I wanted him to unleash everything held back and take me to places I'd never been. *Places even a bent dick couldn't take me.*

He wrapped his tongue around mine and sucked deeply as if he was sucking my clit. My hands pulled at the crop of hair piled on the top of his head. Only the streetlamp illuminated his body, revealing his desire to have me. I'd seen that face before, at my high school graduation, when he tried to kiss me, and Nathan stole our moment. And again, at my college graduation when he finally pressed his soft, pillowy lips on mine for the briefest moment. I remembered his big hands holding my hips with the promise to never let me go. My heart was open to every possibility with Spencer. So many opportunities were presented throughout the years that were shattered for many reasons, but tonight, nothing would stand in our way. Not even my phone ringing.

"Do you have to get that?" Spencer said between kisses, strategically placed down my neck.

"No!" I hissed. "You are mine tonight. The rest of the world could burst into flames for all I care. Nothing will stop us tonight. Nothing! Do you hear me?"

"Loud and clear, Red." His kisses continued their path, kiss by kiss, to my chest that heaved from my aching body. His hands cupped my breasts and kneaded them with just the right amount of pleasure and pain, bringing me joy and rapture.

"Damn, Spence." My thoughts were jumbled, and more eloquent words escaped me. That tongue became weaponized, latching down on my nipple and pulling it tightly between his teeth before popping it off like a lollipop. "Fuck! You need to register that tongue with the U.S. Army. It's a killer."

A loud, boisterous laugh erupted from his throat which made me smile. "A weapon, huh? Wait until you see my missile, Red. You'll want to keep that for yourself."

"Bring on the artillery, handsome. I'm ready for an onslaught." I'd never used an Army metaphor in my life, but this man was on a mission and packing some serious firepower. I suppose being in love with your partner makes everything more intense. My willingness to do or try new things with him was limitless so long as he was at the center of it all.

"You're thinking too much, Becca. I can see it on your face, and your body is tightening." He stopped playing with my tits and looked at my face, concerned.

I felt weepy. I had held back my feelings for him for so long that the floodgates threatened to open. There was so much joy in my heart that I vibrated. It was overwhelming. I could feel every molecule in my body loosening and expanding in a way I couldn't have imagined. How could I say that to him? There weren't enough words to describe how I was feeling at that moment.

My hands pulled his mouth to mine, relishing how he pulled me tighter to his chest. "Sharing this moment with you is rocking my world. For years, I've dreamed about you holding me like this, kissing me like this. I'm in a dream, Spencer, and words cannot express what it means to have you this way. Tell me it's not a dream. I have to know."

He rolled to his back, pulling me with him as he stared at my face. I straddled his hips, and he sat up, supporting me with his strong hands. We kept staring at each other, lost in the moment, weighing the impact of what was said next. He swallowed hard, his Adam's apple rising and falling down the front of his neck.

"This, us, is not a dream. It never was. It will never end. I knew there was something special between us the day I met you, too. I couldn't have told you what specifically. Twelve-year-olds don't have the vocabulary to express anything, let alone words of love. Every time I couldn't put my hands on you was torture. When your prom date got sick, I desperately wanted to drive across three states that night to take you but I knew your mother wouldn't let me in the house. I wanted to call so many times and force you to listen to me, to tell you that I loved you. That you had to love me back."

His eyes closed tightly. I kissed each lid tenderly until they opened again. When they did, a moment passed between us. It was as if a new light in the world burst from our love. I was speechless, but Spencer managed to find his voice.

"Rebecca Strauss. Did you ever wonder why I never could keep a girlfriend? Or wouldn't leave this city? Or insisted that we be friends so that I could hold you and laugh with you until all hours of the night?"

My eyes fluttered with recognition. "You've loved me all these years, too?"

He sweetly kissed my forehead. "Every one of them. Now, can we stop talking? I want to be inside you."

He rolled me over again to my back, quickly stripping me of my skirt and panties. I yanked at his shirt and reached into his sweats, pulling out his hard cock. The one I wanted to fuck three weeks ago. "This is mine, Spencer Weiss," I said, tugging on his most private parts.

"Fuck, yeah, it is."

Spencer used his feet to push down his pant legs, then refocused his efforts on stroking his shaft. "You better be on the pill, or you're going to be pregnant before the wedding."

Holy Moses! I gulped. "I am. Please, for the love of God, shove that huge beast in me."

I didn't know whether to laugh or cry, but when Spencer spread my thighs and kissed the insides of my sensitive skin, I nearly flew off the bed. When his magnificent tongue spread my pussy folds and breathed slow, hot air on my clit, I cursed him for teasing me.

"Be patient, Becca. You'll get everything your heart desires after I tease this sweet pussy into climax. How long can you last, Red?"

I panted erratically, delirious at how he kissed and sucked and dragged his flat tongue from my ass to my hood. He knew what he was doing, and I loved that he took control of our lovemaking. I had to keep myself in control all day, and I was thrilled to let him take me on a magical ride to Orgasm Town. He traced one finger over each fold and crevice and pulled out guttural sounds I'd never made in my life.

"That feels so good. There! Oh! Keep doing that." The way he twirled his tongue around my clit and rhythmically pumped two fingers deep into my pussy was euphoric. He turned his fingers and hit the jackpot. I came so fast, I didn't have time to warn him.

"Fuck! Yes. Oh my God. Spencer. You are the prince of my pussy. Whew! Again." My arms flayed open wide, gripping the sheets as my orgasm pulsed inside me for what seemed forever. Never in my life had I come like that. I guess dreams really do come true.

My whirlwind dating scheme provided some much-needed sexual release, and I was glad to have had such talented, varied men to share them with. I was pleased that each date ended on a positive note, with each guy understanding that it would probably be a one-night escape, except Evan. I learned that having great sex with hot guys didn't mean that I would be emotionally satisfied. There wasn't a mystical connection with any of these men, which helped me to see that Spencer was always the one who filled my heart, soul, and mind. Our decision to push the past aside and focus on our future together made this *beshert* night the best night ever. It gave me hope that whatever we chose to do in our own lives would be championed by a caring, loving person without a hidden agenda. Life was good.

"Prepare yourself, Becca. Relax that sweet pussy, and let me in." He watched as his cock slid into my entrance. My eyes rolled back each time he pressed his thick cock deeper. Inch by inch, he progressed until I could feel his balls resting on my anus, warm and soft, and all Spencer. I wrapped my legs tightly around his waist, finding the best angle to allow him full access. "Yeah, baby. Squeeze me with that tight pussy. So good."

He pulled back slowly, setting me on fire with anticipation. When his crown pulled free of my hot, wet pussy, there was a void I couldn't tolerate. As I began my protest, he slammed his cock again deep inside me, making me shudder with delight.

"Ah! God, Spencer." He thrusted so hard that he forced me up to my headboard. The sound of his balls smacking my ass was erotic and savage. He brought me to my edge over and over until I begged him to push me over the top. "Now, Spencer! Please."

"Rub your clit, baby. Come with me," he commanded.

I slid my hand between us and found my raging bud, circling my index finger over it faster and faster until I screamed, "I'm coming!"

"Tell me you're mine, Becca." He was so close to his climax. I could feel his body tensing and his jaw gapping in ecstasy.

"I'm yours, Spencer."

"Fuck, Becca. Come all over my cock and make me yours." *Fuck, I loved his dirty talk.*

I bucked up, tightening my hold on his waist and exploded over his cock just like he demanded. His release arrived two pumps later with a feral roar. He was beautiful and raw. His strong chest heaved with exertion, and his ironclad arms pulled me up to his chest, eye to eye.

"Every dream I ever had of us fucking never came close to the real thing. You are the sexiest woman in the world, Becca. Everything about you is perfect. Your face, your hair, that big brain of yours, and this body. My God, woman. You'll be the end of me."

I snuggled into his chest, listening to his heartbeat thumping hard. I felt very naughty. I wanted more, and I would get what I wanted tonight.

"How about my mouth, Spence? Is my mouth perfect?" A slow smile crept up both our faces.

"I guess we'll have to test it out," he growled, throwing me back down to the sheets and sliding out of me. He slid off the bed, snaking both arms under my thighs and yanking me down to the edge of the bed.

"Sit up," he ordered, and I obeyed.

He stepped back, pulling my hair through his fingers until he dropped the ends. "Yeah. I think you have the perfect mouth to take all eight inches of me. Shall we try?"

I smirked. Now, he was the gentleman. "We shall."

Chapter 25

Snow blanketed the sidewalks as the sun rose brightly this morning. It was daylight savings and that meant, *oh shit*—I was late for court! I looked at the other side of my bed, expecting to see Spencer there, but he was gone. I felt so empty. I wish I could've spent more time wondering where he went, but I didn't have time. I would have used body wipes and thrown my hair in a bun any other day, but I was covered in sweat and Spencer. *Spencer.*

Enough swooning. I ran into the bathroom, took the fastest shower known to womankind, brushed my teeth, and applied a light coat of makeup before dashing into my closet, pulling a blue skirt and white blouse from the hangers. In my haste to get dressed, I didn't see Spencer leaning on the door frame, holding out a travel mug of coffee and a piece of toast.

"There you are! Uh. God bless you." I grabbed the toast and stuffed the whole piece in my mouth averting crumbs on my blouse. With squirrel cheeks, I kissed him, letting my body walk first and keeping my lips on him as long as possible.

"Later. I'll be back by six. You'd better be here," I called, running down the hall and coming to a halt.

Emily, Danielle, Mona, and Francesca were in my living room, standing there with their coats and briefcases armed for war.

"Hey, uh, what are you all doing here?" I was baffled by their presence. I looked at the clock. It was nine-fifteen. We had to be in court in fifteen minutes. We'd never make it.

Danielle spoke softly, "I got a call from the court officer asking that we meet with the judge at her midday recess. 'Concerned about our allegations,' the judge's request mentioned. We thought we'd meet here and formulate a new plan if this one didn't work out." Her shoulders hung listlessly.

Francesca made a good point. "I cleared out my desk last week just in case I was fired and they wouldn't let me back in the building. Whether we win or not, I'm leaving there. I need a new position fast. My family can't be left hanging." Besides Emily, each of these women had families to support, some without husbands.

I felt for them. They didn't need to be in this situation, which is why they explained they chose to bite their tongues and keep their jobs. It was as though they were indentured without cause. It was time to share my plan, and I hoped they would come on board with me.

Spencer came out of the bedroom clean-shaven and looking delectable. His knowing smile lifted my spirits. After I motioned for the women to take off their coats and have a seat, I walked to the front door and fixed his wool coat collar.

"Thank you for a spectacular evening," I whispered seductively, pressing his lapels flat.

"I'd say the pleasure was all mine, but we both know I'd be lying," he said coyly.

"Six?"

"Six. I'll bring dinner," he supplied. His lips met mine, and I tingled all over, wishing these women would get the hell out of my apartment.

I let him pass reluctantly as he walked out the door without a fuss. I spun around to the room of women and began to share my plan.

"Okay, ladies. Listen up." I walked around the couches where they were sitting and pulled up a deep blue ottoman. "No one will be out of a job. On the contrary, you can join me as I open an all-female law firm if you want. We will be selective in our clientele and even more selective about our team members. That's right. I said team members. Because, with us all working together, not against each other, we will reach our goals while supporting each other as women. As professionals. What do you think?"

Emily clapped enthusiastically, and so did Mona. Unfortunately, the others did not.

"You have questions and concerns. I can see that. Tell me what they are. Let's see if we can work through them," I nodded my head encouragingly.

"Who's paying for the start-up of this company? And, are we expected to pay hundreds of thousands of dollars to have our name on the wall?"

Wow! She went right to the jugular.

"Great questions, Francesca. I've put some thought into this, truly. As we work together to tweak the financial obligations, I would like to front the firm initially. I would ask the three of you to make a ten-thousand-dollar initial buy-in as earnest money; you can pay the rest of your percentage over an agreed-upon time. And," I could see Danielle squirming in her seat, "if you decide you don't want a partnership position, only a place at the firm, I would love to have you. Heck, if you only wanted an equity share, I'd be open to that, too. I know you have families—and big money like that is hard to come by—but I'd like you to own something in this venture. Like an insurance policy for the future. Does that help?" I ducked my head between my shoulders, playfully nodding.

Mona pursed her lips, "You've thought of everything, Becca. I think I can swing the ten thousand. I want in." Her smile was bright and optimistic, and I thought I might cry. Mona was incredibly innovative in real estate law. She'd make an incredible partner.

Francesca spoke next. "With my mom being ill and my husband working a night shift, I can't stretch myself right now. All my kids need braces this year, and I'm concerned I won't make enough to get by the first year if I come on board a start-up. Becca, I want to be on board with all of you, but I'd have to negotiate a firm base to budget accordingly."

I thought this might be the case. I didn't want to lose her, but I did have an offer that might suit her circumstances. "If I could guarantee eighty percent of your current client fees and only ask you to be in the office Monday through Thursday, would that help you decide? If you bring in more business, we can negotiate a higher commission. Please think about it." She nodded, and I smiled encouragingly.

Emily blurted out, "Can I be the office manager? I want to lead people and make more money." Her eyes beamed with the idea of bossing people around.

"If you don't mind being my admin for another year, then, yes, the position is yours." She fell back into the seat cushions, ecstatic. That left Danielle.

"This is a no-brainer for me. I'm divorcing my husband, and I'm taking half of our assets. I'm buying myself a partnership on a ground-floor opportunity. I'll draw up the paperwork, and we'll get this party started." *Divorce? Never saw that coming.* It didn't hurt that she was a divorce attorney and knew how to extract everything she wanted from this guy. I never met him, but I wouldn't want to be him having a shark for a wife.

"Outstanding! This is going to be so much fun."

We got to work sorting out our strategy, and, by eleven thirty, we were loading into my car for the courthouse.

I almost skipped down the hallway to my apartment at ten to six that night. We had won our motion, and the judge insisted that Rutherford, Timmins, and Grovner be present to witness it.

I slowed my roll, checking out a tall, handsome man holding a brown paper sack that smelled of kung pao chicken. "Hey, baby, how about giving me some of that spicy sauce you've got in there," I crooned.

I cracked myself up; dirty food talk.

"Ha! This sauce has nothing on what I can give you. Dare to take me up on that?"

Ooh, this was fun. "No dare needed. Let's eat." Spencer swung his arm around me while I opened the door, and we walked in together.

He took my coat and hung it beside his in the front closet, then shut the door. He kicked off his shoes like he'd lived here his whole life, and I warmed thinking of making a home together. One that lasted a lifetime.

"How did your visit with the judge go today?" He opened the fridge and pulled out two sodas. He didn't need to ask what flavor. He knew everything about me sometimes, even before I did.

"Oh, you're going to love this. Judge Reisler hates the partners at our firm, specifically Rutherford and Timmons. I could see her holding back her joy presiding over this case. She went out of her way to summon all three partners to her chambers just to announce her verdict and see their faces herself. The overwhelming amount of evidence we presented, over and above our motion, was enough for her to approve the motion and agree to combine our single cases into one." I jumped around in a circle, doing a happy dance.

"You're kidding! Can she do that?" Spencer's eyes bugged out with speculation.

"It's called coordination of cases. We didn't have enough people for a class action suit, so this was the next best thing. She moved us up on her docket to tomorrow morning so that we could settle this and start the new year 'fresh.' Her words, not mine."

"Unbelievable. It looks like your Hanukkah lights are burning bright for these women and yourself. I'm so proud of you." He lifted me onto the counter and pushed the food aside. His hands cupped my face and whispered, "I always knew you had the heart of Judah Maccabee. Strong, true, and righteous. You personify the word Hanukkah." He kissed me deeply, taking my breath away. "Dedication. Where would these women be without you?"

That was easy. "Employed?" He smacked my thigh. "You're so bad. If I weren't so hungry, I'd eat you first."

Chapter 26

In all my days as a lawyer, I'd never been in and out of the courtroom as much as I had on our coordinated case. Rutherford's team blustered on and on about how fair and transparent they had been through the years. The "shock" they exhibited was well rehearsed, and the judge dealt with that firmly.

"Gentlemen. Regardless of your claims of a stellar past, it is obvious there isn't now or hasn't ever been a female partner beyond the junior partner status. How do you explain that?" Her stern look sent a shiver up my spine.

"Well . . ." All the blah, blah, blah, didn't sit well with her, and my team and I struggled to keep from laughing.

The judge continued. "I have two boxes of case law specific to gender discrimination right there." She pointed to the Exhibit Table. "I'm sure there is a whole wing of these cases somewhere, but today, sirs, you haven't been able to provide a single piece of evidence that supports your defense. I'm sure during your years of training and practice, you understand that ignorance isn't a valid argument in the courtroom. It is my verdict that Rutherford, Timmins, and Grovner are guilty of the gender discrimination suit filed by Rebecca Strauss, Mona Richardson, Danielle Miller, and Francesca Suarez."

Copious amounts of air whooshed from our team's lungs while grunts of indignation and appeals wafted from their side of the courtroom. Before they had a chance to leave, the judge smacked her gavel for order.

"I have a second motion that has been submitted just this morning for three of the plaintiffs who have suffered lost wages over the past several years in the amount of two and a half million dollars apiece. Ms. Strauss has submitted her own motion for future lost wages due to her discrimination suit in the amount of five-and-a-half million dollars. The total amount of this suit would be thirteen million dollars collectively. Due to the holidays and the courthouse being closed for the next five days, we will reconvene two weeks from today to hear from each side detailing those figures."

The judge scribbled on her docket and looked up. "Any questions?" Timmins looked like he was going to have a heart attack, and Grovner fell to his chair. Too bad Rutherford was still standing because the judge smacked her gavel, closing the session as he opened his mouth to speak.

We won! *Oh my God, we won!* My team hugged it out and promised to meet for dinner after the New Year to celebrate. We set a new precedent in our field by combining our cases and banding together in sisterhood. When this year began, I never would have thought this would be how it would end. I couldn't help but find a correlation between the Maccabees' fight and my fight with my previous partners. Righteousness won again, and I felt vindicated.

As I left the courtroom, I saw Spencer leaning against the wall across the hallway. All broody and sexy in his pea coat, blue knit hat, and dark-washed jeans. *Damn! He even wore hiking boots.* It wasn't every day I got to see him dressed like a lumberjack, but it gave me a whole new repertoire of fantasies to play out in the future.

He pushed off the wall and slinked closer to me, keeping his hands securely in his pockets. I could feel his warm breath on my face when he stopped just short of my body, looking down with those lusty eyes. He didn't reach for me, nor I him. The electricity that arced between us kept me glued to the floor. We needed to get out of this building and naked as fast as we could. My panties were sopping wet and I wasn't sure I could stand any longer.

"Hey, Red." His voice was like velvet. It made me shiver.

"Hey, Spence," I cooed.

He bent his face closer, his lips almost on mine. "You won, didn't you?" I nodded. "And you want to celebrate, right?" I nodded again. "I'd take you into the bathroom and fuck you hard if they weren't closing the building right now. Next time?" *Fuck, yeah!*

My mouth was dry as a bone. His dirty talk was off the charts—and I loved it. Strong hands cupped my face, and he softly kissed my lips as if I were the most precious thing he had ever held. I tried to push my tongue between the seam of his lips, but he stepped backward, one step at a time, creating way too much distance for my liking.

"Where are you going? Spencer. Stop." He continued several more steps before turning and taking off. There was only one thing to do, and I bolted after him in four-inch heels. I nearly caught up with him when he stopped at the gilded door to the outside and abruptly turned.

"I sure hope you don't have any other plans today because I'm taking you on a treasure hunt." He waggled his brows, loving what was in store for me.

"Does it involve finding things or leaving things willy-nilly across the city?" I batted my eyelashes provocatively, recalling another time I lost my clothes across the city.

He nodded smugly. "I like how you're thinking. Yes. You will be divested of your clothing as we go if that is your wish." I looked at him in shock. *Did conservative Becca want to play a dirty game around the city?* He watched me as I ran through possible scenarios.

"You're thinking too hard. You do. Let's go." He grabbed my briefcase, allowing me to put on my coat, and then he pulled me by the hand into a waiting limousine.

"This is ours? Very nice, Mr. Weiss. You sure know how to treat a lady," I purred. He gathered me in his arms and brought his face close to mine as I prepared myself for a sweet kiss. Shockingly, he dipped me to the left, placing a searing, rakish kiss on me instead. *Tell me again why I waited so long for this guy.*

His smile stretched to his eyes, so happy with himself. "Get in, Red." He tucked me and my coat into the back seat and ran to the other side to hop in.

Our first stop was a giant toy store. He took me to the third floor to build a Lego castle and presented me with a bejeweled scepter.

"Milady, you are and always have been the fairest of the kingdom. You have my full consent to smack me with this scepter before, during, and after sex and whenever I'm a bad boy."

I busted out laughing at the way he went from serious to hilarious in the same sentence. "I can't wait!" He grabbed my hand and pulled me down a short hall to the elevator. We waited not so patiently for a mother and her baby carriage to move out of the way, then jumped into the car, pulling me behind him, and made out until the elevator dinged on the main floor. Even then, as we exited the building, we couldn't keep our hands off each other.

There was more kissing and inappropriate public displays of affection in the costume shop, where I received a tiara and a velvet robe adorned with gold roping.

"Now you look the part of a queen." Spencer took pictures of me waving my wand and acting like a five-year-old girl prancing around the room like a Disney princess. Then, there were selfies next to a lion's head, an alien, and a skeleton placed between us. This was so much fun. Way better than ComicCon.

We stopped for sprinkled donuts and hot chocolate, which Spencer had the forethought to bring a flask with Baileys, and strolled down the street while our limo tagged along behind us.

"Are you finished with your hot chocolate?" he asked sweetly. I nodded, and he threw our cups into a trash bin and turned me around. With his hands on my shoulders, he looked at me very seriously. "Do you trust me, Becca? Because this next stop is going to blow your mind."

I don't think there was a day since I met Spencer that I didn't trust him. I'd felt so many other emotions over the years, but my trust in him was solid. "With my life, Spencer. I love you so much."

He blew out a long puff of air that swirled in the crisp winter afternoon. He was everything I ever wanted. Smart, funny, sexy as fuck, and full of swagger. He was thoughtful and kind, and he even stole the deal when we played euchre. He was perfect.

"Close your eyes. I've got you." I did as he asked. He placed tender kisses all over my face that held the promise of a happy ending to this adventure. Spencer would never let me fall, but he didn't promise that we wouldn't attract a crowd. His tender kisses turned into a full-on dip, causing people to whistle and woot all around us. I giggled, and I'm not a giggler.

He spun me around and guided me into the store right behind us. I wished I could remember what store it was to have some reference of what to expect. He held my hand close to his chest with his other arm around me protectively. Several steps later, he told me to take a step up and then another, backing me into a chair.

"Keep your eyes closed until I tell you. Sit there, and no peeking or you're not getting anything from this store." His threats were weak, especially when he chuckled to himself.

It seemed like forever before he told me to open my eyes, but, when I did, he was kneeling before me with a small black box opened to an enormous emerald-cut diamond outlined with tiny red, ruby stones. I gasped. I knew what this was—and it was finally happening to *me*!

"Rebecca Beth Strauss, I can't breathe another day without you in my life, in my bed, or even a random elevator. I've waited forever to ask you this question. I would wait an eternity if I knew you would say yes. Would you be my wife?"

People say that time stops at moments like these. I blew it off as dramatic. But they were absolutely right! I was in a vacuum, and the only thing I heard was my heart thumping in my head and a calm whooshing all around me. The look on Spencer's face seemed like his heart had stopped, too, waiting for my reply. Locked eyes, pure love emanating between us, and, with nothing in the world separating us ever again, the only answer could be, "YES!"

The crowd around us clapped as Spencer slid the stunning ring on my finger. "We'll come back in a few weeks and pick out bands, but I couldn't wait another day without locking you down."

He stood and took both hands, lifting me out of the chair, then kissed each hand. A clerk returned his phone and a small bag emblazoned with the shop's name. We were back on the sidewalk, sliding into the limo as the driver bowed deeply and shut the door. The privacy wall was up, and champagne lay chilling in a silver ice bucket. Our new life is waiting to be celebrated.

Still stunned by what just happened, I sat quietly as Spencer poured us each a flute of the sparkling wine. "To us."

We clinked glasses and downed the full flute. "Just so we're clear," he said seriously. "You're the one telling your mother we're getting married. I'm leaving town with your brother and father when you do."

I swatted at his chest. He recoiled into his seat, having the decency to look ashamed.

"Not if you want some of this again," I said, pulling open my regal robe and showing him all of me." I bit my lip as I watched his jaw drop.

"Fuck, Red. You really did lose your clothes all over this city. Hang on. Did I just propose to you naked?" He lunged forward quickly as I pulled my robe closed.

"I told you I was a naughty girl." I licked my lips, taunting him, swinging my red curls from side to side."

"So naughty," he hissed.

"You'll be by my side for better and for worse, starting with my mother. No excuses. I'm sorry your mother won't have the satisfaction of knowing you got the girl. I truly miss her. On the other hand, my dad and brother will be overjoyed to have another golfing buddy. Oh wait, they already do." I rolled my eyes for effect.

I let him pull back the velvet material again, exposing my taut nipples and almost bare sex. He spread my folds open, swearing to himself how lucky he was, and I agreed. This man didn't need an appointment for a date. He had me whenever he wanted me. It's a good thing I'll have my own office. I'll have to soundproof it as soon as I find one.

"Red. I'm going on my own treasure hunt. Lean back and let me see what I can find."

THE END

Are you wondering what happened between Marilyn and Yetta at the Mahjong table?

Join my newsletter

https://bethgelman.com/newsletter/

SEE YOU NEXT TIME!

ABOUT THE AUTHOR

The sassy Beth Gelman is a professional pianist and vocalist who loves being a steamy romance author. Authentic, resilient, loyal, and spiritual, she's not afraid to learn, fail, speak her mind, or try new things. She loves writing romances, especially romances that make her readers grow and appreciate their strengths and weaknesses. She loves her devoted husband, children, lattes, yoga, and every dog on the planet. Beth is the author of *The Perfect Series, Socially Satisfied, Always Falling Behind, and Eight Crazy One Night Stands.* For more information, book signing schedules, podcasts, catalog, and store, visit www.BethGelman.com.

ACKNOWLEDGEMENTS

In an attempt to be an independent author who can do ALL things, I am reminded daily that the designation will never be reached. For all I know—I know nothing. Leaning on friends, family, and author professionals to guide me, keep me honest, and lift me up daily—many, many thanks to you all.

To Daryl – My Rock and Sometimes Scene Tester—Thank you, always, for allowing me to follow my many dreams. *You complete me!*

To Evan – Book Structural Engineer—Thank you for opening your mind and silly-sweet side to help me create a dating roster for Becca. Picking names is a hard business, but you made it super fun.

To Samantha—Official Sounding Board—Your openness to hear my rantings and ravings, giggles and cackles, and "educational" tidbits warms my heart—many thanks, Beauty.

To Marsha Tucker—Master Champion of a Deserving Daughter—You are the antithesis of Marilyn. Not meddling but championing all I do. Thank you for all the vocabulary words, even when I didn't know what they meant at the time. All the edits on my schoolwork made me sound older than I was. It all made a difference. Ra-ruv ru.

To Dr. Seymour Ziegelman—Gynological Medical Advisor and Storyteller—Oh, the things we have discussed. I hope you know how important your love, guidance, and medical follies have been to me. You are the father I got to pick. How lucky am I!

To Robanski and Jody-O-Dio—Thank you for understanding and tolerating my passion for writing. It's a full-time gig that fills my heart almost to the point of how much I love you both. You have been some of my finest inspirations. (Robin—be sure to thank Marilyn for me. LOL.)

To Robert "Fun Bobby" McMillan—Title Influencer—When you are properly wound up, you are a wealth of funny one-liners—many thanks for this one.

To Colonel "Kern" Paul Scheidler—Military Advisor—I'm striving, always, to make you proud. Your friendship and support as a BETA reader, commiserator, and authoring buddy, thanks for having my back. It means the world to me.

To Jane Litherland—BETA Reader Extraordinaire—Girl, what can I say? Thank you for always wanting to help me do the heavy editing lifting with kind words, meticulous identification of passages that need improving, and, now, friendship. You're a blessing to me and my writing.

To Dawn Spellman—Newest Beth BETA Reader—Many thanks for your prompt reading and feedback. Your keen eye and helpful comments made a big difference. PLEASE come back and do it again. (*Translated: You're mine forever, and you can never stop helping me. LOL.*)

To Janice Alexis Mekula—Editing Director Emeritus—Be it plural or singular, split infinitive, or just a wacky word—thank you so much for your years of friendship and support. I'm so happy I paid attention in high school creative writing.

To Maggie Edwardtowski—Blurb Officianato—From One Funny Gal to Another Funny Gal—thank you for spinning my blurb on its axis to bring the essence of Eight Crazy Nights to life.

To Caitlin, Tana and Donna—My Greater Detroit Romance Writer buddies—Thank you for your assistance, patience, and authorly-everthing to make me a better writer and publisher. It really does take a Village.

To Lynne Golodner—Champion of Jewish Literature and Writing Buddy—Thank you for your encouragement and openness to share resources; they have been astounding.

To my incredible group of ARC readers—who shared their concerns with me candidly and allowed me to make adjustments that made my story better than before. *Toda Rabah!*

Yasher Koach!

SNEAK PEEK:
Always Falling Behind

CHAPTER 1 – A Quest

ABIGAIL

My dilapidated, once-red Toyota Corolla shuddered under the weight of all the belongings I had stuffed into its every available space. Audible sounds creaked from the suspension while I threw myself on the trunk lid, securing it shut for a journey I couldn't have imagined I'd be taking. First, a call from a lawyer who claims I am the sole living person in a family line dating from 1832, then having to notify my less than stellar boss, bosses actually, that I have to leave immediately to claim an inheritance from someone like me could never be responsible enough to accept. My name may be Abigail Farnsworth-Burton, but my AFB initials spell out my actual life, "Always Falling Behind."

I looked at my apartment building, one last time vacillating from what was great about this opportunity to obstacles known and unknown. I opened the driver's door, threw my tush on the torn, black leather seat, and slammed the door, desperately trying to keep my shit together. In truth, my mood matched the weather perfectly—gloomy. The impossible task ahead of me was well beyond my capacity. With no one in the world to guide me, I put my car in drive and headed out of the run-down apartment building parking lot and prayed to God that taking this risk would be better than the pathetic life I was currently living.

The address the lawyer provided was several states away from where I'd been living. Once a Detroiter, I moved to Chicago with a friend, Seneca, to help her dad start a grocery store. My skills, or lack thereof, didn't give me many opportunities for other occupations, so I figured, "Why not," and made a move. It wasn't that I didn't have potential; I did. My high school art teacher, Mrs. Rose, said I was a gifted artist in many mediums, but what she didn't tell me was that my inability to focus on one thing at a time would be a lifetime nemesis. At the persistent urgings of my teacher, my aunt finally agreed to get me some counseling. After countless surveys and emotional tests, Dr. Hastings proclaimed I had ADHD. Yes, the dreaded Attention Deficit/Hyperactivity Disorder millions of people like me struggle with daily.

"That doctor is a crackpot and has no idea what he's talking about. Besides, who does he think will be paying for all those medications he insisted you needed?" My aunt blustered the whole ride home from that appointment. Did I need medication? Wasn't I doing okay in school? Sure, I was scatterbrained at times, but I was a teenager! We all were that way.

As I entered the I-90 Expressway toward Mystic, Connecticut, my engine rattled in retaliation for the high speeds it was usually not forced to take. Dolton, Illinois, was not known for its extended infrastructure; therefore, "Little Red" didn't have to exert herself often. Fourteen glorious hours of silence were in front of me, and all I had were my thoughts and a cassette player my Aunt Eleanor gave me for the trip, along with her collection of 1980s music she insisted were classics. *Whatever.* My car had wheels with mildly balding tires, torn leather seats, sporadically working windshield wipers, and a snarky engine that spoke when irritated. Beyond that, I traveled on a wing and a prayer.

Tapping out the worn tunes on my steering wheel helped burn off my trepidation about my future. The lawyer was sweet and kind in his words, "You remind me of my granddaughter, full of spunk, creativity, and potential." What the hell was "potential" anyway? Was it a finish line? A magical place where money fell from trees, pool boys brought me margaritas, and I had no cares in the world? That stuff may happen for some people, though surely not for me. That wasn't going to happen, especially given my troubled beginnings.

The whoosh of semis barreling down the road had my hands white-knuckling through Chicagoland traffic. I didn't think I could endure fourteen hours of this, except I had little choice. I'd been driving since I was sixteen, only not on jam-packed roads like these. It was time to turn off into a rest area.

I planned to take two days to get to my destination. It was a great plan. Seven hours each day. No stops, fast food, and lots of hyperfocus. One hour into my trip, I had to rethink my excellent plan. I forgot about bathroom breaks. That would add at least two more hours to my two-day trip. Sleeping, that was another thing. Twenty-minute naps every few hours would have to be enough for me to get to Connecticut. It would have to be because I didn't have money for a hotel, let alone the gas my gas-guzzling car required. Yes, this would be my new plan—finally, a solid path to my nonspecific future. I should probably call my aunt and let her know I was okay. That would be the responsible thing to do as soon as I got back in my car. Except I didn't.

An hour later, I awoke to my phone blaring Journey's "Don't Stop Believin'. "*Shit!* When did a few minutes of shuteye turn into a full-on nap? I dug into my pocket and pulled out my phone, loaded with cracks from when I threw it across the room last year when I lost yet another job. It was my aunt. *Shit!*

"Hey, Aunt Eleanor, I was just getting ready to call you." Yeah, right. An hour ago.

"Hey, yourself. You forgot to call me so I could send you all your medical records. I'm moving in a couple of weeks, and you should have these for your next doctor appointments. Where can I send them?"

My mom's sister, Aunt Eleanor, raised me from age four. She did all the mom things my mother would have done, except my mom died of cancer, leaving me an orphan. Where's my dad? Ha! More like a sperm donor without a forwarding address. I never knew the guy, and I'm not looking now. I had the basics my aunt could afford to provide, along with some sage advice about stuff I can't remember, but I'll know them when I need them.I was sure of it—sort of. That was my plan, and I was sticking to it.

"I wish I could tell you I have an address, except I don't. I'm moving to Connecticut, and the place I'm moving to may or may not be working out for me. Can you give me a few days? I'm sorryI didn't call last week when you left a message. I totally forgot, and then this move came out of nowhere, and now I'm trying to keep it together to get this inheritance figured out." I pleaded for more time. I always did. I knew it annoyed her, but I couldn't help it. Maybe that ADHD thing was real.

"Inheritance? What in the world are you talking about?" she barked at me as if I was an idiot. I may be many things, but I'm *not* an idiot.

"Listen, Aunt Eleanor, I have to get back on the road and can't talk while driving. I'll fill you in on everything later. Bye!"

I promptly pushed the end button, threw my phone on the passenger seat, and shoved my fingers through my loose hair. It was time for a pep talk. I did them daily—several times a day, if necessary—this time to shore myself up for the next leg of my journey.

"You got this, girl. Breathe deeply. Settle your mind. You only have one thing to do: get to Connecticut in one piece," I uttered to assure myself. I huffed air out of my lungs to pump myself up, then threw my gearshift into reverse, squealing the tires as I completed a two-point maneuver back onto the expressway. There was one thing I was very good at, and that was talking myself into anything I wanted. However, thinking through the details of how to get the job done—not so much. As I mentioned before, that was how I gave myself the call name, Always FallingBehind.

I'm the queen of two steps forward, one step back. I chuckled, "If my ancestors who left me this giant inheritance could see the person who would one day claim their legacy, they would have rewritten their trust." Anthony Brickner assured me this trust was ironclad—with one minor adjustment: to claim the one hundred and sixty acres, mansion, and pool; I didn't have to be engaged or married as previous inheritors once had. New legislation made that antiquated statute obsolete; now, all I had to do was claim the deed within thirty days of the bequeath. I spent a whole night searching the internet for what all these words meant. Most were four-dollar words requiring a college degree. I may have graduated high school, and I may not be an idiot, but I didn't have either a college or law degree at twenty-four, and I wouldn't ever have one, to be sure.

Two more hours of nerve-racking trucks and high-speed drag racers, and I was done for the day. My stomach grumbled, my bladder was near to bursting, and the needle on my gas tank pointed at zero. I guess it's Cleveland or Bust. Knowing I would most likely never be in this city again, I pulled into a gas mart three miles down from my exit. Whenever I could focus properly, I could be pretty efficient, this being a perfect example: bathroom, food, and fuel. I was feeling proud of myself after suffering through a disgusting unisex bathroom and stomaching a leathery hot dog spinning on a slow roller from behind a glass partition. Not wanting to make another pit stop in an hour, I purchased a small bottle of water, some Skittles, and a bag of corn chips along the way. Healthy eating certainly wasn't a top priority; for the record, it never was nor had been. I'm a survivalist, I have no ego, and I don't measure myself against any other person—mostly. I grabbed the white plastic bag and walked with my head held high back to my car, pondering where I would stop for the night. Surely, I could keep going for a few more hours?

As I unlocked my car, a young man a little older than I asked if I wanted to give him a ride.

"A ride? I don't think so." I may be poor, but I was taught not to give strangers a ride.

"I could pay for your gas. Come on, driving alone must suck." He prodded, giving me a wink.

He did look sexy in his tight, black T-shirt and ripped faded jeans. His hair flopped over his left eye and pierced through its strands to my chest.

"I'm good, thanks," I replied, quickly getting into my car and locking the door.

As I pulled away, he stood with his hands on his hips, staring at me like he lost his prey for the night. Good! The distinct feeling of dodging a bullet passed through my mind, feeling my mother's presence like I always did when I had a serious decision to make. I didn't know how I knew she was with me, but I did. That protection had never steered me wrong, and her protection was definitely concrete tonight. ThankGod!

GET THE REST OF *"Always Falling Behind" TODAY on:*
Amazon   BarnesandNoble   Goodreads   Bookbub

Don't forget to visit my website and join my NEWSLETTER for great bits, where to find me, birthday treats, and special offerings, and lots more.

BETH GELMAN CATALOG

Don't go!

Start another fantastic Beth Gelman series today! See her catalog below.

Thanks for being a Beth Gelman Insatiable Reader!

<u>CATALOG</u>

The Perfect Series:

The Perfect Voice

The Perfect Lessons

Making Perfect Sense

Dazed and Confused Steamy Romances

Always Falling Behind

Novellas:

Socially Satisfied

Visit my website and see all the good stuff. Enjoy my FREE Newsletter while you're there.

www.BethGelman.com

<u>LET'S GET SOCIAL</u>

Join my Facebook Page

https://www.facebook.com/groups/

Follow me on Instagram

https://www.instagram.com/bethgelmanwrites

Follow me on TikTok too!!

https://www.tiktok.com/@beth.gelman.author